Praise for *Deadly Intentions*

"Lisa Harris never fails to amaze me with her high-intensity, adrenaline-fueled, action-packed plots and beautifully crafted characters racing against time and enemies to find the solution to a looming threat. *Deadly Intentions* starts out with a gasp-inducing prologue and the heart-pounding action doesn't stop until the very end."

Interviews and Reviews

"*Deadly Intentions* by Lisa Harris is a must-read novel. The plot is thrilling, action-packed, and fast-paced. The characters had a way of tearing me up, and then sewing me back whole again. I felt everything the characters did. It was like being there along with them. The scenes were vivid. Overall, I recommend this romantic suspense story to all fans of J. T. Ellison, Karen Harper, Carla Neggers, and Debra Webb. Lisa Harris is a writer whose words are worthy of every reader's attention."

Urban Lit Magazine

Praise for *A Secret to Die For*

"Lisa Harris has done it again! *A Secret to Die For* is a fast-paced romantic thriller packed with twists and turns. High-tension action and well-paced romance—everything you want in a romantic suspense—Harris delivers!

Elizabeth Goddard, award-winning author of the Coldwater Bay Intrigue series

THE
TRAITOR'S
PAWN

ALSO BY LISA HARRIS

THE
TRAITOR'S
PAWN

LISA
HARRIS

Revell

a division of Baker Publishing Group
Grand Rapids, Michigan

© 2020 by Lisa Harris

Published by Revell
a division of Baker Publishing Group
PO Box 6287, Grand Rapids, MI 49516-6287
www.revellbooks.com

Printed in the United States of America

Library of Congress Cataloging-in-Publication Data
Names: Harris, Lisa, 1969- author.
Title: The traitor's pawn / by Lisa Harris.
Description: Grand Rapids : Revell, a division of Baker Publishing Group, [2020]
Identifiers: LCCN 2019028423 | ISBN 9780800729172 (paperback)
Subjects: LCSH: Missing persons—Investigation—Fiction. | GSAFD: Mystery fiction.
Classification: LCC PS3608.A78315 T73 2020 | DDC 813/.6—dc23
LC record available at https://lccn.loc.gov/2019028423

ISBN 978-0-8007-3776-4 (casebound)

Published in association with Joyce Hart of the Hartline Literary Agency, LLC.

20 21 22 23 24 25 26   7 6 5 4 3 2 1

CHAPTER ONE

"WATCH YOUR BACK . . . this isn't over."

Aubrey Grayson tried to bury the ominous warning and instead focus on the clear, southern Texas predawn sky suspended above her. She was safe for now. Lost beneath a million brilliant stars. A rush of happy memories pushed their way to the surface, past the threat, and managed to bring with it the familiar sense of contentment she always found here.

She needed to do this more often. Needed to find time to step away from the frantic pace of life she'd found herself caught up in back in Houston. God had a reason for reminding his people to be still, and three days of trekking through the Texas wetlands in exchange for her high-stress job was exactly what she needed. She took a sip of the steamy coffee she'd brought with her and breathed in the invigorating scent. She'd spend the rest of the morning hunting waterfowl, eating bacon and eggs cooked over a fire in a cast-iron pan, and listening to Papps and his boys swap tall tales from previous trips.

But for the moment she was simply going to enjoy the quiet.

Something splashed in the distance, breaking through her thoughts. She turned toward the noise, immediately feeling a spike of adrenaline, but she couldn't see anything. She shook off the instinctual warning. It was probably nothing more than a duck or a frog enjoying the last moments of darkness, broken only by a thin layer of yellow light now along the horizon.

"Aubrey?"

She let out a sharp sigh of relief. "Papps. I was hoping you'd come join me."

"Sorry . . . did I scare you?"

She motioned for him to sit down next to her. "Just lost in thought."

"I'm not surprised. No matter how early I get up, you always beat me." The former senator sat down on the slice of dry ground Aubrey had found overlooking the wetlands. "I'm glad you decided to come down here. You needed a break."

"You're right, and I'm slowly starting to relax."

"Good, because this is the perfect setting for that. I love the hunting, but I also know how much you love the solitude out here at this hour."

"It's something hard to find back home."

He nudged her with his shoulder. "Which is why you should come down here more often. You know there's always a place at the house, and, next to this setting, the front porch is the perfect spot to watch the sunrise."

She smiled at the offer. "I do need to take you up on it more often."

"I wish you would. The house gets lonely with all the kids gone. With Gail gone."

Aubrey didn't try to fight the wave of sadness that swept through her. "I miss her too."

The former senator Grant McKenna and his family had been a part of her life for as long as she could remember. And Papps, as she'd always called him, had become like a father to her, taking the place of her absent biological father. His residence outside Corpus Christi had become her home away from home.

"Ryan told me you were thinking about selling the house," she said.

"I talk about it every now and then, but I don't think I'll ever bring myself to actually do it. Too many memories. Too much work. And for now at least, it gives you and the boys a place to come two or three times a year."

She reached down and squeezed his hand. "You sound lonely."

"I'm doing okay. Really. Gail's been gone four years now, though it's crazy how it feels like yesterday sometimes. Other times it seems like a lifetime ago."

"How are you doing? I mean really doing?"

"I can't complain. I'm staying busy, and that helps. I'm still volunteering on a couple nonprofit boards, and I'm involved in a Christmas fundraiser next month. On top of that I try to catch as many of the grandkids' sporting events as I can."

She chuckled. "Maybe I'm not the only one who needs to slow down."

"I think about stepping down every once in a while, but staying busy helps. Gail and I had so many plans. So many places we wanted to travel to together. I guess you plan your whole life for retirement with the idea of enjoying it with the person you love, but sometimes . . . Sometimes life doesn't go the way you think it will."

Aubrey heard the regret in his voice. He wasn't the only one who found it hard to believe Gail was gone.

"But enough about me," he said. "You're the one I'm worried about. You seem tired this trip. More tired than usual."

She stared out across the water as the sun continued to slowly bathe the horizon in yellow and gold. She was tempted to tell him about the threats she'd received, but she wasn't going to add to his worry. "Things never seem to slow down, but moments like this remind me how much I need a break."

"You could always transfer and get a job down here. I understand they're hiring game wardens. It's got to be calmer than what you're doing in Houston."

She took another sip of her coffee. "The job has its ups and downs, but I love it, and can't imagine doing anything else."

"Meaning your promotion to detective?"

She nodded.

"I remember when you first started talking about law enforcement. You were probably ten, maybe eleven. You always had this desire to serve your country."

"And you were one of my biggest influences. If it wasn't for you and your family, I'd be in a different place right now."

"I don't know. You've always been strong, no matter what life throws at you. Besides, I think I'm the one who should be thanking you. I love my boys, but we needed a bit of softness to balance out all the testosterone. We all love it when you're around."

She laughed, loving how he always made her feel like she was one of his own. "You've definitely got that between Ryan and the twins. But now that Kyle and Mitchell are married, it's a bit more balanced."

"True. And don't get me wrong. You know how much I love my daughters-in-law, but you'll never catch them out here duck hunting."

"You do have a point." She watched the rays of light start to edge their way across the marshland, the yellows and oranges of the sunrise reflecting across the water. Renee and Kim had no idea what they were missing. "Mitchell told me they took advantage of their husbands being gone and are Christmas shopping in Houston."

Even her mother had never understood how she preferred camping and hunting to a weekend shopping trip, but she'd choose time out in the middle of God's creation over shopping any day. It always helped lower her stress and calm her mind.

Papps squeezed her knee. "I'm glad you're here, but there's something you're not telling me, isn't there?"

She glanced at him. The morning glow on the water gave her just enough light to read his worried expression. "You always know when something's going on, don't you?"

"It must be a sixth sense. In case you forgot, before I got into politics, I was a father, counselor, and youth pastor."

She let out a slow breath. "I'm just learning how to deal with some of the aspects of my job, but it's nothing really."

"Were you threatened?"

She closed her eyes for a moment, wishing she could permanently erase the image of the dead bodies on the living room floor. And the chilling expression their suspect had given her when they arrested him. But what she'd experienced was part of the job. Part of her commitment to making the world a safer place. And nothing anyone could say or do was going to change that.

"Empty threats," she said. "The man's now sitting behind bars and looking at life in prison."

"If you ever feel like you need extra help, please tell me. I've got friends who work in security—"

"I can't run every time someone threatens me." She shook her head. "I've got a partner who watches my back and a supportive captain. It has unsettled me some, but I'll be fine."

Papps sighed. "Sometimes I forget you're not a little girl anymore, begging me to take you to the aquarium every weekend."

She laughed. "I still love the aquarium."

"I'm not surprised, but if you change your mind . . . seriously—"

"I appreciate it, but like I said, I'll be fine."

She would. She just needed to shake off the alarm. Nico was in prison and couldn't hurt her. Or anyone else, for that matter.

"What frustrates me the most is that even though he's finally behind bars, there are still more out there." She pulled up the zipper of her jacket a couple more inches to block the wind. "The work to get people like him off the streets never ends."

"No, but your job isn't to catch all of them. And everyone you do take off the streets is one less criminal who can hurt someone. That's all you can do—one at a time."

"You always know exactly what to say, don't you?"

He laughed. "I try."

She smiled, reminded once again of how much she enjoyed being with him and his sons. How they'd become like a second family to her after her mother passed away. And how the emotional and spiritual encouragement they gave her was exactly what she needed. She didn't have to worry about Nico. He couldn't touch her here.

"You ready to get in a few hours of hunting?" Papps asked. "I hear Ryan has thrown down a challenge to see who can get their day's quota first."

Aubrey laughed. "Why am I not surprised?"

"You know me and the boys. We always like a bit of competition."

They stood up and started back toward the duck-hunting blind. All three of his sons shared their father's love of hunting as well as his competitive spirit and had made this weekend an annual event. Aubrey just enjoyed the feeling of belonging.

A second later, a muffled shot echoed off the water, followed by the flapping of wings, shifting her attention to the right.

"Aubrey . . ." Papps sucked in a sharp breath and grabbed her arm. "Aubrey . . . I think I've been hit."

"What?"

He stumbled beside her, then collapsed onto the ground, as she tried to decipher what had just happened. A second later another shot rang out, slicing the air next to her as she knelt beside him. She stuffed down the panic, needing to keep them both out of the shooter's line of sight. Water seeped into her rubber boots. In this position, there was no protection beyond the tall grass surrounding them, but what terrified her even more was that she was certain this wasn't an accident. Not only had the shot been suppressed with a silencer, it didn't seem to have been aimed at any birds.

But motivation didn't matter right now. What mattered was

getting Papps out of here alive. The problem was that they were too exposed, and trying to call for help would only expose them further. Staying low, she managed to pull Papps into the outcropping of muddy, tall grass behind them.

"Where were you shot?" she whispered.

"My side."

She pulled back his shirt, but in the low light of dawn, it was impossible to tell how much damage had been done.

"I have to try to stop the bleeding," she said, "but you're going to have to stay as still as possible."

She untied his neck bandana, folded it quickly, then pressed it into the wound. But stopping the bleeding wasn't going to be enough. They needed medical help. Mitchell was a doctor and only a few hundred yards away, but hunting hours had just started, and even if anyone had heard the shot, no one would think twice about it. As crazy as the idea sounded, she was going to have to try to take down whoever was out there.

Keeping her hands pressed against Papps's side, Aubrey shifted her position slightly to the right, then raised her head. Marsh grasses rustled around her. Duck calls and the boom of shotguns sounded in the distance. A flash of sunlight glinted off a gun as she caught sight of the silhouette of a man.

Bingo.

She glanced back at Papps. She'd found the shooter, but her options were still limited. She was irritated at herself for not bringing her weapon with her. All she'd wanted to do was catch a few moments of quiet before the sun rose. Now that had turned out to be a deadly mistake.

No doubt the retired senator had a score of enemies, but he

wasn't the only one who'd been on the receiving end of death threats. There was simply no way to know at this point which of them was the target. She glanced back down at Papps's side. The bandana was already soaked, but she was unsure how much was blood and how much was water. Her heart pounded. A dog barked in the distance. Butch, Papps's Labrador, was already retrieving ducks at their hunting site, and no one had any idea what was going on.

"Stay with me, Papps," she said. "I'm getting you out of here. Can you hold this against your side?" She pressed his hand against the cloth.

"I'll try."

"I'm going after him," she said. "Right now we're pinned down."

"Aubrey, don't . . ."

She caught the panic in his voice, but she didn't have a choice. She kept low, her boots pressing into the mud as she headed toward where she'd seen the shadowy figure. He was still out there. Waiting. Stalking. She stopped behind a large clump of marsh reeds, not moving, barely breathing, and tried not to shiver. Even with her waterproof gear she could still feel the cold seeping through to her skin.

Show me what to do, God. Leaving Papps could mean he bleeds out, but if I go back . . . If I don't stop this person . . .

Aubrey caught movement to her right and turned toward the figure, but she was a fraction of a second too late. He grabbed her, slamming her onto the ground. She groaned as she landed on her back, opened her mouth, and tried to fill her lungs with air, but the muscles in her chest refused to work.

"Don't scream." He stood over her, gun pointed at her head. "Don't make a sound, or your friend is going to end up with another bullet hole."

"What do you want?" she asked.

"You're coming with me."

He dragged her toward the water where a small boat bobbed next to the shoreline. The familiar sounds of duck hunting surrounded them while the sun continued to slowly move above the horizon. So Nico had made good on his threat. She had no idea how he'd found her here. She hadn't mentioned to anyone except a couple of close friends where she was going.

She felt the barrel of his gun jab into her rib cage. "Get in the boat, on your knees. Now."

She hesitated before obeying, knowing if she got on that boat and left with him, she was as good as dead. The bottom was wet with an inch of cold water, but that was the least of her worries. If someone didn't find Papps quickly, he was going to bleed out and die. And if she didn't get away, his family would eventually find her body floating in the water. If she was going to get out of this alive, she had to escape.

She spun around and jammed her elbow into the man's Adam's apple. He countered by throwing a wild punch at her, but she managed to duck, then block his punch. She screamed as he swung at her again. This time, she prayed Papps's boys would hear her. She leveraged her weight to her advantage and blocked another punch, then struck the guy hard beneath his chin. But she wasn't the only one trained in self-defense. A second later, he swung the butt of his weapon against her temple, and everything went dark.

CHAPTER TWO

JACK SHANNON PULLED INTO the parking lot in front of the restaurant located a couple blocks from Oso Bay where he'd agreed to meet his brother. At 7:00 a.m. the place was buzzing with the breakfast crowd, though he wasn't surprised. The hole-in-the-wall eatery had the best fish tacos he'd ever tasted, both in and out of Corpus Christi, and had been one of his favorite go-to places back in high school after basketball games.

He and his brother had been close back then, but over the years they'd managed to drift apart. He always made a trip home for the holidays—most years anyway—to their parents' house in Dallas where the couple had retired, but after he'd left Corpus, things had never been the same between him and Adam. And a big part of him still regretted letting that happen.

Adam was heading toward him as Jack stepped out of his car. His brother looked younger than his thirty-two years and still just as fit as he'd always been.

Jack glanced at his watch. "I'm not late, am I?"

"Early, actually. But we've got a problem. I'm sorry to bail on you, but I just got a call from the local sheriff."

"What's going on?"

Adam's jaw tensed. "Grant McKenna was shot, out duck hunting this morning about an hour out of the city."

"Senator McKenna?"

"Yes."

Jack frowned at the news. It wasn't the first time he'd heard about an accidental shooting. Every year there were cases of both stray and self-inflicted pellets, where hunters were shot—sometimes even killed—with their own weapons. It was one of the reasons Adam had gotten involved in the area's hunter education programs, promoting safe hunting outside his job as a game warden. But this surprised Jack. He knew the senator was not only an excellent marksman but also a stickler about safety.

"Is he going to be okay?" Jack asked.

"He's in critical condition and en route to the hospital." Adam's gaze shifted past him. "But there's something else, Jack. They don't believe this was an accident."

"What do you mean?"

Adam hesitated. "He was hunting with his boys, one of his grandsons, and Aubrey Grayson."

"Wait a minute . . ." Jack's fists clenched as he leaned back against his car. "Bree?"

"You were the only one she let call her that, but yeah . . . I thought that might get your attention."

"What was she doing there? I thought she was living in Houston."

"She is, but she still comes down here at least once a year to go hunting with the senator's family. According to Senator

McKenna's son, there were six of them who went out. They got there early to set everything up, and the senator went with Aubrey to watch the sunrise before the hunting started, where he was shot." Adam glanced at his phone. "Officers first on the scene tried to talk with him, but he was pretty out of it. They're life flighting him back here and have a team of surgeons waiting, but we're not going to know anything for a while."

"What does Bree say? I'm guessing she was a witness?"

"All we know at this point is that the senator took a bullet to his side, and Aubrey . . ." Adam hesitated. "She's missing, Jack."

"Missing?" His brother's words felt like a punch in the gut. "Wait a minute . . . Why would she be missing?"

"That's what we're trying to find out."

"So you have no idea where she is right now?" Jack asked.

Adam shook his head. "Unfortunately, no. We're thinking abduction."

"How long has she been missing?"

Adam glanced at his watch. "They found the senator twenty minutes ago."

Which meant if she'd been abducted, she could be anywhere along the coastline or even miles inland. Jack frowned. They needed something else. A clear insight into the motivation behind the attack. The most logical explanation was that this was related to the senator, but they couldn't make any assumptions yet.

"What can I do to help?" Jack asked.

"I figured you'd ask that. I could use your help. You know both Bree and the terrain around here as well as I do."

"Of course. What's the plan?" He didn't hesitate with his

response. He'd find a way to work around his current case with the FBI, because there was no way he was walking away from helping to find Bree.

"You can come with me now," Adam said. "I've called in the search and rescue team, and they're organizing a grid search near the spot where she was taken. We can join them there."

"Then let's go."

Jack slipped into the car next to his brother, remembering every detail about one of the last times he'd seen Bree. They'd left campus and gone cycling along the coast, something they'd been doing together for years. But on that day, somehow the sunlight brought out the highlights in her reddish-brown hair more than usual, and her laugh had him wanting to kiss her.

Which at the moment seemed crazy.

They'd known each other since they were both eleven years old and had gone to the same junior high and high school together. They'd always been comfortable hanging out, but while they were close, they were never more than friends. Until one day in college, everything changed for him, and he found himself wanting more than just a friendship with her.

But there was a problem. Three months earlier, Bree had started dating Adam, and not only had Jack suddenly realized he was in love with her, he was lost to know how he fit into the picture anymore. He ended up transferring to the University of Texas at Dallas in order to pursue a degree in criminology. Career-wise, it was a smart move. But relationship-wise, in trying to guard his heart, he'd misjudged the situation.

He thought Bree and his brother would eventually end up married, but six months after he left for Dallas, they broke things off and went their separate ways. Jack never said anything to anyone about how he felt about Bree, and now, all these years later, too much time had been lost, as far as he was concerned. Turning back the clock at this point wasn't possible, even if he wanted to.

He shifted his thoughts from the past and back to the situation they were dealing with as Adam sped down the highway. Any feelings he'd once had for Bree didn't matter at this moment. Finding her alive did.

"Is there anything else we know at this point?" he asked.

"Not really." Adam's fingers gripped the steering wheel. "No one knows exactly what time she left camp, but the senator told his oldest son he was going to join her to watch the sunrise, then they'd both return. About twenty minutes later, the senator's son heard a woman scream—presumably Aubrey—and started looking for them. They found the senator with a gunshot wound to his side. Bree was nowhere to be found."

"And they weren't able to get any information out of him?"

"Just that she had gone looking for the gunman."

Jack frowned as a string of regrets surfaced. Back then, he'd decided it wasn't worth fighting his brother over a woman. He'd ended up with a master of science degree in criminology, eventually joining the FBI and moving to Denver. The past—and Aubrey Grayson—eventually faded into the background. But in all these years, no one had come close to taking hold of his heart like she had.

"Is it possible she fell into the water?" Jack spoke out loud as half a dozen possible scenarios ran through his head. "Maybe she was shot as well?"

"They've searched the immediate area where the senator was found, and so far, there's no sign of her. According to his sons, there have been a number of threats to their father over the past few months, though that isn't unusual. He's still a high-profile figure even though he's no longer in office."

"So you think this is somehow politically motivated?"

"I don't think we can jump to conclusions. But with her missing, I think it's pretty safe to assume this was no accident."

"Agreed, but why take Bree if they were after the senator?"

"That's what we need to figure out."

Jack stared out at the ocean as they sped toward the crime scene. Palm trees framed the blue waters in the distance. He loved the familiar feel of city and surrounding wetlands where he'd grown up along the miles of beaches and shallow flats with their year-round fishing, and winter duck hunting with his family. He swallowed hard, feeling the need to stuff the past back where it belonged. In the past. But there was still one thing he needed to say.

"Listen, Adam. I know there are things that need to be said between us. I know it's been too long since I've been here, and too long since we spent any time together."

"Forget it." Adam shook his head. "I'm pretty sure you'll agree that nothing matters right now except finding Aubrey."

Jack nodded. His brother was right. This wasn't the time to dig up any grievances between the two of them, even if it was simply to try and patch them up. There would be time for that later.

They rode the next fifteen minutes in silence. He'd planned on catching up with Adam about his brother's wife and two little girls over breakfast with a dozen questions he wanted to ask. But at the moment he couldn't stop thinking about Bree and what might have happened to her.

"We'll be at the meeting place in just a few minutes now." Adam pulled off onto a dirt road that ran parallel to the water.

"How are you doing with this?" Jack asked.

Adam glanced at him. "You mean because I used to date her?"

Jack shifted uncomfortably in his seat. "Just because the two of you didn't end up together doesn't erase the fact that you once cared deeply about her."

"No, and I still do. I'd hate to see anything happen to her. But what about you? She was your best friend."

Jack felt a jolt. He hadn't just fallen in love with any girl. He'd fallen in love with his best friend. How had he let the past decade come between them?

"She was, and that's why I'm here with you right now."

In another couple of miles, Adam pulled off the road where a circle of law enforcement vehicles had gathered.

A heavyset uniformed man in his late fifties approached as they exited the car. "Adam Shannon . . . thanks for coming. I was told you were taking over the case once you arrive. You know these wetlands better than anyone here."

"And I've brought reinforcements. My brother knows this area as well and is willing to help."

Jack held out his hand to the older gentleman. "Jack Shannon. I'm glad to be of help."

"We're glad you're here. I'm Sheriff Matt Daniels. You're with the FBI, aren't you?"

Jack nodded. "I'm down here investigating a case, but I know both Aubrey Grayson and the senator."

"We can use all the help we can get," the sheriff said.

"Update me on what's been done so far," Adam said.

"We've searched the immediate vicinity where the senator was shot, looking for Detective Grayson and any evidence of what happened, but so far there is no sign of her. We're currently expanding the search and have just sent the first two teams out on the water."

"I've arranged to have drones and a K9 unit here in the next thirty minutes," Adam said.

"Good."

Jack walked over to the hood of one of the law enforcement cars where a map of the area was spread out. "Can you show me where they were hunting?"

"Here." The sheriff jabbed the map with his finger. "About fifty yards to our east, at the edge of this small island of mangroves."

Jack frowned. One of Bree's favorite spots.

"And where did they find the senator?"

The sheriff pointed to a spot highlighted in yellow.

Memories of a brown-haired girl with big brown eyes and a dash of freckles across her nose and a fondness for dark chocolate, pizza, cycling, and country music flooded through him. He was surprised he remembered so much about someone he'd tried to forget for so long. He forced himself to switch gears, shoving the memories aside, and instead worked through a list of probable scenarios. He knew the area from his own time on the water growing up. He and Adam had spent hours duck hunting, fishing, and boating, and the majority of the time, Bree had been right there with them.

What he couldn't forget, though, was that she was no longer the fresh-faced teen he'd grown up with. She was a well-trained police detective, smart and capable. Whoever had taken her had better be on their guard, because she wouldn't go down without a fight.

But even that knowledge didn't take away his anxiety.

Jack zoomed in on the map. "If someone took her, they'd probably head east by boat toward the main waterway here. That would be the quickest way out if someone was trying to avoid being seen."

Adam nodded. "Agreed."

"Okay then." The sheriff pulled out his radio. "We'll send out two more teams and have them spread out toward that point."

The plan was solid, but Jack knew they were looking at miles and miles of terrain. If they were off the mark at all, finding her would be almost impossible.

"I want to go out there on the water," he said.

"Done," Adam said. "We've got two more boats ready to go. I'll send an officer with you, so you can concentrate on finding her."

"Good."

"And Jack . . ." Adam caught his gaze. "Thank you."

Jack nodded, but he wasn't doing this for his brother. He was doing it for a best friend his heart had never forgotten. And not only because he'd once loved her. As anxious as he was to find her, he'd come to terms with her not being a part of his life. He'd moved on, and he had no doubt she had as well. But none of that would ever take away the place in his heart she'd once held.

A minute later, he was introducing himself to his pilot, a young game warden named Christopher Beckett, who didn't look a day over twenty-one. They quickly went over the route he wanted to take, then Officer Beckett started the engine of the Majek boat. Jack scanned the familiar terrain as the boat headed out onto the water, looking for anything that seemed out of place.

We've got to find her, God . . . Please . . .

A wave of guilt surfaced. The night he'd told her he was transferring schools, she'd said that, as much as she was going to miss him, she couldn't blame him for jumping on the chance to follow his dream. She'd probably have done the same thing if she'd been in his place. And yet, he hadn't missed the disappointment in her eyes.

On top of that, he'd always regretted not telling her the truth about how he felt that day. But would it really have mattered? His best friend was falling in love with his brother. Staying wouldn't have changed anything. It would only have put a wedge between them.

Which was exactly what had ended up happening anyway.

He stared out along the slow-moving waterway that had been his backyard growing up. Signs of life were everywhere throughout the marshy bay, but there was no sign of a second boat. No sign of Bree.

He held on to the grab rails in the middle of the boat next to Officer Beckett, trying to imagine what Bree would have done.

If she could, she would have left some kind of clue. Something that would point them in the right direction, like Hansel and Gretel's bread crumbs. And yet nothing but the morning sunlight reflected off the waters.

Where was she?

They continued chugging through the choppy water, the banks flanked by reeds and the gray horizon in front of them.

He signaled at Beckett, then shouted above the motor. "Slow down. What's that up ahead?"

Beckett shifted the boat into neutral. "Looks to me like it's the sun reflecting off something in the water."

Jack tried to swallow his disappointment, but the man was right. His stomach tightened. The problem was that every minute they were out here meant she was another minute farther away.

Beckett maneuvered the boat down the middle of the waterway. "Did you know the missing woman?"

"I did. She was . . . an old friend of mine."

"I don't know her, but I met the senator a few times. He's a good man. One of those politicians that from what I could see always tried to do what was right for his constituents."

"He is a good man. I met him a couple times as well and always liked him. She was like a daughter to him. We need to find her."

"Keep looking. We will."

He wanted to believe that, but the reality was that whoever had taken her had enough of a head start that they could be miles away, depending on which direction they had taken. By land, they could be on the way to Houston, Laredo, or San Antonio, but there was also the port that was filled with vessels going in and out constantly. They needed to find a way to narrow down the search.

Adam's voice crackled over Jack's hand radio. "Anything yet?"

"No. What about on your end?"

"There's no sign of another boat. It's like she simply vanished."

Jack frowned, refusing to believe that. "She's out there, and we're going to find her."

"You're right." Adam paused. "I do have an update on the senator. They just took him into surgery. He's still not out of the woods, but at least they've been able to stabilize him."

"That's good news."

"I'm hoping as soon as he wakes up we'll be able to get more information from him. I have an officer there now waiting to talk to him, but also to ensure his safety in case he's the target of all this."

"Roger that."

He searched the horizon for signs of a boat. He was grateful the senator was safe, but they still weren't any closer to finding Bree, making his heart battle with emotions he wasn't sure how to deal with. How could she still manage to affect him? He'd dated other women over the past few years, but any relationship never went further than a handful of dates before he managed to find a reason to walk away. He'd told himself it had nothing to do with Bree and that he certainly wasn't comparing them to her.

But his feelings toward Bree had nothing to do with this moment. The only thing that mattered right now was saving her before it was too late.

CHAPTER THREE

AUBREY LEANED BACK AGAINST the side of the boat, working to loosen her hands while her captor steered the boat through the narrow inlet. Her head pounded, and she'd sliced her leg on something, but at least she was still alive. She couldn't say that about Papps. If his family hadn't found him by now, she knew he would have already bled out.

A sick feeling snaked through her as her mind continued to replay what had happened and what she could have done differently. But they'd been ambushed by a sniper. She'd done what she'd been trained to do—try and neutralize the threat. Having failed that, the only thing she could do now was pray that Papps's sons had heard her scream. But her captor had timed his dirty deed well. Duck hunting wasn't like deer hunting, which was more of a solitary pursuit. And for the McKenna family, it had always been a social event. It had been the same every year for as long as she could remember.

She knew exactly what had been going on at the blind. Until the birds landed, there would be no shortage of conversation. They'd watch the sunrise break through the morning fog while

Mitchell and Ryan told jokes and started breakfast. Any activity that combined guns, water, and the cold included an element of danger, but they wouldn't have been listening for the deadly shot of a sniper.

She continued to work to untie the twine securing her wrists as she formulated a plan. They'd been gone at least forty-five minutes, winding their way through the grass flats and channels. She'd spent time in these wetlands, but before long, the scenery began to look the same. Miles of water and vegetation with no idea where they were going. Memories of days spent on the water with Papps teaching her about the ecosystem of where the water met the land flooded through her. A place filled with cattails and other grasses, along with birds, fish, and sea turtles, where she could momentarily forget about the stresses of her work.

But today, she'd walked into a nightmare, and what she didn't understand was what the objective had been. Papps had been shot, but if he was the target, why grab her? The twine cut at her wrists as she continued to slowly loosen it. Nothing made sense, but she didn't have to understand the motivation to realize her life was in danger. The only way she was going to survive this was to escape. A search party had probably been assembled by now, but with no clues to know where to look, she couldn't expect rescue anytime soon. And in the meantime, she needed to get as much information as she could.

"Where are we going?" She shouted above the noise of the motor, making sure she memorized the features of the man who'd taken her. He was Asian—probably Chinese—short and thin, yet muscular, with a one-inch scar running across his temple.

"You'll find out soon enough. We're almost there."

"Where? Are we meeting someone?"

He frowned at her. "Stop with all the questions."

"I will, if you tell me why you shot the senator. You could have just grabbed me and left him alone. Unless he was the target all along." She paused, praying for some feedback, but the man said nothing.

"Nico paid you to snatch me, didn't he?" she asked.

The man didn't answer.

"Or was the senator the target? If they weren't able to get him to a hospital, there's no way he could have made it. And if you're convicted of capital murder, you could easily be looking at life in prison without parole."

He caught her gaze. "I told you to stop talking."

He turned away from her again, but she wasn't ready to stop probing.

"What I don't understand is—assuming the senator was the target—why grab me? Who are you working for?"

"Did you not hear me?" He stepped away from the steering wheel and backhanded her across her cheek. "I said shut up!"

She bit back the sharp sting of pain from the blow, irritated that she'd allowed herself to push him too far. Put him across the table from her in an interrogation room where she was in charge of the situation, and she knew she could pull the truth out of him, but she wasn't going to get anything out of him. Not now. She studied the coastal waterway surrounding her. The truth wasn't what mattered right now. What mattered right now was getting out of here alive.

She twisted her wrists. She needed a few more minutes to

undo the loosened twine, but then she would have to find her way out of the miles and miles of swampy waters without him catching her.

If that was even possible.

More memories flooded her of time spent in the marshlands with Papps and his family and growing up with Adam and Jack Shannon. So much had changed over the past decade. Adam had a family now and worked as a game warden. Jack had moved away years ago. She'd made peace with Adam after their breakup, and while it had stung at the time, looking back she knew it was the right decision. They never would have been a good match. Thankfully they'd finally realized it, and in the end, they both moved on. Adam found the perfect woman, got married, and had two adorable girls.

But Jack . . . Jack was a different story.

She kept working at the loosening cords, ignoring the cramping in her wrists. Something had hurt him, she knew that, but to this day she wasn't sure why he'd left so unexpectedly. Maybe it was nothing more than a career move, but at the time she'd been convinced there was something else.

Her eyes swept the boat for signs of the rifle. No sign of it, but the man had a handgun holstered on his side. Her captor's phone rang, and he picked it up off the console in front of him.

She listened in on the conversation, still working on getting loose, as he and the caller tried to communicate with an apparent weak signal. She caught the name Rudy, and after some muffled conversation, him confirming that he'd meet them. But for what? That was the question she couldn't answer.

Yet.

She shifted in her seat, almost free now, planning her next move because she was only going to have one chance. Her heart raced, knowing that the odds were against her. He was armed and she wasn't, plus he had at least thirty pounds on her. Which meant she was going to have to outsmart him.

The cord slipped off her wrist.

He dropped the phone into the storage console in front of him, clearly distracted. It was now or never.

She lunged at him from behind. Her left hand covered his face and pulled back on his head while her right hand gripped his right arm. A fraction of a second later, she slammed her knee into the back of one of his legs, shifting her weight into him and forcing him to collapse. He stumbled, momentarily disoriented, then sprang back to his feet. His elbow rammed into her jaw, throwing her back against the metal railing of the boat.

Aubrey ignored the pain and threw her weight into her next move, sending him over the edge and into the water. Knowing she had only seconds at the most to press her advantage, she glanced around the bottom of the boat for his weapon, hoping it had fallen during the attack. But he must have managed to keep it with him when he went overboard.

She could hear him flailing in the water and shouting at her as she rushed to start the motor that had died. A shot rang out, hitting the console, just missing her. She ducked and tried a second time to start the boat. Nothing. She could barely feel the panic, so strong was the adrenaline pumping through her. Much of the Texas marsh was like a spiderweb, connecting grasslands with areas of open water that spread out all the way to the Louisiana border. All she needed was to get out of here and disappear.

Seconds later, he was pulling himself back onto the boat, trying to keep his gun aimed at her. This time she had to win, which meant she had to disarm him. She charged at him and grabbed his wrist, then quickly spun the gun away from him, breaking one of his fingers in the process. He cried out in pain and tried to regroup, but it was too late. She now had control of the gun, and him. She moved quickly again, tackling him and pinning him to the bottom of the boat with the gun aimed at his head.

"I wouldn't move if I were you. Turn over onto your stomach. Now."

A second later he complied. She pressed her knee into his back, unwilling to take any chances as she tied his wrists securely behind him with the same twine he'd used to secure her, then sat him down and secured his hands to the metal handle on the other side of the console.

"This isn't over," he said, still struggling against her. "You need me. You'll never find your way out of here."

"I grew up around here, so I think I can manage," she said, trying to start the boat.

"Maybe, but you won't make it far. And how are you going to manage when my boss shows up?"

"So the plan was for you to take me to your boss?" She didn't buy that lie. She'd heard him say he'd meet them, but what if they could track him if he didn't show up? She tried to work through what she knew, but it wasn't enough. Who were they and why did they want her? If this didn't have to do with Nico, then maybe they were planning to use her as leverage for some reason, but again, why? She wasn't worth anything financially, and if they were looking for a ransom payout from the McKennas, it would have made more sense to take a family member.

"Why were you supposed to grab me?"

"Don't know. Don't care. I just did what I was told."

So he'd been hired to do the dirty work. But there was no more time for questions. She needed to get the boat going and out of here, because if he was right, it wouldn't be long until "they" found her.

She tried to start the engine again. The boat emitted a loud grinding noise, then nothing. Seconds dragged past. Her heart hammered inside her chest. Papps had taught her how to drive these shallow-bottom boats, but dealing with a bullet embedded in the controls had never been in the instruction manual. And, on top of that, there was another problem she had to deal with. Someone out there wanted her, and she needed to make sure she avoided them at all costs. If she couldn't get out of here now, what was she supposed to do?

She glanced around. To the right was an endless field of marshy wetlands. To the left she could see the ocean. If they had found Papps, the authorities would be looking for her by now, but what if the men after her found her first? Here in the open she felt like a sitting duck.

She grabbed his phone and tried to place a call to 911, but there was no signal. If she couldn't use the phone to her advantage, she needed to make sure it wasn't used against her as a tracking device. She ripped off the back, pulled out the battery, to ensure the phone couldn't be traced, then put them both on the console in front of her, still trying to plan her next move. She could wade a few feet to a small island and wait there. One of her fears was that the phone wasn't the only thing that could be tracked. More than likely the boat had its own GPS tracker as well, often mandated by insurance companies. Which meant that staying with the boat was just as risky as leaving it.

She caught the flash of sun reflecting on metal and felt her stomach clench. The familiar sound of a motor roared as it sped across the water toward her. She didn't know whether it was friend or foe behind the wheel. She needed to see them before they saw her. She stuffed a gag into her captive's mouth to keep him quiet, then used the fiberglass push pole to move the boat deeper into the thick reeds.

Seconds later, she slid out of the boat into the cold water that was almost waist high and started for the embankment, still needing to know if it was a local patrol boat or someone else before she caught anyone's attention. The drawback of leaving the bad guy in the boat was that there was always the possibility he could eventually get away and she'd lose him as a bargaining chip, but that couldn't be helped. She held the gun tightly in her fingers, praying that whoever was driving the boat was someone who would help her and not someone who wanted her dead.

CHAPTER FOUR

JACK STUDIED THE TERRAIN around them from behind the helm of the flat-bottom Majek boat, then signaled to Beckett to slow down again. They'd already covered 75 percent of the grid they'd been assigned to, and what scared him was that the longer the search took, the lower the odds were of finding Bree.

A flash of light to the left had caught his attention. Maybe it was just the morning sunlight bouncing off the water again, but he wasn't going to take any chances of missing her if she was out there.

"Did you see that?" he asked. "Something's flashing in the water, and this time I don't think it's just the sunlight."

Beckett slowed down the boat. "I think you're right. I'll move closer so we can see what it is."

Seconds later, a woman wearing camo emerged out of the grass at the edge of the embankment. He caught the familiar face in the sunlight as the boat pulled up next to her. Reddish-brown curls spilled over her shoulders, while light brown eyes stared back at him. He'd been right.

Bree.

"Jack!" She untangled a reed from her hair, then made her way through the water toward the boat. "What in the world are you doing out here?"

He caught the surprise in her eyes. "I was about to ask you the same question."

He took the gun she was holding from her, handed it to Beckett, then hoisted her into the boat. He pulled her shivering body against his chest and wrapped his arms around her, trying not to panic. She was shaking, and her clothes were wet and covered with blood. There was a cut on her forehead, and a bruise was forming on her left cheek.

He took a step back. "Bree . . . you're injured."

"It's Papps's blood." She tugged at the red stain at the bottom of her insulated jacket. "They shot him, then took me. Please tell me you found him."

"They did. He's the one that gave us a heads-up that you'd been taken. They life flighted him to Corpus."

"Do you know how he is?"

He shook his head. "The last report I was given was that he was in surgery and was currently stable. I'm sorry. I wish I knew more."

She blinked back the tears as she pulled off her boots and dumped out the water. "But he's alive. You're sure of that."

"As far as I know, yes." He took off his coat and wrapped it around her shoulders hoping to warm her up, then dug into the first-aid kit and pulled out an emergency thermal blanket for an extra layer of heat. He needed to get her dry and warm as soon as possible.

"How'd you find me?"

"Mitchell and Kyle went looking for you when they heard a woman's scream, figuring it had to be yours. They found their dad and eventually pieced together that you'd been kidnapped." He glanced down at his bloodstained jacket. "Are you sure none of this blood is yours? You've got a goose egg on your forehead next to a cut. You look like you've been in a fight. If there are other injuries . . ."

"There was a fight, but I won. He's in the boat."

Jack looked where she was pointing and caught sight of another boat partially hidden in the grass. A man was tied to one of the boat's metal rails. He glanced back at Bree. He wasn't sure how she'd done it, but he was impressed. She'd somehow taken the armed man down.

"When I heard your boat, I wasn't sure if you were the good guys or the bad guys. I decided not to take any chances until I knew for sure who was behind the wheel."

"That was a smart move."

He sat her down on one of the seats. They needed to deal with their suspect, but first he wanted to check her for injuries and signs of shock. Clammy skin, rapid pulse, enlarged pupils . . .

"I'm fine, Jack. Really."

He frowned. All he could see were a few bumps and bruises, but he was still going to insist she get checked out by a doctor, because her physical well-being wasn't the only thing he was worried about. Not only had she just survived a kidnapping, she'd also witnessed the shooting of someone close to her. And that in itself was traumatic.

Jack signaled to Beckett. "Try to maneuver closer so we can transfer the suspect into this boat."

"Yes, sir." Beckett started the engine again. "I've just informed our search base that we found her, along with the suspect."

"Good."

Bree pulled the blanket tighter around her shoulders as the boat started to move. "Whoever he was planning to meet is still out there. He spoke to a man named . . . Rudy. He was planning to hand me over to them."

"Well, that's not going to happen on my watch."

"His phone is in the console of the boat. I'm hoping there's a good chance there's evidence on it as to who's behind this."

He glanced out across the water, listening for the motor of another boat. He was impressed with how many details she was able to recall. With many victims, details disappeared because of the trauma. But he wasn't surprised. No doubt it was her attention to detail that had pushed her to the top in her class at the academy and eventually promoted her to detective.

He waited until they were close enough for him to step into the other boat, where their suspect sat tied to one of the metal handles, his jaw tense, and looking as if he was ready for another fight. Jack used his pocketknife to cut him free from the rail, then escorted him to the other boat.

"Search him, then secure him," Jack said to Beckett. "Is there a way to tow the boat back with us so we can keep any evidence secure?"

Beckett handcuffed their suspect to a seat, then picked up one of the boat lines. "I can rig a single bridle line and make sure we don't go too fast and overload the engine. We'll just have to make sure we spread the load, so we don't put too much of a strain on this one."

"Do it. I've got the boat's hull identification number, so they can start tracing it now."

A moment later, he was back in the police boat with the suspect's phone and a photo of the boat's ID. He put in a radio call to his brother.

"I just heard you found her," Adam said.

"I did, and I've also got a suspect in custody. Apparently he was planning to meet someone and hand her over to them. I don't have any details, other than another boat out there was planning to rendezvous with him."

"Copy that. Get back here as soon as you can. We'll put out an updated APB and find them."

"I'm texting you a photo of the boat's identification number so you can start tracking the boat's history. See what you can find."

"Do you know who he is?"

"No, but I plan to find out."

Jack ended the call as the two boats glided through the shallow water.

"Jack?"

He bent down next to Bree. "What can I get you?"

"Nothing." She glanced toward the bow at their suspect. "He wouldn't answer any questions, but I want to give it another try."

"He'll be questioned, I promise, but not by you."

Her frown deepened. "Why not? He shot Papps. I can't just let it go."

Jack squeezed her shoulder. "I'm not asking you to let it go. I'm just asking you to let me handle it right now."

She nodded, but her hands were shaking in front of her.

"Tell me what happened," he said.

"I'd been so excited about taking some time off and being here with Papps and his family," she said. "You know he's always been more of a father to me than my own father. We were just starting to head back to camp, and then . . . I heard a gunshot, and he went down. There was blood everywhere . . . all over him . . . all over me."

He took her wrist and felt her racing pulse. Her chest heaved as she fought for a breath.

"Bree." He squeezed her hands. "You're having a panic attack. I want you to take a slow, deep breath. I'm right here with you, and you're safe."

"He can't die, Jack."

"You know the doctors are doing everything they can to save him. As for the man who shot him, we'll get him to talk and find out what's behind all of this, but for right now, Bree . . . you're still shaking." He rubbed her arms, trying to get her circulation going again. "You need to get warmed up. Breathe slowly for me—long deep breaths—and let me handle things for now. Please."

"Then go talk to him. The sooner we get answers, the sooner we can find out who else is involved and put a stop to this. We need to know who they're looking for."

"I will, but you come first right now—"

"I'm okay."

He hesitated, not wanting to leave her. "Do you recognize him?"

"No. I've never seen him before." Bree rubbed her hands together. "Do you think an assassination attempt is what happened? Someone who doesn't like the senator's political positions?"

"That could be an explanation, but if that's true, why take you?"

"I haven't been able to put that together. I've had threats against me, but so has Papps. There are those who hate him just because he's in politics."

He opened the first-aid kit again, grabbed an antiseptic wipe, and started dabbing at the blood on her forehead. She winced at his touch but didn't pull away. Memories of the last time he'd seen her surfaced, but this wasn't the time or place to dig up memories of the girl he used to go biking with in Oso Creek Park and fishing with in the summertime.

Or the girl he'd started falling in love with.

He put on a dab of antibiotic cream and frowned. He'd always wondered what would have happened if he hadn't left. If he'd stayed and risked seeing what could have happened between them. But none of that mattered right now. What mattered was finding out who was behind all of this so he could keep her safe.

"Tell me again exactly what happened."

He could see the fear in her eyes, and the exhaustion. But there was a determination as well. He knew her well enough to know she wasn't going to just walk away from this. She was going to fight until she found out the truth. She was switching modes—from victim to survivor. Which meant that, as much as he wanted to protect her, she would want to be in on taking down whoever was behind all of this. The first step was to take her statement while everything was fresh on her mind.

"I was out before sunrise. The sky was beautiful with the stars. Papps knew where to find me. It's quiet, and he knows I like to soak it in before the day begins. We sat and talked for a while before it was time to go back to the blind. We'd just started walking when I heard a shot that sounded like it came from the northeast. It sounded close. At first I thought the hunt had officially started, but then Papps told me he'd been hit."

"Did you think it was simply an accidental shooting?"

"That was my immediate assumption. That it had been a stray bullet. But things didn't add up. It was a rifle instead of a shotgun, and the man who shot Papps not only used a silencer to muffle the sound, but definitely wasn't shooting in the direction of any waterfowl. Then when he grabbed me . . . I knew it hadn't been an accident. He'd shot Papps on purpose."

"What we don't know is why," Jack said.

"What's the working theory of the authorities at this point?" she asked.

"I'm not sure they have one. At least not until they're able to get your statement and question the shooter. Do you know anyone who would want to kill Senator McKenna?"

"I'm sure Papps has a list of enemies, and I think that's the right place to start, but I have no idea. He's enjoying retirement. His sons will know more specifics, but he's never mentioned any concerns to me about his safety." She reached out and grabbed his hand. "If you won't let me talk to this guy, then you go talk to him. Find out who he is. The more information we have, the quicker we'll be able to move on this."

Jack hesitated. "Are you sure you're okay?"

She nodded. "Shook up, yes, but I'm fine."

He stepped up next to Beckett at the wheel. "How much longer till we get back to the search base?"

"I'm having to take it slower than normal with the tow, but I'd say . . . ten minutes tops."

Jack moved to the front of the boat where Beckett had secured the man. Bree was right about one thing. The sooner they identified who he had planned to hand her off to, the easier it was going to be to find them. With dozens of boats out on the water on any given day, finding the second boat without having that information was nothing more than a shot in the dark at this point.

Jack sat down on the edge of the port side. "What's your name?"

The man stared out across the boat, ignoring him.

"Who were you planning to meet on the other boat?"

Still nothing.

"In case you aren't aware, we have in our possession the weapon that I believe will prove that you shot Senator McKenna. Which means you're going to be arrested not only for kidnapping, but for attempted murder as well. And if the senator dies . . ."

The only reaction was the slight tightening of the muscles in his jawline.

"From what I know so far, they hired you to either murder the senator or kidnap her, but unfortunately for you, neither sentence will have you out on parole for a very long time."

There was still no response, but this wasn't over. They'd

get him to talk *and* find out who was behind this. It was just a matter of time.

They were quiet the rest of the way, with only the familiar buzz of the flat-bottom motor rumbling beneath them until a dozen vehicles lining the shoreline came into view. Jack helped her out of the boat and onto the ramp where Adam was waiting for them.

"Bree . . . I am so, so sorry this happened. Are you okay?"

"I'm fine," Bree said, "but I need an update on the senator."

"The latest news I have is that he's stable and in surgery. I'll pass on anything else as soon as I hear it."

Adam signaled for a couple of the officers to secure the suspect and the boat, then turned back to them. "Anything out of your suspect?"

Jack shook his head. "He's refusing to speak right now."

"Here's the question we all have," Adam said. "Why shoot the senator and grab you?"

She shrugged. "I wish I knew. I've run the scenario over and over in my mind, and it always comes back to my connection with the senator. Leverage . . . ransom . . . I don't know. If this was a for-ransom kidnapping, I'm not worth anything financially on my own, but my relationship with him is no secret. Papps was like a father to me."

"As far as I know," Adam said, "there have been no ransom demands, but his sons as well as his office are putting a list together of potential enemies that we've already started going through."

Jack frowned. "That could be a long list. The man was in politics. No one gets away unscathed in that business, even in retirement."

"At least it gives us a place to start and hopefully something we can work with," Adam said.

Jack took a step back and caught Bree's gaze. "What if you were the target? You were the one grabbed, and you mentioned threats against you."

Bree hesitated before answering. "It is possible that everything that's happened is my fault."

"Your fault?" Jack asked. "Why?"

She drew in a deep breath before answering his question. "The threat I received was from a man my partner and I arrested a few days ago."

"Who was it?"

"You've probably heard of him. He's been in the news. His name is Nico Graves. He killed his wife and two children."

"I've been following his story," Jack said. "It was a sad case, though I didn't know you were one of the detectives involved. He's a guy who needed to be off the streets."

She shook her head. "The way he looked at me as they were taking him away, like he could see right through me. Like he hated me and planned for me to be his next victim."

"Did he say anything specifically to you?"

"He said he was going to send people over to my house to finish me off. He also claimed to know where a couple of the other detectives involved in the case lived."

"That's definitely not something we can ignore," Adam said.

"He's behind bars, but that doesn't mean he can't hire someone. And if Papps dies because of one of my cases . . ."

Jack heard her voice catch, and he reached out and squeezed her hand, wishing he could help her shake the guilt. "Don't even go there." He knew from experience that wasn't a place she needed to go. He turned to Adam. "Let whoever's in charge here know about Graves and get them to investigate that lead right away."

Adam nodded and walked away.

"If nothing else," Bree said, "with the gun and the phone, there's leverage to get him to cooperate. I started to question him, but he refused to talk, which means right now we need to—"

"Hold on, Bree." Jack held up his hand. "Before you come up with a long to-do list, the first place you're going is to get checked out by a doctor. You're going to need stitches at a minimum."

"Fine, but I need you to promise me one thing."

"I'll do my best."

"I want in on finding whoever's behind this."

Jack shook his head. "I can't make any promises."

"More than likely, they're going to rope the FBI into this, which means you'll have plenty of say. Not only was someone I love just shot, I'm trained to handle situations like this. There's no way I'll just sit around and watch this go down."

"You always were stubborn."

"Funny. I'm serious, Jack."

Shots rang out. Someone screamed.

"Gun!" Jack shouted, searching the shoreline for the shooter. "Everybody down, now!"

CHAPTER FIVE

JACK GRABBED BREE'S ARM and pulled her behind a large cement block, then glanced around it, trying to determine where the shots were coming from. There was only one response in a situation like this for law enforcement and first responders, and that was to locate and disarm the shooter. But Jack was pinned down and helpless. He watched a speedboat carry the gunman past the dock as he emptied another round of bullets. People screamed as they scrambled for cover. Then a second later, the shots stopped as suddenly as they had started.

Bree scrambled to her feet a split second before him. "They just shot our only lead."

Jack moved beside her out into the open. The boat had reversed course and was heading back out into deep water. And their prisoner lay motionless on the ground.

Adam was shouting into his radio for an ambulance. Another officer hurried to the fallen man and started assessing him while a pool of blood gathered beneath his head.

Bree ran for the shoreline and the police boat they'd just been in. "We need to go after them."

There was no time to make a plan. She was already halfway up the boat ramp. Jack followed her, determined she wasn't going to go after them alone. She was right that they needed to find the men behind this, but they also needed a strategy. He still had his weapon, but she was unarmed, shifting any odds against them. Ten seconds later, he was following her orders and untying the stern and bow lines while she started the engine, thankful someone had already untied the boat they'd been towing.

Adam jumped into the stern of the boat as the engine roared to life. "Go!"

Bree maneuvered away from the dock, then sped across the water in the direction of the shooters.

"What just happened back there?" Adam shouted above the noise of the motor.

"I have no idea, but our suspect got caught in the middle."

"Or maybe, like you and the senator, he was targeted."

There was no way to determine the motivation at this point—other than someone had to have wanted to silence the man—but from what Jack had seen, he was pretty sure the perpetrators had swept in and done exactly what they'd planned to do before leaving. And that was to kill their suspect.

Bree gripped the helm. "How fast can this thing go?"

"You should be able to get at least sixty knots out of it. Which is hopefully faster than their boat."

Jack stood beside her, surprised at the feelings of protection sweeping through him at the sight of her stepping into danger. He didn't want her out here risking her life, but he knew he was wrong to be worried. Bree wasn't the teenage best friend he remembered from over a decade ago. She was trained to handle a situation like this and knew exactly what she was doing. He remembered her as being carefree and even a bit impulsive, but her instincts had almost always been dead-on.

But as proficient as she was, he also knew she'd been through a trauma this morning. Not only had she watched someone shoot her father figure right in front of her, she'd been grabbed and kidnapped. What she'd gone through would disturb even a seasoned law enforcement officer. He glanced at her and caught the determination in her face. She'd be okay, but at some point she would have to face what had just happened and the emotional repercussions she wouldn't be able to ignore.

Adam stood to the side, holding on to one of the grab rails while talking with his supervisor and requesting another boat along with a helicopter for backup. They skimmed across the water with the enemy boat racing ahead of them in the shallow waters. Law enforcement used these sleek boats because of their lightweight design, speed, and maneuverability in both shallow and rough waters, but it was going to take skill to catch up with the other boat and ensure no one was hurt in the process. But if anyone could outmaneuver the enemy, Bree could.

He turned to his brother. "Are they sending backup?"

"There's a second boat behind us, and the chopper's five minutes out."

Jack shook his head. "That won't be good enough. They'll be long gone by then if we don't get them first."

"Then we better be prepared for a confrontation."

Adam unlocked one of the storage compartments and pulled

out a handgun and two rifles. He shoved the handgun into his back holster and set one of the rifles next to Bree.

"Glad you're on our team," he said.

She glanced down at her camo jacket and pants. "I might not be in uniform, but I'm ready for a fight."

Jack stared out across the water. The other boat had vanished. "Do you see him?"

"He slipped out of view," she said, "but he should be just beyond that next bend."

They sped along the water, still with no sign of the other boat. Jack felt his neck muscles tense. There were miles of inlets in this area, and many of them didn't allow motor-driven boat traffic. Which meant the sound of a motor should stand out.

Jack squeezed her shoulder. "Turn off the motor."

She nodded, then shut it down and let the boat coast across the water. They listened for the other boat. There were dozens of inlets and coves where a boat could slip in and disappear. The familiar sounds of ducks and other birds played out around them. Finally, he heard the sound of a motor humming ahead of them. Jack signaled toward the east.

"Got 'em."

Bree maneuvered across the water toward the sound. She'd always been the outdoor type, and clearly that hadn't changed. She was still just as smart and competent. And just as beautiful.

He thrust aside the thought as she pushed on the throttle and upped their speed. He grabbed the binoculars in front of him, equipped with a digital camera, and turned on the image stabilizer.

"Can you see them?" Adam asked.

"I found them."

He studied the horizon, then zoomed in, looking for any kind of distinguishing marks that might lead to identifying either the boat or its driver.

"We need to get closer, but I've got two males in my sites. Both Asian and both armed."

"Any markings on the boat?" Adam asked.

"Nothing identifiable from the back. It's an older model . . . a Sanger flat bottom. There's no way to read the hull identification number at this distance. But wait a minute . . ."

The boat was turning slightly, following the route of the narrow waterway. "There's a number and name on the side of the boat. Two . . . five . . . seven . . . And the name is *White Pearl*."

"Got it." Adam passed on the information to his captain back on shore, along with an update on their position. "Now we just have to hope the boat's not stolen."

Jack stared through the binoculars. The men were shouting at each other, arms flailing, like they were in a heated conversation. One of them stepped to the bow of the boat and pulled out a couple of automatic weapons.

"What have you got?" Adam asked.

"They've taken at least two more automatic weapons from their storage hold," Jack said.

"What do you want me to do?" Bree asked.

She waited as Adam relayed her question to his captain.

"Captain McClure wants us to hold our position. Keep them in our sites but wait for backup before we engage with them."

"Roger that."

Jack steadied himself beside her, still keeping tabs on the men through the binoculars. But he was worried about her. There hadn't been time for her to process anything that had happened this morning. And in reality, she needed to be at the hospital right now, being checked out, not chasing their suspects. He glanced at her and caught her tense expression. She had to be exhausted mentally, but also emotionally.

Jack kept his gaze on the enemy boat but his attention on Bree. "Do you think they made the wrong call?" he asked. "Having us wait for backup?"

She shook her head. "I know they're right. If we go in now, someone's going to get hurt. But I just . . . I just can't stop thinking about Papps. He was losing so much blood. I'm afraid he's not going to make it."

"I know. And I'm so sorry."

As much as he wanted to, he couldn't promise her Papps would be okay. Or that any of this was going to turn out okay for that matter. There was simply no way to know. What he did know was that she was strong, and as hard as the situation was, she was trained for it—facing the enemy instead of running away.

"But the bottom line is that even if Nico is behind this," he said, "this is not your fault."

"I know." She frowned. "On one level at least. I just can't stop seeing Papps's face after he'd been shot, and wondering how he is."

"We'll get you there as soon as we can. I promise."

"Jack . . ." They were still at least a hundred yards behind the second boat. Close enough to monitor them, but far enough away to ensure they were safe until backup came. "What are they doing?"

He held up the binoculars again and studied the boat. One of the men was opening up a storage console in the stern of the boat. He pulled something out, then hoisted the weapon up onto his shoulder before turning around and facing them. Jack's heart pounded as his mind unscrambled what he was seeing. This wasn't just another automatic weapon. And they were aiming at the boat.

"Adam . . . Bree . . . they've got some kind of grenade launcher."

"A what?"

"We need to jump—now!"

He heard a whizzing sound streaming toward them. Bree jumped away from the console and into the water. He was right behind her, but a second before he hit the water, the boat exploded into a ball of flames.

CHAPTER SIX

AUBREY STUMBLED TO FIND her footing on the seabed as she broke the surface of the shallow water. She drew in a deep breath, then let it out slowly. She could feel the heat of the burning boat as she tried to orient herself, but everything around her was spinning. She shook her head, needing to stop her ears from ringing from the explosion, while at the same time trying to blink away the burning in her eyes from the smoke.

With the waves lapping at her waist, she widened her stance a few inches in order to help keep her balance and stared out across the water, her vision finally starting to come into focus. Smoke spiraled upward from their boat, still burning on top of the water. There was no sign of the boat they'd been after, but that didn't surprise her. She didn't expect them to stay around and watch the spectacle. No doubt they were long gone.

Adam shouted from behind her. "Aubrey! Are you okay?"

"Adam." She turned around, then looked down to where he was staring at a long trickle of blood running down her forearm. "It's nothing, where's Jack?"

"I don't know."

She turned slowly in a circle, searching for him. A few seconds ago, he'd been beside her, warning her of what was about to happen—and saving their lives. But now . . . Where was he?

"Jack!" she screamed as she searched the water in front of her and the thick reeds bordering the shoreline. "Jack!"

Panic bubbled up inside her. He had to be here. Had to be okay. Debris from the boat floated past her as flakes of black ash rained down on them. Her vision was getting better, but there was still no sign of him.

"Adam . . . I don't see him."

"I don't either."

The panic in Adam's voice reflected her own. She bit her lip and fought to breathe. This couldn't be happening. Papps had been shot, and now they couldn't find Jack. If he'd been hit by the grenade, was somehow still on the boat . . . On the boat. That's where he had to be. If the grenade had hit before he could jump clear—

She shoved away the terrifying possibilities, focusing only on finding Jack. She shouted at Adam, "We've got to check the boat."

She trudged through the water toward the boat, a thickening, heavy smoke burning her eyes. She was shaking, as much from fear and shock as from the cold. Twenty yards away, the remains of the boat continued to burn, flames licking around the console as the fire spread vigorously across the fiberglass frame.

She pulled her drenched neck gaiter up around her mouth and nose in an attempt to block the smoke. He had to be nearby.

He'd been right behind her when she jumped, and she thought he'd gone over with her.

"Aubrey!" Adam shouted. "He's here . . . near the shoreline."

She shifted direction. She'd dumped the water out of her boots when they'd arrived back on shore, but now they were filled again, making walking through the water awkward. She slipped them off and swam hard for the shoreline.

They found him wedged against the shoreline, his body twisted while he fought to keep his head above water.

"Jack . . . Jack, are you okay?"

"I'm okay, but my leg's caught on something, and I can't get loose."

"Hold on." She dove beneath the water to investigate. A few seconds later she came up for air. "It looks like it's caught on some fishing lines in the underbrush. I'll go back under and try to untangle you."

Jack caught her gaze. "Just be careful. Please."

She turned to Adam. "Have you got a knife?"

He dug into his front pants pocket and pulled out a Swiss Army knife. "Always."

She glanced back at the boat burning behind them. Orange flames licked at the structure as she opened the knife. "We've got to hurry. If the flames hit the gas tank . . ."

She didn't have to finish her sentence. They all knew exactly what she was thinking.

"How much time do you think we have?" Jack asked.

"I don't know." Adam shook his head. "The fire's moving fast."

And the growing fire wasn't the only issue. The current was

strong, and it wouldn't take much to pull their feet out from under them, especially in places where the bottom was slippery.

She drew in a deep breath, then dove beneath the surface of the water. Her eyes burned when she opened them. Sediment floated in front of her, making it hard to see. She reached for Jack's leg and felt the thin line that was entangled around him on one end and a fallen log beneath the waterline on the other end. She unfolded the blade, then started to cut the line away from his leg, pausing as her fingers hit a fishing hook stuck into his calf. She felt his muscles flinch as she carefully pulled out the metal barb. A few seconds later, he was free.

She came up for air, then motioned for Jack to follow her away from the boat that was still burning.

Adam helped steady her. "Are you okay?"

"Yes." She glanced back at the burning boat. "We need to get out of here."

They swam downstream another twenty yards, then stopped. Adam climbed up onto the shoreline and helped both of them out of the water.

She sat down in the soggy mud between Jack and Adam, thankful that at least she was out of the water and that they were farther from the burning boat. A moment later, a second explosion rocked the boat as the gas tank ignited. Debris shot into the air again along with more thick smoke.

Jack pulled her shivering body close to him as she stared at what remained of the boat. "That was way too close for comfort. Are you okay?"

She nodded, trying to stop her teeth from chattering. "Wet and cold, but okay. What about your leg?"

He reached down and pulled up his pant leg. There were five or six scrapes and a bloody hole where she'd pulled out the fishing barb, but nothing that had to be dealt with right now. "How far behind is the second boat?"

"Last I spoke with them," Adam said, "they were about five minutes behind us. And no doubt they saw the explosion."

"You still think Nico Graves is behind this?" Jack asked.

She shook her head. "We certainly can't rule him out, but I can't see him arranging something this complex, especially when it would be easier to get me in Houston."

"I can't either," Jack said. "But from the little I know about the case, he got away with murder for a long time, and the extent of his criminal involvement is still unknown."

"That's true."

But everything that had happened over the past few hours had seemed planned and thought out. Nico wasn't like that. The paid sniper, a grenade launcher . . . Clearly there was more involved in this than they presently understood.

"What about security for the senator?" she asked, turning to Adam.

"A detail's already been arranged."

Jack squeezed her hand. "He's going to be okay. And we're going to get to the bottom of this."

The sound of a motorboat broke into their conversation. The backup police boat approached the shore. Moments later, she was climbing into the bow in front of Adam and Jack. Smoke still filled the air as the fire burned down.

"I'm Lieutenant Perez and this is Sergeant Lowe."

Adam quickly made the introductions.

"We just saw the explosion. What happened?"

"The boat we were after hit us with some kind of grenade launcher."

The lieutenant took a step back. "A grenade launcher?"

"Apparently, we got too close," Jack said, "and they decided to take us out."

"The three of you are lucky to be alive."

"Tell me about it," Adam said. "What about our suspect?"

"A bullet grazed the side of his head, and he's still alive. He's being transported as we speak for observation, but the paramedics on the scene believe the damage is minimal, barring any complications like a concussion."

"Have you been able to identify him yet?" Aubrey asked.

"No, and he's refusing to talk."

The sergeant took the helm while the lieutenant handed each of them a first-aid blanket. "We're sending the helo out to do an aerial search, but it's not going to be easy to find them. Did you get a good look at any of them?"

Jack wrapped the blanket around his shoulders. "I doubt the binocular photos are recoverable, but I got a good look at the men and the boat. Both men appeared to be Asian. At least one had tattoos down his arm."

"Any identifying marks on the boat?"

"We called it in earlier. It was named the *White Pearl*."

"Hopefully that will help us find it."

A flood of emotions rose to the surface, but she managed to push them aside and settle into the seat next to Jack.

He nudged her with his shoulder. "We make a pretty good team."

"Losing suspects together?"

"Well, if you insist on looking at it that way . . ."

She smiled. He'd always been able to make her smile. It was a reminder of how much she'd missed him. Made her wonder why she hadn't tried to stay in touch.

He tugged on the edge of her emergency blanket, pulling it tighter around her shoulders. "I haven't thanked you yet for saving my life."

"Honestly, it was a tough call, but I decided I couldn't let you stay out there all tangled up in that fishing line. There aren't a lot of gators in this area, but I know there are stingrays, and they can be pretty painful if they get ahold of you."

"Very funny. And I was just about to pay you a compliment."

"Which was?" she asked.

"Hmm . . . I'm not sure you deserve a compliment after that."

She laughed. She'd even missed his constant teasing.

"I was just going to say that I've noticed you haven't lost any of your spunk," he said. "You were the one who took off after those guys before anyone else had barely reacted."

Her eyes widened. "Spunk? Really?"

"Wrong word?" he asked.

"Maybe it was the right word back when I was fourteen, but now . . . yeah, it seems like the wrong word. I was doing my job."

"I've never seen you in action, so what I should have said is that I'm impressed."

"Impressed?" She shot him a broad smile. "Maybe embarrassed is a more appropriate word, since you had a hard time catching up with me when I ran for the boat."

"Now I'm the one who needs to question your choice of words."

"I'm just saying, I did have to wait for you to get on board." She laughed, but her smile turned serious. "Have I told you that despite everything that has happened today, how good it is to see you?"

"I agree, though if someone told me I'd run into you today, I never would have believed it. I've missed you, Bree. It's been too long."

"It has."

"Maybe when this is all over . . . maybe we can catch up. Hang like we used to."

"I'd like that."

She tried to interpret whatever it was that was passing between them. Or maybe it was nothing, and her imagination was working overtime. But she didn't ever remember him looking at her that way, and she wasn't sure what he was really thinking.

Jack cleared his throat and shifted his gaze to her forehead. "You need to get to the hospital and get stitched up. You look like you've been in the boxing ring."

"How bad is it?"

"Well . . ." He leaned forward. "Your eye's a light shade of pink, but I'm sure within a day or two it will be purple. You could always add a bit of eye shadow to the other side, so they match. As for the cut, I'm sure a couple stitches should be enough."

Her hand automatically went up and touched her forehead. She winced.

"Does it hurt?" he asked.

"Only if I touch it."

"At least it stopped bleeding."

She shifted her gaze and stared out across the water. It seemed crazy how just a few hours ago she'd been quietly watching the sunrise, thankful for a few days off, and now everything had spiraled out of control. She had no idea who was after her, or who had shot Papps. But what she did know was that she was glad Jack was here with her.

She watched the dock come into view as the driver slowed down and eased the boat alongside the wooden structure. There were still several police cars, at least two unmarked ones, as well as an ambulance waiting along the shoreline.

She grabbed the arm of the captain who was waiting for them at the dock, as he helped her out of the boat. "Do you have an update on the senator's condition?"

"All I know is that he's still in surgery. They were expecting it to take a couple hours."

She dropped her arms to her sides, frustrated at the lack of information. But at least he was alive.

Thank you for that, God.

"What about his family?"

"They're all either there or on their way."

"And our suspect that was shot?" Jack asked.

"The doctor wants to keep him a few more hours for observation to make sure there's no concussion before he's transferred to the jail."

"I want to talk to him," Adam said.

"We'll get to that, but at the moment, I want each one of you checked out by a doctor at the hospital. That was far too close a call."

CHAPTER SEVEN

AT HALF PAST TEN Aubrey examined the stitches on her forehead above her left eyebrow in the emergency room bathroom, hoping they wouldn't leave a scar. But a scar seemed insignificant at the moment. All she cared about right now was seeing Papps and making sure he was okay. She pulled a jean jacket over the white shirt and black jeans Adam's wife had brought for her, along with a pair of short boots, then tossed the bloody clothes she'd been wearing in the garbage. A sickening feeling washed over her as she stepped away from the trash can. The ruined clothes weren't reminders she needed right now.

She stepped out of the bathroom, surprised to see Jack standing there. "I wasn't sure if you were still here."

"I wanted to make sure you're okay."

"How do you like my battle scars?" She pulled back her hair to reveal three even stitches.

"Let's just say I'd hate to tangle with you in some dark alley. You always could hold your own and today proved that."

She chuckled. "What about you?"

"Beyond a couple scrapes on my legs from the fish hook, I'm fine."

Her smile faded. "Have you heard an update on Papps? One of the nurses promised to check for me, but I'm still waiting."

"I spoke with the nurse liaison on my way here."

Her pulse picked up. "How is he?"

"He's out of surgery and in his own room. They recovered the bullet, repaired the wound, and made sure there's no further internal bleeding. The next twenty-four hours will be telling, but the doctor is optimistic that he'll make a full recovery."

She sighed with relief. "He's a fighter. He'll make it."

Because he had to. Grant McKenna was the closest thing to family she had. And losing him . . . well, that just wasn't an option.

"Can I see him?"

"I asked about that as well, and you can, but only for a few minutes. I'll also see if he recognizes our shooter at the same time, since they're wanting to limit his visitors for the next twenty-four hours."

"Thank you for finding out for me."

"Of course. His family is gathered in the waiting room up on the third floor right now. You can see them after you visit Papps." Jack cupped his hand around her elbow as they started for the row of elevators. "They wanted me to assure you if you needed anything else to let them know, and that you're welcome to stay at the house as long as you want."

"I appreciate that. They've always been so good to me."

Jack pushed the button for the third floor, and she leaned against the elevator wall, facing him.

66

"How are you doing?" she asked him. "This has been a tough few hours for you too, even though it could have been a lot worse."

"I know. For both of us. And I'm fine."

"I almost lost both you and Papps."

He reached out and squeezed her hand. "But you didn't."

She blinked back the tears, hating the feelings of vulnerability she was trying to combat. "It's strange being on the other side. I'm used to being the one helping the victims. Now I *am* the victim, trying to work out in my mind what just happened, and why they took me."

"I know you're strong, Bree, but don't dismiss the impact of what just happened. It's easy to suppress trauma in our profession. If we do, it will end up affecting our lives, our careers, and the lives of those around us. And when it's personal, like this was . . ."

She glanced at him and met his gaze. "I know, and I won't."

"One other thing. As soon as we're done here, I've been asked to escort you down to the police station so they can get an official statement from you."

"You know I want to do anything I can to find out who did this, but an FBI escort?" She shook her head. "Isn't that a bit excessive?"

"You can call this an unofficial escort if you'd like, but you were kidnapped, Bree. Even if the senator was the target, you're still involved. And until we know what's going on, I, for one, am not willing to take any chances. Besides, once you're done there, I thought it might give us a chance to go out for lunch and catch up under more . . . normal circumstances."

Normal. She let out a low laugh. Today had been anything but normal. "I'd like that."

But she couldn't shake what he'd said. People who dealt with trauma on a daily basis—like law enforcement, the military, and emergency personnel—often struggled to erase the images they'd seen, only to find themselves replaying the violence over and over in their minds. Still, it was hard to interpret her own feelings. Her nerves were on edge, and she couldn't press down the adrenaline that was still running through her. But just because this was personal didn't mean she could let fear take hold.

The doors opened on the third floor. She stepped out of the elevator and followed Jack down the hallway. It was a fine line she was determined to stay on the right side of—the one that separated being a victim from being a survivor.

She glanced at Jack's lean profile. There was an added air of confidence to the strong, down-to-earth personality she remembered. She'd always known he'd go far, and he'd clearly excelled. She still wasn't sure how they'd grown so far apart after all the years they'd spent as best friends. Her memories of high school and college were late-night study sessions and hanging out on weekends when he always managed to make her laugh so hard she snorted.

And then she'd started dating Adam.

That was when the shift had begun.

At the time, she wondered what Jack would think about her decision and even confronted him about it one afternoon over a box of macaroni and cheese. He shrugged any concerns off like it was no big deal and told her she'd always be his best friend, and who she dated wasn't going to change that.

But he was wrong. Nothing was ever really the same between them after that. He decided to move away, and eventually their communication became less and less. She broke things off with Adam, but while she and Adam managed to salvage their friendship, she always felt as if she lost Jack in the process. Something she always regretted.

She stopped next to him in front of Papps's room, knowing she was going to have to leave the past where it belonged. All of what happened between her and Jack had taken place years ago, and while she was thankful for a chance to catch up with him, he would make sure she got to the police station safely, then go back to work on the case that had brought him down to Corpus in the first place. And that's the way it should be.

Jack waited in the doorway while she walked inside the room where Papps lay. Machines beeped quietly behind him. His face and lips were pale, and they'd put him on oxygen. But he was alive. It was hard to believe that only a few hours ago they'd been sitting out beneath the night sky, talking about the past and looking forward to a morning of duck hunting. Now he was lying here, fighting for his life. *I need to find out who did this, Jesus. Please show me what to do.*

She sat down on the bed and took his hand, noticing the age spots and prominent veins. He'd always been a rock to her. Someone who knew how to stay grounded no matter what was going on around him. Today reminded her that he was as vulnerable as anyone else.

He looked up at her and smiled.

"Papps . . . I'm so, so sorry."

"Me too." He drew in a slow breath. "Thankfully, they were

able to patch me up and they told me I should make it, but what about you? I heard you scream—"

"I'm fine. Really."

"You don't look fine." He reached up and brushed her hair away from her forehead where the stitches were. "What did he do to you?"

"There was a fight, but I won."

"Did you find out who he is?"

"The authorities are still looking for answers, but he's in custody." She was worried what would happen if Papps started getting worked up. In order to recover, he needed to rest, and getting agitated wouldn't help. "They'll figure out what happened."

"I talked to the police right before I went into surgery," he said.

"You don't need to worry about that right now."

"But I do. I'm to blame for what happened out there to you. This is my fault."

"This is anything but your fault." She shook her head. "I'm heading down to the police station right now to give my statement. I'll be back later. I promise."

"I just don't want anything to happen to you. You're like a daughter to me."

Aubrey blinked back the tears. "And you've been a father to me. You've always made me feel like I was a part of your family. Always made me feel like I had a place to belong. But for now, all that matters is that you're alive, and that the doctors are expecting a full recovery."

"Senator McKenna?" Jack had stepped up next to her, holding his phone. "I'm glad to see that you're out of surgery and recovering, sir."

"It's good to see you again, Jack. I heard from someone that you're an FBI agent now?"

"Yes, I am, sir. I wondered if I could ask you a couple quick questions."

"Of course."

"I understand you spoke briefly to the police before you went into surgery, but that you weren't able to remember much of anything."

"That's true."

"Have you been able to remember anything more since then?"

Papps shook his head. "I wish I could have told them more, but I never saw anything. One moment we were enjoying the sunrise and the next moment I realized I'd been shot."

Jack nodded. "I understand. They're not going to let us stay much longer, so I just have one more question. Do you recognize this man?" He handed the senator his cell phone.

"Is that the man who shot me?"

Jack nodded.

Papps studied the photo. "He doesn't look familiar. I'm typically good with names, but I've come into contact with so many people over the years . . ." He shook his head. "No, I don't recognize him."

Jack slipped the phone back into his pocket. "That's okay. We'll figure out who he is."

Papps caught Aubrey's gaze. "You've never seen him either?"

She shook her head. "No."

"My sons are working to provide the police with a list of potential suspects, but it's going to take a while."

Jack held up his hand. "The authorities have a couple of leads and are searching for whoever is behind this, so all you need to think about right now is getting better."

"I agree." One of the nurses stepped into the room and stopped at the foot of the bed. "I'm sorry, but I have to ask the two of you to leave. The senator needs to rest."

Aubrey glanced at Jack. "Of course."

Papps reached for her hand and squeezed it. "Just promise me two things before you go."

"Anything."

"Be careful, and until they find out what's going on, don't take any risks."

She kissed him on the cheek, then smiled. "You know I'll do both."

"Take care of her, Special Agent Shannon."

"Yes, sir. I will."

They left the room and headed toward the waiting room where the family had gathered. Aubrey sighed. "It's hard seeing him so weak. He's always been such a rock to me and now . . . and now he almost died."

"You were right. He's a tough old man. I have a feeling this isn't going to stop him for long."

"Jack . . ." Adam strode through the waiting room door toward them.

"Hey, Adam, what have you got?"

"I have some news. We've just identified the senator's shooter. His name is Thomas Hwang. It'll take some time, but we're working to identify the contacts in his phone." Adam handed Aubrey a piece of paper. "In the meantime, I need to know if you recognize any of these names. I'll have the senator look through them as well."

She scanned the page, then shook her head. "I don't recognize any of them, but I would like to cross-reference them with my recent cases so I don't miss something."

"Of course. You can keep this and get back to me if you find a connection."

Jack took a step forward, his hand out. "Can I look at them?"

"Sure." Aubrey handed him the paper.

"You said Thomas Hwang?"

"Yes," Adam said.

"His face wasn't familiar, but I recognize the name."

"Who is he?" Aubrey asked.

"He's wanted for questioning by the FBI. He's suspected of being part of a network that recruits US citizens in order to steal intelligence and military secrets." Jack's brow furrowed as he handed the list back to her. "Thomas Hwang is a spy, and one of the reasons I'm here."

CHAPTER EIGHT

JACK'S MIND SCRAMBLED to put together the pieces of the bizarre coincidence as Adam pulled them into the empty prayer room filled with a dozen padded chairs and a stained-glass window in the front. The connection between his case and Bree was something he wanted to dismiss, except the facts were staring him in the face. Thomas Hwang was the man who'd shot the senator and snatched Bree. And he was on the list of suspects he'd come here to find.

Jack had worked the case for the past thirteen months. Two days ago, they finally caught a solid lead, and he ended up flying here in order to chase it down. So while he had no idea how the two cases were related, there had to be a connection.

"Jack . . . Jack?"

Jack's attention shifted to his brother. "Sorry."

"I'm just trying to figure out what you're saying. You believe there's a connection between the case that brought you here and what happened this morning?"

"I know it sounds crazy, but yes. He's part of what we call the Albatross File."

"What's that?" Bree asked.

"We've been working on a series of threats where the Chinese are targeting US intelligence. We discovered a spy ring that's using a secure source-messaging browser to share files and documents. The setup is actually a bit old school, but they create a chatroom and have other users join them. The chat names and usernames are always birds."

"Thus the Albatross File," Adam said.

Jack nodded. "Once we discovered how they were communicating, we started working on a way to decode what they were doing. Tracking them down has been difficult, but a couple days ago I got a lead that several of them were here in Corpus. The problem is, we don't have real names or any photos."

"So you came here to see if you could track them down," Bree said.

"Yes, but when I met up with Adam for breakfast, and he told me you were missing . . . I couldn't exactly leave when I found out."

"Have you thought that it could simply be a coincidence?" Bree sat down on one of the cushioned chairs and rested her arms against her thighs. "There's got to be dozens of Thomas Hwangs. And you mentioned selling secrets, and spies, but I can assure you the senator is no traitor and would never get involved with someone like that."

Jack paused before continuing, not ready to make any assumptions at this point. "I'm not implying he's involved, but I do believe it's possible he was in the wrong place at the wrong time. Maybe both of you were. I'm just looking at the facts. Just like we can't yet rule out the possibility of Nico being involved. But if there is a connection with the Albatross File, and if we can finally get our hands on a list of names through Hwang's phone . . ."

He hesitated again, the worry in Bree's eyes evident. He knew how much the senator had meant to her and her mother growing up, and she'd never believe he could betray his country unless the facts were indisputable. He just needed to ensure they looked at all the facts before coming to any conclusions.

"Let's look at what we do know." She leaned back in the chair, clearly exhausted, and yet not ready to back out of the fight. "All of this has seemed targeted and planned. Shooting Papps, my abduction, and even the drive-by at the dock."

"I have to agree," Adam said. "You were off the beaten path when the senator was shot, but it definitely seemed planned."

"What about the boats?" Jack asked.

Adam frowned. "Unfortunately, both boats they used were stolen."

Jack could tell Bree was trying to distance herself from the situation and look at it objectively, but that wasn't possible, and they both knew it.

"What about the photos Jack took?" Bree asked. "Were you able to identify the men?"

"Not yet. The pictures are being run through facial recognition software."

Jack made a quick decision. "I need to talk to Hwang. Alone."

Adam shrugged. "I'm not sure I'm the one who can arrange that. Technically, I'm not in charge anymore."

"Then I can arrange it." He pulled out his FBI badge and held it up. "If there's even a hint that he's connected to my case—which there is—the FBI is officially getting involved."

TWENTY MINUTES LATER, Jack walked into the room where their prisoner was handcuffed to the metal frame of his hospital bed. The intended kill shot had missed its target and was going to leave a nasty scar, but at least he wasn't going to die from it. Which Jack was thankful for. He also hoped that any pain medicine the man had been given wasn't going to impede his memory or his judgment.

Jack sat down beside the bed. There was a bandage covering the spot where the bullet had struck and a bruise on Hwang's cheek where Bree had managed to hit her target. After his day, the man was lucky to be alive.

"I'm FBI Special Agent Jack Shannon. We met out on the boat a couple hours ago after you kidnapped Detective Grayson."

The man's jaw twitched, but he just continued staring straight ahead.

"Here's the thing," Jack said. "You might believe, like you did earlier on the boat, that keeping silent is somehow going to make all of this go away, but you're wrong. We know you shot the senator, and we know you kidnapped Aubrey Grayson. There's no question about either of those. On top of that— you're going to think this is humorous, or at the least a crazy coincidence—I've been looking for you in connection to a Chinese spy ring. So if I were to do a bit of calculating, I'd say that the charges that are about to be brought against you will probably add up to life in prison. Not to mention the fact that someone tried to assassinate you this morning. With all that against you, I'm not sure silence is your friend right now."

Piercing black eyes stared straight ahead. "You don't know anything."

"That's where you're wrong. I actually know quite a bit about you, believe it or not. I've just had trouble tracking you down. I know how you've been working to grow your government's network of contacts in the US and how you've passed on hundreds of trade secrets of classified projects to your superiors."

That got his attention.

"Surprised to hear that?" Jack asked. "You're not as anonymous as you think you are. What I didn't know—until this moment—was how to find you. But my lead paid off and here you are, handcuffed to a bed with the DA ready to charge you with both attempted murder and kidnapping, and I'm ready to add to the charges."

"You're lying."

Jack moved directly into the man's line of vision. "Your code name is Blackthroat, and your boss uses you to do his dirty work because he trusts you implicitly. You're what we call a lackey. What I want to know is, why Aubrey Grayson?"

Hwang shook his head, but Jack didn't miss the beads of sweat running along his forehead. "You've got it all wrong. I was out duck hunting, and I saw this girl. She stumbled and almost fell into the water. I was trying to get her help. I don't know anything about the man who was shot."

"And that nasty bruise on your cheek? How did you get that?"

"She fought me."

"I'm not buying your story, and neither will the DA. So let's cut to the chase."

Hwang turned his head and caught Jack's gaze. "Like I said,

you don't know anything. I was just an innocent bystander trying to help."

"The problem with your story is that we have evidence that links you to the shooting. A bullet from your gun and gunpowder residue on your hands."

"This is nothing more than a setup."

"We both know that's not true." Jack stood up and leaned over the bed, letting a long silence fall between them. "You've got yourself in quite a lot of trouble. And if there is any chance at all of you spending even a day outside of prison before you die, now's the time to start talking. I know a lot about you, but you're not the one the FBI really wants. If you'll agree to cooperate, I can see about getting you a deal."

Hwang's knuckles turned white where he was gripping the sheet. "I don't need a deal."

"Really? Because we also both know someone wants you dead. That was no accidental shot out there on the pier. That was an assassination attempt, and I'm assuming someone you work for wants you silenced. If they hadn't missed, you wouldn't be here, you'd be in the morgue. But we can always put you out there on the streets and see who comes for you again. You might not be so lucky the second time."

Hwang tugged on his handcuff, clearly worried.

Jack had just found the man's vulnerability.

Now he needed to find out how Senator McKenna and Bree were involved.

"Maybe I do need police protection."

"Finally we agree on something. But you can't possibly think I'm going to give you police protection without you giving me something. It doesn't work that way. If I were you, I would seriously start thinking about my current situation and my need to start cooperating."

Hwang drew in a slow breath and caught Jack's gaze. "What do you want to know?"

"Two things to begin with. Who do you work for, and what did they pay you to do?"

"I was sent to grab her."

Jack noted the evasion of question number one. "So the senator wasn't the target?"

Hwang shook his head.

"Then why shoot him?"

"That wasn't a part of the plan. She was alone at first. When I got into position, the senator showed up—except I didn't know who he was. I knew the hunting day was about to start and thought no one would notice anything unusual. I just wanted to get the woman and get out."

Jack felt his patience begin to ebb. "Explain. I need to know how she's connected to all of this."

"A few months ago, we discovered a problem with some of the intel we were buying from a certain asset. If you know the men I work for as much as you say you do, you'll know as well that if you betray them, they'll hunt you down and kill you."

Jack worked to put things together, but nothing made sense. He could no more believe that Bree was involved with selling government secrets than the senator. And yet for some reason she was in the middle of all this.

"Our asset's handler needed to confront him, so he set up a

rendezvous like they had dozens of times before, but this time the asset didn't show up."

"And you were sent in to ensure he showed up."

Hwang nodded. "If he intentionally double-crossed us . . ."

They'd hunt him down and kill him.

"What's this asset's name?"

Hwang hesitated.

"Do I have to remind you again that I'm your only friend right now?" Jack said.

"His name is Charles Ramsey. If he's smart—and we know he is—he'll have an escape route already charted."

"Does he have a code name?"

"Junco."

Jack frowned. That name had been on their list. And if he was planning to disappear, they needed to find him before he could. His options were limited, but if he had the right documents—a social security card or other form of ID—how hard would it be for someone who had spent years in intelligence to simply vanish? But at the moment, Jack was more interested in Bree.

"You still haven't told me why Detective Grayson was your target."

Hwang hesitated. "We needed something to, let's say, *persuade* the asset to come to a meeting."

Jack gripped the rails on the side of the bed and put his face inches from Hwang's. "What does that have to do with Aubrey Grayson?"

Hwang laid back on his pillows. "We took her for leverage."

A sick feeling spread in Jack's stomach. "Why?"

"Aubrey Grayson is Charles Ramsey's daughter."

CHAPTER NINE

AUBREY SAT IN A PADDED CHAIR in the front row of the small chapel and stared up at the stained-glass window. She'd spent the past fifteen minutes praying. For Papps and his family, for Jack, for answers . . .

Jack.

Seeing him again reminded her of the things she missed about him. His smile, his sense of humor, his dedication. It seemed crazy he'd been the one who found her out there on the water, and even more crazy that he thought there was a connection between her abduction and his FBI case. How was that even possible? All she could do was keep praying that Thomas Hwang had answers for them.

"Aubrey?"

She turned around to see Adam walking in with a couple bags of fast food in one hand and a drink carrier in the other. "Hey."

"I heard you were still here. Thought you might be hungry."

She stood up and started down the short aisle. "I suppose the security officer standing outside the room was also a giveaway as to where I was."

Adam shot her a smile. "That did help narrow it down. You okay?"

"I will be. The shower and clean clothes, thanks to Renee, did wonders, and I was also able to talk to the senator's family for a few minutes." She glanced back up at the stained glass. "I guess I just needed a quiet spot to sort through everything that's happened."

"I can't blame you. It's been a long day, and it's barely noon." He held up a bag. "Think you can eat in the meantime?"

"Sorry, but I don't think so." Her stomach turned as she sat back down on one of the chairs, a mixture of fatigue and worry overshadowing the need to eat. "Is Jack still in with the suspect?"

Adam nodded. "I expect he'll be done soon, and as soon as he's finished, I'll see that Hwang is transferred to the jail. While I'm doing that, Jack is planning to escort you down to the FBI's satellite office where you will file an official statement."

"Do you really think I need an escort?"

"Until we know why you were grabbed this morning, it can't hurt. And the FBI is officially involved now."

"I just hope Jack gets answers out of this guy."

"You know Jack. He will."

"True." She chuckled at the comment. Jack had always been both determined and stubborn. She looked over at him, still smiling. "I was trying to remember how long it's been since I've seen you. I heard you have two little girls now."

"I do, and they're growing like weeds. Michaela turns four next week, and Cora is seven months. I know I'm biased, but they're the sweetest, most beautiful girls in the world."

"I'm sure they are. I'd love to see them and your wife again. The last time I saw you, Michaela was just a baby."

"It's crazy how time flies. You know you're welcome to stop by anytime you're in town."

She shifted in her chair, thankful that her heart had healed years ago over anything that had once gone wrong between them.

"How often do you see Jack?" she asked.

"Not as often as I'd like. We both try to make it to Mom and Dad's in Dallas at the same time at least once a year, but he's pretty busy with his career."

"I always felt like something came between the two of you when we started dating. I hope that's not part of it."

"None of that was your fault." He sat down across from her. "Even I'm not exactly sure what happened, but I guess it's natural for people to grow apart. We're not exactly teenagers anymore, and we live different lives in different places. It's just the way it is."

"So he's never married?" Aubrey winced as soon as she asked the question, wondering why she'd headed in such a personal direction. A decade ago, she'd known Jack's favorite songs, movies, and foods. Today, he seemed more like a stranger, and she wasn't even sure how it had happened.

"I know he dates some, but the last time I asked, he didn't even have a girlfriend." Adam glanced toward the door. "Speaking of my brother . . ."

Aubrey looked up as Jack walked into the room. She had no idea what had happened with their suspect, but from the look on his face, the interrogation hadn't gone well.

"I brought lunch for you," Adam said, standing up, "but something tells me you're not hungry either right now."

"Actually, I'm not. I need to talk to you, Bree."

"Okay." She unsuccessfully tried to push back the alarm that had settled in her stomach.

Jack sat down across from her. "I don't know how to say this, so I'm going to just spit it out. Have you ever heard of a man named Charles Ramsey?"

Charles Ramsey.

Aubrey felt the air whoosh out of her lungs as Jack held up a driver's license on his phone. The room started spinning, and a wave of nausea swept through her. All this time she'd wanted to believe that she'd been in the wrong place at the wrong time, but not now. She swallowed hard, wanting to ignore Jack's clear implications. This couldn't have anything to do with him. It was all some mistake. The FBI wasn't looking for her father. There had to be more than one Charles Ramsey in the world.

Except the picture was of him. She stared at the photo. He'd aged since she'd seen him last. His hair had turned white and receded, and he'd lost weight, leaving a hollowness in his eyes. She almost didn't recognize him, but there was enough of the man she remembered in the photo to know it was him.

She felt her hands begin to shake. For a second, she was back at her ballet recital, waiting impatiently for her father to show up, then pretending she wasn't disappointed when he didn't. The memories were few and scattered over the years, always filled with disappointment and sadness. Always leaving her feeling like a child with a piece of her heart missing.

Jack dropped his phone back in his pocket and took her hands, trying to steady her. She bit her lip.

"Charles Ramsey's my father," she said. "Though something tells me you already knew that."

He squeezed her hands. "I'm sorry. I just needed to confirm it. I thought your father's name was Charlie, but you have a different last name."

"My mom changed her name back to Grayson after their divorce. Mine as well. That was before I knew you." She blinked back the tears threatening to erupt. "But I still don't understand. How does what happened today have anything to do with my father? What did Hwang say to you?"

"Your father's been on the watch list of the FBI for over eighteen months, and recently we tracked him here, but until now, I didn't know his real name."

"I thought you were here for Hwang?"

"Your father is involved as well."

"Wait a minute . . ." She looked up and caught his gaze. "Before you went in to question Hwang, you told me he's a spy."

"Yes."

"And you believe my father is involved? That he's some kind of spy as well?"

"Yes, I do."

She shook her head, still trying to process everything he was telling her. Though maybe it shouldn't surprise her. Not really. Hadn't her father spent his life selling out people he loved—or at least claimed he loved? Why would he pass up the opportunity to get paid for it?

Still . . .

She pulled her hands away from him, stood up, and started pacing the short aisle. "My father has done a lot of unscrupulous things, but I'm having a hard time believing we're talking about the same person. Adultery doesn't exactly equal selling government secrets. And betraying his country . . . I don't want to think he'd do something like that, no matter what I think about him personally."

"What do you know about him?"

She let her mind reach back into a place she didn't want to go. "I know he spent most of his career in military intelligence. He retired five, maybe six years ago. He remarried, though they've now divorced." She drew in a slow breath, knowing she was going to have to shove aside any personal feelings she had at the moment in order to look at the situation objectively. "What do you know about him?"

"All we know so far is that his code name is Junco, which interestingly enough is one of the most common birds in North America."

"His job was to blend in," Adam said, stepping into the conversation.

"Exactly. We have evidence that he's sold thousands of classified documents that he gained access to while he was still working for the government, as well as ones he's managed to procure more recently since his retirement."

"What kind of documents?" Adam asked.

"Weapons technology, counterintelligence . . . whatever he could get his hands on."

"You're talking about treason," she said, not even trying to identify her emotions at the moment. She'd deal with them later.

Jack nodded.

"Okay," she said. "I'm struggling to process all of this, but my biggest question is, why would they come after me?"

"According to Hwang, they needed leverage. He told me there was a problem with some of the intel your father recently sold to the Chinese, but they haven't been able to get him to meet with them to discuss it."

"So Papps was the one in the way, and I was the leverage."

"Exactly."

"Here's the problem." Aubrey turned to face them. "My father's been out of my life for years. I can hardly believe that my being captured would bring him out into the open. There are no real ties between us, and there haven't been for years."

For the most part.

"That might be true, but what if they don't know that?" Jack said. "All they know is that you're his daughter."

"It makes sense, Aubrey," Adam said.

"I know. It's just hard to process."

"How often did you see him?"

She didn't want to go there. Back to a past that was filled with hurts and disappointments. It was a place she rarely visited, because it always managed to break her shattered child's heart all over again. She sat back down and pushed the thought away as she drew in a breath, then let it out slowly. She was looking at this all wrong. That wasn't who she was anymore. And if she forgot that, she was only letting him control her. That wasn't going to happen.

She worked to pull herself out of the equation to look at the situation like an outsider. Just the facts. No emotion. She had a lot of practice with that. A lot of practice with people she loved walking out of her life. She glanced at Jack, then shook off the familiar pain that passed over her. Jack was different. And besides, their relationship wasn't the one in the spotlight right now.

"Every couple years he'd show up on my birthday or on Christmas, but beyond that there wasn't a lot of communication between the two of us. Once I was in high school, I rarely saw him."

"Did you ever meet him?" Adam asked Jack.

"Once. He showed up at one of my senior basketball games, then took us out for pizza afterward." Jack caught her gaze. "When's the last time you saw him?"

"Two . . . maybe three years ago, and that was only because he had a question about a baseball card of his he thought I might have. We don't keep in touch." She forced the memories to resurface. "I know he started his own security company. Remarried a few years ago. I heard she ended up leaving him, but like I said . . . we don't really keep in touch. I'm not even sure where he lives."

"We're going to figure this out, Bree, but I'm going to need your help."

"You know I'll do anything."

"I'll need to ask you some more detailed questions about your father. I'm hoping you'll be able to help us track him, but I'd rather do it at the FBI office."

She nodded. "Adam told me you were going to take me there."

"I've arranged a driver to pick you up downstairs in about fifteen minutes," Adam said.

"I really don't need the escort, Jack. I'm sure you have a million other things to do."

"Then do it to humor me," Jack said.

Ten minutes later the two of them headed down the hospital corridor toward the car Adam had arranged. Everything about today had left her feeling off-balance. She was used to being a protector, not the victim, and the uncomfortable switch had thrown her off. But she wasn't going to let feelings of vulnerability take root.

She followed Jack into the elevator, then watched as he pushed the button for the hospital basement. "I'm guessing you chose the basement because it's the most direct route?"

"Are you kidding? I chose it for the scenery."

She laughed at his comeback as the elevator doors slid closed, realizing how much she'd missed that humor. On the basement level, the dingy hallway smelled of chemicals and antiseptic. Footsteps echoed down the hallway as a woman in scrubs slipped through a doorway. Aubrey automatically checked for her side arm, then remembered she didn't have it.

"I'm not sure I like the scenery down here."

"All of this is simply a precaution, but I don't plan to take any chances until we know what's going on. You're one of our main witnesses, so you've just become valuable to both sides, including the FBI." He turned at another long, narrow hallway. "There's a curbside exit down by the morgue not too far ahead, where our driver is waiting."

She quickened her pace. Trusting him wasn't the issue. If she were honest with herself, it was her being forced to dredge up the past that was leaving her feeling exposed.

"So how long have you been a detective?" Jack's question pulled her back into the present.

"Eight months and counting."

"You like it?"

"It's hard work, but I feel like I'm doing what I was made to do."

"I remember you always talked about going into law enforcement."

"I think that's why this morning shook me up so much. I'm not used to being on the other side of a case."

"That's not the only reason you're so shook up. I told you, you can't just brush this off. You watched someone you love get shot. That's enough to rattle even the most veteran officer."

He was right, but now wasn't the time to worry about her mental health. She planned to do anything she could to make sure they found whoever was behind the shooting. Which meant she was going to have to be involved, no matter how she was feeling.

Footsteps on the tiled floor echoed behind them. A shiver slid through her. She was being paranoid, which wasn't like her. She turned around. Two men hurried toward them, both carrying side arms.

"Two men with guns at our six," she said quietly to Jack.

"I have a feeling this is about to get ugly. Stay behind me."

Jack turned around, his weapon drawn. "FBI—weapons on the ground and hands in the air. Now!"

A woman wearing scrubs stepped out into the hallway, momentarily shifting Aubrey's attention.

"Bree, get her inside!"

One of the men fired off a shot. The bullet slammed against the wall beside them as Aubrey grabbed the woman's arm and pulled her into the nearest room. A man and another woman wearing scrubs stood over a body bag, staring at them. Frustration snapped through her as she glanced around the morgue. Rows of metal cabinets lined one of the gray walls. Four body bags lay on metal tables. She needed to get the three of them to safety so they didn't end up in body bags too.

If the gunman entered the room, there would be nowhere to hide. A bullet would slice through the metal tables. She should have insisted someone bring her her side arm before they left.

"I'm Detective Aubrey Grayson. Is there another way out of this room?"

"There's a walk-in cooler." The man pointed behind him.

She made a snap decision. "Get in there now."

The second woman stood immobile next to the body.

Aubrey ran toward her. "Go, go, go!"

CHAPTER TEN

JACK FIRED HIS WEAPON in response, then pressed his back against the wall. At the moment, he had only two objectives in mind: ensure the safety of Bree and everyone else in this hospital, and take down the shooters. One of the men shouted, then they both turned around and ran down the hallway before slipping around the corner and out of sight. Had he winged one of them? He wasn't sure. What he was sure of was that he needed to stop them.

He pressed on the surveillance earpiece Adam had set him up with. "Adam . . . I need you to lock down the south wing of the hospital immediately, as well as all exits, and call in backup."

"What's going on?"

"We've got two active shooters just outside the morgue, heading south down the corridor toward the maintenance wing. I think I clipped one of them, but I can't be sure."

"Copy that. I'm going to send out backup immediately and coordinate the hospital's emergency lockdown plan. Are there any injuries at your location?"

"None that I'm aware of. The morgue technicians are inside with Bree and safe at the moment."

"Contain the situation if possible, then wait for backup."

He agreed with the call, but his options were limited. He was armed, but clearing the wing solo was extremely risky, and there was no way to ensure an employee didn't end up in the line of fire.

"Jack . . ."

He glanced behind and saw Bree running toward him. He frowned. "You should have stayed in the morgue. You're unarmed."

"I'm counting on you having a backup weapon. And that you weren't planning to go after those guys alone."

He reached down and pulled a Glock 23 from his ankle holster. His primary job might be to keep Bree safe, but she was no ordinary assignment, and she wasn't going to simply retreat.

He handed her the weapon. "I was still hoping you'd stay back there."

"We need to get these guys, Jack," she said. "You need me."

She was right. Going after them together was far more advantageous than a solo act, but he still didn't like it.

"Where are they?"

"Ahead and to the left."

They moved forward cautiously, needing to avoid a gunfight. He'd already run through the scenario a dozen times. They had to believe that the Chinese thought Bree was worth taking. But they wouldn't do it on his watch.

"What do you think their plan is?"

"I think they assumed they could pull a quick ambush, but now that that didn't work? I don't know. We need to sweep this floor and try and flush them out. I've already spoken to Adam, and he's working with the hospital to lock down this wing as we speak, as well as any other exits from the rest of the hospital."

"What's ahead of us?"

He'd memorized the layout of their route, even though he'd hoped they wouldn't run into any resistance. "Maintenance is to our left, and there's an outside exit beyond that."

His tactical training came back automatically. He would have preferred a four-person team charging down the narrow hallway, but the two of them would have to do. He paused before the hallway intersection, an automatic danger zone, grateful he trusted Bree and her instincts implicitly.

He slowed down as they came to a T-junction, then signaled for her to go low and work the left side. He'd remain standing and work his side of the opening. They called a situation like this a fatal funnel because if the enemy was waiting around the corner for them, they'd become an open target. Something he couldn't let happen. But neither was he going to just sit back and do nothing.

He leaned slightly to the right in order to see down the hallway. The response was a spray of bullets from around the corner that slammed into the wall inches above his head. Jack pressed back against the wall.

"Bree—"

"I'm fine."

Seconds later, footsteps pounded against the ground and faded into the distance, followed by an eerie silence that filled the corridor. He slowly cleared the corner a second time, aware of his line of fire. This time the hallway was empty. Where were they?

"If they're trying to avoid the exit, where would they go?" Jack spoke again into his com.

"Give me a minute," Adam said. "I'm going to get someone on the line that's more qualified to answer."

Jack felt his heart pounding in his throat as he waited. They didn't have a minute, but neither did he want to end up pinned down by a miscalculated plan.

"Agent Shannon, this is Bill Mathers, the hospital's chief executive officer. There's a lab to your right and maintenance to your left. Both rooms have exits into the main hallway, but they are also locked."

"You're positive about that?"

"It has been confirmed that both are locked down."

They walked toward the maintenance room, and Jack tried the handle. The man was right. It was locked.

Jack tugged at his communicator again, hating the game of cat and mouse. "Do you have anyone guarding the south exit?"

"We're waiting for confirmation, but that door is locked from the outside only, so they would be able to get out."

"Then they have to be heading for that exit, hoping they avoid resistance. They are armed. Backup needs to be ready."

"Roger that."

Bree followed him down the narrow hall to the south exit, then stopped beside him at the door. If they weren't careful, the men would be able to pick them off. But something told him their plan wasn't to kill them. Or at least not Bree. They wanted her alive and had taken a huge risk to find her.

He only hoped he was right.

He pushed open the door, knowing the threat from outside

could come from any angle, and breathed in the humid salt-water air just in time to see the men drive off.

"I need backup at the south entrance immediately!" Jack shouted into his com. "Shooters are driving away in a white Dodge Durango."

On the sidewalk a woman was screaming hysterically.

"Ma'am . . . are you okay?" Bree moved in front of the woman, her hands on her shoulders, and looked her in the eye. "Take a deep breath and talk to me. What happened?"

"Jack." Adam's voice came through the earphone.

"They just carjacked a vehicle," Jack said. "Give me a second."

"They took my babies," the woman said, her chest still heaving. "They . . . they're in car seats in the back. They pointed a gun at me and pulled me out of the car. I tried to stop them, but I couldn't—"

An unmarked car pulled up, dash light flashing, shifting their attention momentarily.

Bree glanced up at Jack. "We need to go after them. Now."

"Detective Gerome?" he asked, running to the driver's door.

"Yes." The man stepped out of the vehicle, its engine running. "What's going on?"

"I need your car."

"I thought I was supposed to escort you—"

"Plans just changed." Jack headed for the driver's seat. "Two men just carjacked this woman's vehicle. Her two children are in the back. Get the details from her and issue an Amber Alert immediately."

"Yes, sir."

Jack threw on his seat belt as Bree slid into the passenger seat, ignoring the confused look still lingering on the face of the detective. A moment later they were exiting the hospital parking lot.

"Do you see them?"

Bree leaned forward and braced her hands against the dashboard. "They're about four cars ahead of us in the left lane."

"Got 'em."

He pressed on the accelerator and started weaving his way around vehicles to catch up with them, thankful traffic wasn't too heavy this time of day. He knew the dangers of a police chase. Knew the risks of a crash, of innocent-bystander injuries and deaths. But there were two children in that car who needed rescuing.

His com crackled. "Jack, I need an update."

"There are two kids in the back of the vehicle they stole."

"Do you know where they are now?"

"We have them in sight. We're heading west away from the hospital. The detective is with the mother, getting details from her now so we can put out an Amber Alert on the children as well as the vehicle."

"Maintain pursuit, but do not engage. I'm coordinating now with the local police."

Bree stared out the windshield, her fingers gripping the dashboard. "I can't believe this is happening, Jack. Those babies . . . if anything happens to them—"

"We're going to make sure nothing does."

A van pulled out in front of their vehicle, then slowed down, blocking his view.

"Can you see them?" he asked.

She gestured. "You need to get over."

"I'm trying." Jack bumped the siren for a short burst in order to get the van to move. "Get out of the way . . . get out of the way . . ."

He flipped on his blinker, waited for a Jeep to pass them, then sped around the van.

"Jack . . . they just turned again. The mall parking lot to your right."

Jack pushed on the accelerator, then turned into the mall entrance, trying to figure out where they were going. The mall was busy this time of day. How hard would it be to disappear into a crowd? And the woman's children? If the shooters were smart, their plan would be to leave them behind and run. The children would only slow them down.

"Where are they, Bree?" His focus was divided between looking for the car and ensuring he didn't hit a pedestrian.

"I lost them. Take a left. They had to have gone that way."

He searched for the white vehicle. There were dozens of cars that all looked the same. "They've got to be here, Bree, but I don't see them."

"There was an 'I'd rather be at the beach' sticker on the back window," she said, trying to narrow it down. "Wait a minute . . . next aisle. Looks like there's been a wreck."

She was right. The stolen car had rear-ended another vehicle.

Her seat belt was off by the time he stopped the car. "They're gone. We lost them."

"Our first concern is those children. You check on them, I'll call this in and check on the other vehicle."

A woman groaned from the front seat when he approached the car.

"Ma'am, are you okay?" Jack asked.

"I think so. This car came out of nowhere, ran into my car, then the driver and passenger just ran off."

"We've called 911, and someone will be here in just a minute." Jack headed toward the other car.

"You think they're okay?" he asked Bree.

She nodded. "I don't think they have any idea what happened."

A baby was crying behind the driver's seat.

"Can you get the little one out, Jack?"

He pulled open the back door of the vehicle, then fumbled with the car seat buckle before slipping his hands around the baby and pulling him out.

He spoke into his com. "What are the kids' names, Adam?"

"Harper is two and Oliver is six months. Their mother wants to know if they're okay."

"They're a bit shaken up, but it looks to me like they're going to be just fine."

He started rocking the baby.

"Is he okay?" she asked.

"As far as I can tell."

Oliver snuggled up against Jack's chest.

"I don't think I've ever seen you with a baby, but you seem to have the touch."

He smiled, but was relieved when two officers came to take over the scene. He needed to get Bree out of there.

"We need to go."

"I'd rather wait until the mother gets here."

He shook his head. "They'll be fine. I promise."

"And the other woman?"

"She's talking with an officer now, and she said she wasn't hurt. I've let the mother know that her babies are fine. They're going to be transported back to the hospital and meet her there. In the meantime, I want to get you somewhere safe."

"Where are you thinking?" she asked.

"Adam's been talking to one of the senator's sons. I think the safest place to take you right now is his father's house. It's gated and secure . . ." Jack hesitated at her distracted stance. "Bree . . ."

She wasn't listening to him.

"I've arranged for both of us to stay there for the next couple days . . ." He moved in front of her and caught her gaze. "Bree . . . you okay?"

"Yeah, but I can't stop thinking if something had happened to those children . . ."

"But it didn't, Bree. They're going to be fine. It's over."

She shook her head. "Except it's not. We've got to find my father and put an end to this before someone really does get hurt."

CHAPTER ELEVEN

JACK STEPPED OUT ONTO the large brick veranda that surrounded the swimming pool with a tray holding a pot of hot tea, a couple of mugs, and a plate of lemon bars. He'd seen the fatigue in Bree's eyes and hoped he could convince her to go upstairs and take a nap. They'd decided that the senator's two-story house was the safest location at the moment with its walled yard and built-in security system. A couple of plainclothes officers outside the front gate added another layer of protection. He had asked for the most seasoned officers because until he had a grasp on the situation, he wasn't going to take any chances.

The seven-bedroom house looming above him was impressive with its cathedral ceilings, grand foyer, and stunning waterfront view of the bay. But even the added security of the property clearly wasn't enough to settle Bree's nerves.

Bree stood against the metal railing surrounding the pool, staring out across the bay. Until this moment, she hadn't had a chance to process everything that had happened the last few hours. And once she did, it wasn't going to get any easier.

Jack filled a mug. "I brought you some tea and lemon bars."

The only response was the sound of the wind blowing through the palm trees edging the property.

"Bree?"

She turned around and faced him before crossing the veranda and sitting down in one of the deck chairs. "Sorry. I know I'm distracted. I'm just trying to figure all this out. I'm having a hard time taking everything in."

He sat in the chair next to hers. "I don't blame you for being distracted. All of this has to be a lot to process." He slid the mug of hot tea in front of her. "It's chamomile. It's supposed to have a calming effect."

"Thank you." She wrapped her hands around the mug and took a sip. "What's the latest update on the guys from the hospital basement?"

Jack shook his head. "Nothing yet, but there's a BOLO out on them."

She took another sip, then set her mug down. "I've made a list of all the phone numbers and email addresses I have for my father for you. I've tried calling and left messages for him, telling him I need to speak to him, but so far I haven't got any response."

"That's a good start."

"I'm also trying to figure out the complex web my father's got himself tangled up in. I don't know how the spy game works, but do you think he knows they're after me? Do you think they've told him?"

"We have no way of knowing. We were able to get a bit more out of Hwang. Hwang said your father promised his Chinese handler a piece of intel worth hundreds of thousands of dollars.

But if he turned around and betrayed them, either by reneging or giving them false information, they wouldn't be happy."

She nodded as Jack continued.

"We're going to find the truth, but like I said, it's a lot to process. Give yourself some grace. This isn't just another case you're trying to solve. This hits close to home."

"Way too close. Ryan called me a few minutes ago. He told me they're keeping Papps in ICU overnight, but he's still stable."

"He's in good hands."

"I know." She fiddled with the zipper on the end of her jacket and stared across the table past him, toward the bay. "It seems strange that I have more memories of Papps than my own father."

He sat back in his chair, waiting for her to continue at her own pace. Healing what had already happened was going to take time, and yet he knew that this was far from over.

"I remember him taking my mother and me to the opening of Whataburger Field. I was so excited I hardly slept the night before. I was worried he wouldn't show up, but he did. I'm sure I drove him crazy. The field was spectacular, and seeing the *Lexington* and the aquarium from the stadium was amazing. I loved baseball, though I'm not sure how much of the game I saw. I remember eating burgers and ice cream until I was almost sick. The best part was that my parents were both sitting beside me. For those few hours we were a family and everything was right in the world. And then the next day, he was gone. I didn't see him again for months, or even hear from him other than a couple postcards. I always knew deep down that the fun we had that night wouldn't last, but for the moment—for that one night—everything was perfect."

Jack caught the sadness in her voice. She'd grown up since that night at the ballfield, but he knew there would always be regret for what she'd missed. Part of him wished he could whisk her away from all of this, so she didn't have to deal with it, but as hard as it was—if they were going to find her father—they needed her. But first he wanted her to rest.

"What do you need from me right now?" she asked.

"Right now? I want you to go lie down for a couple hours. When you get up, we'll order some dinner, then you can help us work on a plan."

She shook her head. "I need to find out the truth of what's going on. I can sleep later."

Jack sighed. He'd known it was a long shot. "Okay . . . then tell me more about your father." He leaned forward, not wanting to push her, but she was right about one thing. They needed answers, and at the moment she was their best lead. "Anything you can think of, no matter how obscure, might help. Anything that would help me understand how he thinks and acts and how he might respond to this situation."

She picked up her mug and held it in her cupped hands. He could read the mixture of sadness and frustration in her eyes. He knew she wanted to help, but there had to be a measure of guilt running through her, because no matter what he'd done, Charles Ramsey was still her father. And what he was asking her to do was help him bring the man in. Which meant his job was to walk the fine line between being an agent and being a friend.

"I know this is hard to talk about, Bree."

"Our relationship is . . . complicated. Mainly because he hasn't been a part of my world for a long time. To be honest, he never has been a part of it." She put her mug down, then pressed her palms against the table as she formulated her words. "Maybe this doesn't make sense, but as strained as our relationship has always been, I still don't want to believe he would do something like this. It just seems like some bad movie. In the span of a few hours, I found out that my father is a spy and a traitor. It's just . . . it's going to take time for all of this to sink in."

He appreciated her focus and willingness to move forward even though he knew it was difficult. "Do you have any idea where he might be?"

She shook her head. "I haven't spoken to him for a couple years. I'm not even sure where he lives anymore. I've got an address, but it's probably not up-to-date. I have a feeling that your FBI file will have more information than I do."

"That's okay. Just tell me what you do know."

She sighed as she worked to dredge up memories he knew she'd rather forget. "I know he was in the military and that he worked in intelligence after he got out. Not long after he turned fifty, he went through some sort of midlife crisis. He divorced my mom and a few years later ended up marrying a girl half his age. By that time I was nineteen. She was twenty-nine. He traveled the world for a few months with his new wife, then he started some tech business. After he divorced my mom, I rarely saw him. He never demanded visitation rights, never seemed to want a relationship with me, though he always paid his child support on time. All of which was fine with me. I preferred to live with my mom than one of his girlfriends or later his wife."

"You said his second marriage ended in divorce also," Jack said. "How long did it last?"

"Five . . . maybe six years. That was the point where a lot of things fell apart for him. After he lost Rachel, his business started failing."

"Did you ever hear from him?"

"He typically sent me postcards a couple times a year, mainly from when he traveled overseas. I tried to respond for a while, to keep in touch, but after my mother died, the connection between us dissolved, and eventually I decided there was nothing left for me to give."

"And where did the senator and his wife come in?"

"They were always like surrogate parents to me. They made sure I had a place to go for holidays, both me and my mother. Never missed a birthday or an important holiday, and then there was duck hunting and fishing. Papps taught me clay pigeon shooting and how to tie fishing lines to a hook while Gail taught me how to make pies and macaroons. But the best thing he did was treat me like a part of his family."

"You needed that."

Bree smiled for the first time. "I did. I was hungry for attention and a father figure, and that's what he gave me."

"Now I know why you were always so multitalented." He studied her body language, pleased that she was finally starting to relax. "How did you meet them?"

"Believe it or not, he and my dad were best friends in college. It's hard to believe how different they are today. I think my father became resentful of my relationship with Papps and his family."

"Does your father have any other relatives still alive? Siblings? Parents?"

"No siblings, though there are a few cousins I've never met. My grandmother, his mother, is still alive."

"I remember you talking about her. Where is she now?"

"In a nursing home in San Antonio. She's the one person in his family I've ever been close to. Or at least was close to. She has Alzheimer's now, and most of the time she doesn't even recognize me. But she was a wonderful woman who'd be horrified to know what her son has done. I don't even think she remembers my parents divorced."

"I'm sorry. I know from experience with my own grandfather how hard that is. When's the last time you saw her?"

"Last month. I try to visit her as often as I can get away from work."

"So sometimes she remembers you?"

"It depends on the day, but most days she's lost in the past. The only good thing is that she's always her same sweet self I remember from when I was growing up." Bree drew in a deep breath, then let it out slowly. "Nana is so different from my father. She worked hard her whole life and yet she always had time for me. She knew how to make me laugh, made the best chicken and dumplings, and loved sending me handwritten letters all through college."

"What is your father's relationship like with your grandmother?"

"I have a feeling he doesn't go very often, which is sad. She loved him fiercely despite his neglect. She's always had a place for my mom and me in her life."

Jack studied her while she spoke, struck—not for the first time—by how one person's actions could affect so many people. Both positively and negatively. In this case, how one father's selfishness destroyed a family and left the daughter to be raised by a single mom. Charles Ramsey had taken off and apparently never looked back.

"I have a question," she said. "You know how all this works better than I do. Why would my father have been recruited in the first place? He had contacts, but it's been a while since he retired from government work."

"It's not an unusual approach. They look for people struggling financially, or who worked with contractors or are currently working as a contractor with connections in intelligence circles."

He wished there was a way he could take her out of the equation, but even if he could somehow do that, he knew she wouldn't want him to.

She pulled her sweater tighter around her shoulders. "Ever since he walked out on my mother and me, I've thought he didn't love me enough. But now . . . now I wonder if he was trying to protect me in his own misguided way by staying out of my life, though maybe that's just what my heart wants to believe."

"So if he knew that the FBI was after him—along with the Chinese—where would he go?" Jack asked.

She shook her head. "I can't narrow it down, but I would think close enough to be able to keep an eye on things and still be in control, and yet far enough away so no one could easily find him."

"Then let's start there. Everyone has habits. That place of familiarity. What was familiar to him?"

"He'd avoid the familiar, but that was his way. He loved visiting new places. I told you he used to send me postcards when he traveled. I remember daydreaming about how one day he'd invite me to come with him on one of his trips. We'd travel to Berlin, Morocco, Paris, and Beijing. But of course that never happened."

"So you think he'd head somewhere unfamiliar."

"I think so." She tapped her finger on her lips. "I remember once, when I was about fourteen, he told me he planned to retire somewhere like Belize or Ecuador."

"If he had the correct paperwork and enough cash, that would be the perfect place to disappear."

"What if he's already left?"

"It's possible, but I don't think so. I think there's something else he needs from the Chinese. I think if he'd gotten it from them, he'd have left a long time ago."

"Money."

"Exactly. Enough to disappear for the rest of his life." Jack tried to put himself in the man's shoes in an attempt to figure out what he would do. "What about a weakness?"

Bree hesitated before answering. "My grandmother. If he is planning to disappear, he'd want to tell her goodbye."

"Even if she doesn't know who he is?"

"I think so."

Jack scooted back his chair, a plan of action finally starting to form in his mind. "We need to call the assisted living home where she is and instruct them to tell us immediately if your father stops by. We can put the local authorities on alert as well."

"I can do that," Bree said. "What else?"

"I've got something." Adam walked up to their table. "I just received a call from local PD. Your father was just spotted here in Corpus."

CHAPTER TWELVE

HER FATHER WAS HERE?

A wave of nausea swept through Aubrey. On any other day, a visit to Papps's house would have had her soaking up the afternoon sun on the back veranda of the senator's large house. She'd always loved the warm winter days and the line of palm trees and the blue ocean spreading out in front of them. But instead of enjoying the incredible view, she was caught up in her father's messy decisions.

She sat back in her chair. "Where is he?"

"With the BOLO out on your father, someone at the local PD found video surveillance of him at the Omni Hotel while investigating a separate incident. They followed up, but he didn't check in, and there's no evidence he met anyone."

Her mind worked through the possible scenarios, and only one stood out. "He had to have been meeting someone. Maybe whoever it was didn't show up."

"It's very possible."

"If his ex-wife lives here, like I think she does, he might be here to see her," she said.

"I think it would be worth paying her a visit," Adam said.

"I agree." Jack turned to her. "Do you know how to find her? With the new information we're gathering, we're still updating our files."

"She shouldn't be hard to track down." Aubrey opened her laptop that was sitting on the table. "As far as I know, she still lives around here after remarrying. I don't know her new last name, but her maiden name was Brook."

Aubrey searched for Rachel's Facebook page. Fifteen minutes later, she found the page that was filled with a sprinkling of energetic selfies and beach shots. "Looks like I was right. She remarried and lives just outside of Corpus with her new husband."

"You're good." Adam leaned forward and studied the page. "What else can you tell us about her?"

Aubrey dug through another pile of memories she would have preferred to keep buried. But this wasn't the time to let the past drag her under. "The last time I spoke with her was right after their divorce went through. She needed something from my father and wanted me to talk to him for her. It was clear from the tone of her voice that she was relieved to be rid of him."

She remembered feeling sorry for her father at the time. Sorry that he was still searching for something and had ended up failing at another marriage. Sorry that she and her mother hadn't been enough for him.

Adam flipped through a few of the photos. "She seems like a bit of a gold digger."

"I've thought the same thing, though unfortunately for her,

my father looked better with his expensive car and clothes than he did on paper. Which is why, I'm assuming, she ended up walking out when she found out the truth. He was always more flash than substance and spent more than he made." She blinked back the emotion. "All of this makes me miss my mom, though on the other hand, it makes me so glad she's not here. I know that when they married, she loved him, and to be fair, he loved her, but things changed. He changed. I would have hated to see her having to deal with the fallout from all of this."

Adam nodded. "I always loved your mom. She had a way of making everyone feel at home no matter who they were."

"She was always like that. Loved having a full house. She could whip up a meal for guests in thirty minutes that made you think she'd slaved over the stove for hours."

"Her spaghetti and meatballs was my favorite," Jack said. "I'd finish off my plate and she'd pile on another helping."

Aubrey laughed at the memory. "For some reason she always felt like she had to fatten the two of you up."

Jack reached out and squeezed her hand, making her wish for the moment that they could go back in time. That he could drive her to her mother's house for spaghetti and meatballs with chocolate cake for dessert like they used to when everything in life seemed so much simpler. When the biggest concern she faced was passing Mrs. Gunther's science test and what she was going to wear to school the next day.

"What if Rachel hasn't seen him?" Aubrey asked. "What next?"

"We'll go to plan B," Jack said.

"Aren't we well beyond plan B?" She pulled her hand away

and took a sip of her tea that was now lukewarm, trying not to be frustrated. "I understand you've been at this for months."

She might not be close to her father, but she knew if he didn't want to be found, it wasn't going to be easy to track him down.

"You're going to start making me feel like I'm shirking my job."

She shook her head. "Not at all. But I will say this about my father. He's been disappearing and shirking his responsibilities for as long as I remember."

"We're going to find him, Bree." Jack stood up. "It's just a matter of time."

"I'm going with you."

"Bree, I brought you here to keep you safe."

"And you need me. Rachel will talk to me before she talks to the FBI."

Jack frowned. "I'm not going to argue with that, but we need to be careful."

It didn't take long for them to drive to the house, which sat on a large piece of land overlooking the ocean with a dozen palm trees. It had to be worth at least a couple million dollars. Maybe Jack had been right about Rachel being a gold digger. She also couldn't help but wonder if her father had felt any of the same loss that she knew her mother had felt when he'd left them. A single mom, struggling to pay the bills and keep food on the table. She'd risen to the occasion, but even as a young girl, Aubrey had seen that it hadn't been easy.

It wasn't as if Aubrey really knew her father's second wife. She'd only spoken with her a couple of times. The first time had been the day her father had insisted on bringing Rachel to meet her just days before they drove to Vegas to tie the knot. The whole time it seemed more like an opportunity for him to absolve the guilt he had to have felt. To get her to give him the approval he seemed to want from her. Why, she'd never quite understood. He never cared what she thought about anything else.

She'd given him nothing. How could she approve of the way he'd walked out on her mother, especially when he was marrying a woman barely ten years older than she was. But what had hurt the most was that he never asked about her mother that day or any other day. He probably didn't even know when the cancer came back again with a vengeance and the doctors didn't expect her to live more than a few more months. And why would he? As far as he was concerned, Mary Grayson was a piece of his past, and Rachel was the woman who was going to make him feel young again.

The memories pressed in around her. She'd seen the fire in her father's eyes that day. The lilt in his voice as if he'd struck gold. And in the end, Rachel had only been another step toward his ruin.

She dragged her mind back to the present as she walked beside Jack up the long brick walkway in silence and focused on trying to ignore the ball of nerves in the pit of her stomach. Thoughts of her father were something she was used to dealing with, but she thought she'd buried her feelings about him years ago. No, erased them. But clearly, she was wrong. The last few hours had resurrected emotions she'd rather forget, leaving her feeling small and vulnerable.

She studied Jack's profile as he stepped onto the porch. It

seemed strange, seeing him after so many years, and now they'd been thrown into working a case together. He'd always been a calming presence in her life, and somehow that hadn't changed at all. He was still that grounding in the midst of the chaos swirling around her. She drew in a long, slow breath. She could do this. There was a higher purpose at stake, which meant she couldn't let personal feelings get in the way.

Jack stopped in front of a pair of massive wooden front doors and rang the doorbell. A man in his late thirties wearing shorts and a T-shirt opened the door with his cell phone in his hand.

"It's about time." His frown deepened as he stared at them. "Except you're not the plumber."

Jack shot Aubrey a side glance. "No . . . I'm FBI Special Agent Jack Shannon, and this is Detective Aubrey Grayson. You're Corey Porter?"

She recognized the man from Rachel's Facebook page as her husband.

He, on the other hand, clearly didn't recognize Aubrey or her name, which shouldn't surprise her. She had a feeling Rachel didn't share details about her ex-husband's family.

"FBI?" He took a closer look at Jack's badge and frowned. "What's going on?"

"We need to speak to your wife, Rachel. Is she at home?" Aubrey asked.

"Give me a second." He told whoever he was talking to that he would have to call them back, then turned to Jack. "Listen, I don't know what this is about, but unless you've got some kind of warrant, you're going to need to tell me what's going on."

"Your wife isn't in any kind of trouble. We're looking for some information she might have."

He hesitated a few more seconds. "Information?"

"About someone she used to know. Just a couple of questions, that's all."

"Fine. Rachel . . ." He shouted from the entryway for his wife to come to the door.

They heard the click of heels against the wood floor and then, "Aubrey . . . wow . . . it's been a long time." Rachel glanced at her husband, then back to Bree. "I guess you met my husband, Corey."

Aubrey smiled at her. "Yes. We have."

Rachel hadn't aged since the last time she'd seen her, though from the look of her slightly frozen brow, tanned skin, and bleached hair, she'd had some help keeping her face timeless.

Aubrey felt a sudden wave of discomfort, just like the first time she'd met Rachel. She was only ten years younger than the woman who, for whatever reason, decided to marry her father. The arrangement had always bothered her.

"You know each other?" Corey asked.

"We've met," Aubrey said, leaving it at that. "Not in regard to police business, of course, but socially, though it's been a long time."

Corey looked confused but didn't say anything. Neither did he move away from the door. Clearly Rachel had never told him about the daughter of her ex-husband, which could make this situation even more awkward. "I'm assuming this is police business, judging by the FBI badge?"

"We are here on official business." She flashed her own badge.

There was clearly an issue between Rachel and her new husband, but there was no reason Aubrey needed to disclose their former relationship. "I'm sorry to disturb you, but we're looking for a way to contact Charles Ramsey."

"Charles?" Rachel's gaze dropped. "Is he in trouble—"

"Wait a minute . . ." Corey grabbed the doorframe with one hand. "Your ex-husband?"

"The FBI needs to talk with him," Jack said, leaving it at that. "We're having trouble tracking him down. We thought you might know where he is."

Aubrey tried to read Rachel's expression as she glanced at her husband. Annoyance? Fear? She wasn't sure.

Rachel sucked in a sharp breath. "You have to understand that when I walked out of his life, I walked out for good. I haven't talked to him since the divorce was finalized, and I don't want to. He was a mistake I'd like to forget."

"So you have no way at all to contact him?" Aubrey asked.

Her gaze shifted again. "I just said I haven't talked to him since I signed the divorce papers, and I'm married again, so . . . there was never a reason to keep in touch with him. And honestly, I'd like to leave the past in the past."

"I understand. I'm sorry to bother you." Jack handed her his business card. "If you do happen to hear from him, please give me a call. It is very important that we get ahold of him."

"Of course, and I'm sorry I couldn't be of any help."

She was simply another victim in the wake of her father's destruction.

Aubrey started back down the driveway with Jack, feeling his irritation. "There was something about the way she answered that made it seem like she knows something she's not telling us," she said.

"I agree, but why?"

"The number one reason would be her husband. He could be the jealous type. We have no idea how much she's told him about her ex, and if she's seen him . . ."

"Is there anything else you can think of about her that might help?"

"Honestly, I don't know her well. I never did. She eloped with my father. He brought her to meet me a few days before they got married. He wanted my approval, but I tried to act like I didn't care. The bottom line is that there was never a relationship between the two of us. To be honest, I never wanted any kind of relationship with her, and I'm pretty sure she didn't either. The few times I was around her felt awkward, especially to a kid who just wanted to spend time with her father. Not with his new wife."

"So you think she's seen your father?"

"I'm not sure why she would, but it's possible. Something seemed off with her answers."

Jack started to open his car door, then stopped. "You up for a walk and a bit of fresh air to clear your mind?"

"Where to?"

He shot her a grin, then started walking. "It's not far."

"Okay."

She hurried to catch up with him, wondering what he had in mind. But maybe it didn't matter. The weather was perfect, views of the winter beach were stunning, and the company wasn't bad either.

"You know, a few years ago, you wouldn't have questioned my suggestion or missed a chance to go to the beach," he said. "It was your favorite place. There's a food truck set up nearby, so I was thinking some mini tacos and a bit of sunshine might be on the menu before the sun sets."

Ten minutes later she was sitting at one of the picnic tables that overlooked the beach where a family was playing in the sand. It wasn't the first time they'd sat in this very same spot. Back then they would have grabbed takeaway and headed out on the beach with some of their friends in time to catch the sunset. She held on to the memory as he made his way to the table and set down a couple packets of tacos in front of her.

"I didn't think I was hungry, but I was wrong," she said, taking the drink and food he offered her. For the moment, anyway, she was content to just enjoy his company. "It doesn't get much better than this. Seventy-two-degree weather, a couple mini tacos—"

"And don't forget the company."

She couldn't help but laugh. "You can't get much better than this, can you? I confess, I've spent far too much time working and not near enough enjoying what's around me."

"Hazards of the trade, and on top of that you were supposed to be on your vacation right now."

"Some vacation." She added some fresh pico de gallo to her taco, then took a bite. "I'll have to ask for a few more days to make up for this one."

But as much as she enjoyed his company, she couldn't get her father off her mind—how he could be a traitor to the country she loved and served.

"Bree." Jack met her gaze. "You need to know that many people who are recruited don't start out planning to betray their country."

He could still read her thoughts. "Meaning my father didn't wake up one day and just decide to become a traitor?"

"It usually happens gradually," Jack said.

But how he got there wasn't the point. She knew it was greed that had kept him on the path.

Jack's phone buzzed and he pulled it out of his pocket. "Now this is interesting."

"Who is it?"

"A text message from Rachel."

Aubrey frowned. "Really?"

"She says she wants to meet up with us in town in thirty minutes."

"Does she say why?"

"No, but it seems pretty clear that she's wanting to talk to us without her husband standing there."

"So we were right." She caught Jack's gaze and frowned. "She was hiding something."

CHAPTER THIRTEEN

TWENTY-FIVE MINUTES LATER, she and Jack slipped into a coffee bar on the south side of town with colorful tables and chairs and an eclectic mixture of pictures on the walls, including coffee quotes, local sports team paraphernalia, and a few signed celebrity photographs. Even in mid-November, Christmas music was already playing, and the owners had a lopsided Charlie Brown Christmas tree in the corner, decorated with coffee-themed ornaments. Not really the kind of place she could imagine her father's ex-wife hanging out, but maybe that was the point. If she was hiding something—and Aubrey was certain she was—this was a perfect meeting place.

Aubrey studied the busy room, where most of the tables were already filled and half a dozen customers sat on comfortable chairs, glued to their laptops. But there was no sign of Rachel.

"Do you want something to drink while we wait?" Jack asked.

She glanced up at the long list of specialty coffees. "I could use some caffeine."

"So could I. You still prefer your latte with extra milk and two sugars?"

She smiled. "You remembered."

His hand brushed hers as he started for the counter. "It's not been that long."

"The place is filling up, so I'll get us a seat."

A strange stir slipped through her at his unassuming touch. Familiarity? Wistfulness? She couldn't put a name to it, nor was she sure what just passed between them. It brought up memories of carefree Saturdays at the beach she'd always thought would last forever. But nothing ever really lasted forever. She'd come to accept the reality that there were new stages of life, things changed, and that was okay. What she didn't expect was for her feelings to be so strong at seeing him again.

She slipped into one of the last booths in the back of the room that gave her a clear view of the front door. If she were honest with herself, she'd thought about Jack often over the past few years, wondering why they'd let their friendship drift apart. She really couldn't blame either of them completely. After he moved, they called and exchanged text messages frequently at first until one day she couldn't remember the last time they talked. It happened so gradually, and life was so busy, she realized she hadn't even noticed. Which made her sad.

It felt strange to watch him ordering coffee while she sat waiting for him. She almost expected him to return to the table and start talking about classes and what they were going to do over the weekend. Their relationship had always been strictly friendship. He was her best friend since sixth grade, which was all she wanted. And she'd made an effort to keep it that way. The handful of times she'd felt something more try to trickle in between them, she'd managed to force those feelings to disappear, because she'd been terrified that if they stepped into the water of a relationship, everything they had would change between them. And if they broke up, they might have lost it all.

Like what had happened between her mother and father.

The comparison wasn't new to her. She knew that was where her fear of a relationship with Jack had originated. Her parents' relationship had made her gun-shy, but she couldn't compare her relationship with Jack to her parents'. Her mother and father had been good friends during college, then, two months before graduation, they both realized that they wanted more out of the relationship. Her mother confessed once that she wondered what would have happened if she had taken the scholarship for a master's degree in musical performance at Guildhall in the UK, but her father had somehow talked her into staying and teaching at a small school on the Gulf Coast, eventually settling in Corpus.

Was that really the only reason she'd always made sure nothing romantic developed between her and Jack? It wasn't the first time she'd asked herself that question. What if she'd been wrong? But then when Adam asked her out, for some reason she said yes. She always enjoyed Adam's sense of humor and his love for the great outdoors, but Adam had never been Jack. Not long into their new relationship, she realized Adam wasn't what she wanted. He wasn't Jack.

But by that time, telling Jack—or Adam for that matter—seemed too late. And besides, by then Jack was already gone. Telling him how she felt would have made things even more awkward than they already were.

She glanced up and saw him maneuver his way through the

busy café with the two drinks in his hands and a small paper bag, making her suddenly wish they weren't working on a case but were simply here to catch up on the past few years.

He set her drink on the table, then slid into the booth across from her.

"Thank you."

"The tacos were great, but I couldn't resist the macaroons."

She laughed. "You never could. You've always had an incurable sweet tooth. Don't think I ever saw you turn down any dessert."

"You know me too well."

"Dipped in chocolate?"

"Of course."

He held her gaze for a moment, then reached into the bag, pulled out one, and handed it to her before grabbing another one for himself.

"I still have a love for the water and street tacos, and you still love macaroons," she said. "Maybe time hasn't changed us as much as it feels like sometimes when I look in the mirror."

Jack laughed. "Trust me. You haven't aged a day since I saw you last."

"And you are just as charming."

"What about the bucket list you were always going to finish by the time you turned thirty?"

She took a sip of her coffee, then sat back, wanting for a moment to forget the reason they were really there. "For starters, I finally did the sixty-mile Tour de Houston this year and took my first cruise in the Caribbean with the McKenna family. What about you?"

"I went skydiving on my twenty-fifth birthday."

"Not bad. I've still got that on my bucket list."

"What about traveling?" he asked. "Besides the cruise. I know you always wanted to go to Italy and Australia."

"Went to Italy and France two years ago. Still hoping for Australia, though it might not be before I'm forty."

He smiled at her with that broad, familiar grin. Coming from a dysfunctional homelife that had done a number on her self-esteem, she loved the way he'd always made her feel safe and cared for. Somehow, with him involved in this case, she felt just as safe.

The bells on the front door chimed, dragging her attention back to the reason they were here, and it had nothing to do with macaroons or future trips to Australia. Rachel walked through the door. She'd changed into workout clothes and a light jacket. She slid into the booth next to Aubrey, clearly uncomfortable with her surroundings. Or maybe she was just uncomfortable meeting with the FBI.

"I told my husband I was going to the gym, but then again, I didn't exactly tell you the truth either."

Aubrey wrapped her fingers around her drink. "Maybe you should explain."

"I . . . I saw your father a couple days ago."

"Here in Corpus?"

She nodded. "He called me up out of the blue and asked me to meet him for lunch at the Omni Hotel."

"What did he want?" Jack asked.

Rachel hesitated before answering. "He needed to borrow some money."

"How much?"

"Ten grand."

Jack's brow rose. "And did you give it to him?"

"No. I'm well off, thanks to my husband, but even he'd notice that kind of money disappearing out of our account. I told him he was going to have to go find someone else. He tried to assure me it was just for a couple weeks and that he could pay it back with interest, but I told him I didn't want anything to do with him."

"Did he say what he wanted the money for?" Aubrey asked.

"He said he needed to leave the country and had run short on funds he could access quickly, though he promised me he had a big payout just around the corner. Then again, he was always talking about the next big deal that would change everything. I just figured he had to be pretty desperate to come to me. I also know that he could talk most people into anything, but I already learned my lesson."

Rachel was right. Her father knew how to be a chameleon and fit in wherever he was. He could give the impression he was rich whether he had a dime in the bank or a couple grand in his back pocket. And she had no doubt that he'd given that impression when he snagged Rachel initially.

"What else did he say?" Jack asked.

"He said he was in some kind of trouble but wouldn't tell me what. And now the FBI's looking for him? I guess he was right about being in trouble. What has he done?"

Jack took a sip of his coffee. "I'm afraid that will have to stay classified for now."

"So why didn't you tell us this back at your house?" Aubrey asked.

"Because Corey has always been the jealous type. My sister

says I ignore it because he has money, but for whatever reason, I know I don't want him finding out I spoke to Charlie."

Her response confirmed Aubrey's lingering suspicions that the woman had only been after her father for his money. More than likely, he hadn't been the only one good at spending beyond his means. "Do you know where he's living or how we could get ahold of him?"

"No." She shook her head. "The number he called me from came up unknown. He told me he had to go off the grid for the next few weeks. That he was involved in something important for his country, but there were some very bad people after him and he needed to disappear for a while."

"And you believed him?"

"I have no idea if he was telling the truth or not. You know how your father is as well as I do. He could make you believe anything and everything he does is for the greater good." She tapped a set of manicured nails on the table. "I really think he's in trouble this time. A part of me feels bad I didn't help him, but I have no plans to get involved with him ever again. I learned my lesson being married to him."

Aubrey leaned forward. "If he needs money, who else would he go to?"

"I have no idea. From what I saw, the man hasn't changed at all. I'm not going to be dragged into his web again. And if Corey found out I agreed to see him . . ."

"We appreciate your meeting with us," Jack said. "Can you think of anything else?"

"No. I'm sorry, but I thought I should come clean. I don't want to get in trouble for withholding evidence or anything."

"That was a good decision."

"Is he really in trouble?"

"Yes, he is. But if we can talk to him, we might be able to help him."

Rachel grabbed her purse off the seat next to her. "I have a lot of regrets in life, and unfortunately, your father is one of them. When we first met, I was mesmerized. I'd just ended a bad relationship, and he managed to waltz into my life and sweep me off my feet. He was full of crazy spy stories that made me laugh, and somehow I lost my head for a while. Until I realized that beneath the surface was someone completely different than the person he always tried to portray."

Aubrey frowned. "Thank you for telling us."

"You have my card," Jack said. "If he contacts you again, I need you to let me know."

Rachel nodded, then slid out of the booth before catching Aubrey's gaze. "I know this is going to sound crazy, but I really did love him. Or at least loved who I thought he was. Turned out I was wrong, but for a while, he made me happy. And for what it's worth . . . I know now how much he must have hurt you and your mother, and for that I'm truly sorry."

Aubrey watched her walk away, feeling sorry for the woman for the first time. She supposed the same thing had happened to her own mother. She'd fallen in love with the man she thought he was, and in the end had never stopped loving him, no matter what he'd done. Love did that sometimes. Made you stay when you should run.

CHAPTER FOURTEEN

JACK STARED OUT at the ocean where the moon cast a streak of white across the water. He'd spent the evening working with Bree and two other agents as they scoured FBI notes, updated files, and input data, all in hopes that they could find a way to put an end to this. With news that the senator was asleep and stable, the family had gone to bed after an exhausting day. Bree had been close behind them. He was enjoying some time alone, sitting out on the veranda of the senator's house, drinking decaf coffee and working through the data they'd compiled one last time before finally turning in for the night.

He pushed back his computer, dropped his chin to his chest, and slowly moved his head in a circular motion, trying to work out the kinks in his neck. He was thankful the McKenna family had offered him a room at the house so he could stay close and protect Bree. Today had taken him by surprise. He'd been impressed—though not surprised—at how she'd responded to her situation. But he wasn't sure about the other feelings he was having, seeing her again after all these years.

He'd spent years trying to forget her, telling himself it was okay to leave her in the past. But seeing her again had resurrected all those feelings he thought he'd managed to bury. And now that he was here—with her—he had no idea what to do with them.

The back door of the house creaked open, and his brother stepped out on the veranda.

Jack looked up as Adam crossed the stone flooring. "I thought you'd left to go home."

"I was almost out the door when I got a call from CCPD. The judge denied Hwang bail. I thought you'd want to know."

"Good. I'm still going through the contact information on his phone."

"Anything?"

"Maybe. One of his contacts is Peter Cheng, who was investigated by the FBI about five years ago for Chinese espionage." Jack sat back in his chair and looked up at his brother. "Surveillance of him went on for almost a year, but in the end, the agents failed to come up with enough evidence to prosecute him, which unfortunately made many believe it was simply an example of racial profiling. But while that might be true of some investigations, I know the agent who led that one, and honestly, I can't see him bending his principles just to arrest someone. With what I'm finding, I think there's a good chance the investigation was right on. Cheng could be Bree's father's handler."

"That would be huge."

Jack nodded. Ramsey's handler would be the one he passed information on to, primarily through encrypted communication tools, emails left in draft folders, and possibly even in person. In return, Ramsey would be compensated financially. And Ramsey wouldn't be Cheng's only asset.

"But we're still missing something," Jack said. "We don't know specifically what her father did that made the Chinese want him eliminated."

"Well, my suggestion is that you put it aside for now and try to get some sleep. It's been a long day, and all of this will still be here in the morning."

"I know. There's just so much information to go through."

"Like I said, it will all still be here in the morning." Adam sat down in the matching wrought iron chair next to him. "You remember that big kingfish I caught the last time you were here?"

Jack glanced up at his brother, surprised by the shift in conversation. "The one you were always exaggerating about its size?"

Adam laughed. "It wasn't an exaggeration, but yes."

"You'll never forget that, will you?"

"That's just my way of telling you I miss you," Adam said. "You need to come back more often. A day out on the water arguing over who's going to make the biggest catch of the day would be nice."

"I miss you too. I just wish it wasn't so . . ." Jack searched for the right word. "Complicated."

"What's complicated about coming back here more often? Shoot . . . if I had it my way, you'd move back here. The pace is slower, and family is closer, and I've been dying to try out your H&H Magnum rifle on the range again."

Jack laughed. "So now the real reason comes out for your wanting me to come back."

Adam smiled, but his grin quickly faded. "There are other reasons. Mom and Dad are less than three hours away, you're near the ocean where you can go boating, windsurfing, hunting, and eat the best seafood for miles. Or if for no other reason than we can hang out together more than once a year."

The comment stung. He'd been gone for too long, but that didn't mean moving back here was the answer.

"You're right about coming back more often," Jack said. "But I like what I do. I like where I am in life."

"I just miss having you around. I can hardly remember the last time we just hung out."

Jack took a sip of his coffee. "I'll make a deal with you. We'll set a date before I leave. We'll see if we can borrow the senator's boat and take it out for a few days. Just the two of us. We'll see who can make the biggest catch of the day, eat way too much beef jerky and trail mix, and catch too much sun."

Adam smiled. "I'd like that."

"I have to admit, despite everything that's going on, it's good to be back. I miss the warm winter, the ocean, and you and your family, of course."

"You still need to come to dinner before you leave. Kristy's going to be upset if she doesn't see you."

"I have a feeling I'm going to be staying a bit longer than I originally planned."

"Does any of that have to do with Aubrey?"

Jack hesitated. He'd never told Adam about his feelings toward Bree and, as far as he was concerned, never planned to. That wasn't a road he wanted to go down right now.

"It's been a long time, and I hadn't realized how much I

missed her. But I bet you're enjoying seeing her as well. There doesn't seem to be any awkwardness between the two of you like I would have expected."

"We worked things out years ago. Our breakup was mutual, and we've managed to stay friends. She's even come by the house a couple times and met Kristy."

Jack swallowed the last of his coffee, then pushed it aside. "I'll be honest. Being back does make me question why I left sometimes. There was a time when I planned to grow old and retire here. I'll always consider it home. I miss the beaches, the sunshine, and a taqueria on every corner."

Adam leaned back in his chair. "In case you're still in doubt, I know why you left. You were in love with her."

His brother's words took him by surprise. "With Bree?"

"That is who we were just talking about, isn't it?"

Jack set his empty coffee cup on the table. He hadn't expected the conversation to go in this direction. He'd barely admitted his feelings to himself, let alone to anyone else. And that was years ago. Nothing was going to change now.

"If I remember correctly, you were the one in love with her back then, not me," he said.

"That's where you're only partially right. I thought I was falling in love with her—for a while—but you were the one who was in love with her."

Jack pushed back his chair, feeling the urge to cut their conversation short and leave. His brother had always had a tendency to exasperate him.

"Come on, Jack. You might not have thought anyone else knew, but it was pretty obvious. Maybe not at first, but the day you left . . . I don't even remember now what you said, but I realized why you were leaving, and it had little to do with that job you took and far more to do with Bree."

"You never said anything."

"Maybe I should have, but what was I supposed to say? She was my girlfriend at the time, and I didn't want to lose her. I just never thought I'd lose you instead."

Jack's frown deepened as he shook his head. "You never lost me. We might not be as close as we used to be, but you're my brother, and that will never change, even though I'm not around as much as I wish I was. And as for Bree . . . We were close friends, but that was it. At least for her. She had no ties to me romantically, and the two of you . . . Things were very different back then. I didn't want her to know how I felt. Definitely didn't want you to know."

"Why not?"

He leaned forward, not sure why they were even having this conversation. "Because she was in love with you, not me. And you felt the same. I figured the two of you were going to get married and live happily ever after. What would have happened if I had said something to her? I couldn't ask her to leave you. To choose between the two of us. That wouldn't have been fair to you or her. So in the end, leaving seemed like the right thing to do."

"But we didn't end up getting married, and I've always been convinced that part of the reason we broke up was because of you."

Jack turned back to his brother. He was exaggerating the situation—just like one of his fish stories. "Why would you think that? We were never anything more than friends."

"Maybe not, but I always believed she felt the same way about you."

"Adam—"

"The two of you were close friends, and I think you were both so afraid of anything going wrong and messing up your friendship that you missed what was right in front of you. I bet you anything that she was in love with you too. I probably should have said something back then once I realized things weren't going to work out between the two of us. Looking back, I think your leaving was the wake-up call that she'd chosen the wrong brother. I think that's when something changed in our relationship. But by then . . . I don't know . . . we both ended up losing her."

Jack frowned, working to put his emotions back in place. With his brother's OCD tendencies, once he got fixated on an idea, there was no stopping him. But *this* was nothing more than another one of his brother's tall tales. Except this time, it hit on a far more personal level.

Jack shook his head. "You're wrong. She was never in love with me. I would have known it."

"Would you have?"

Jack shifted in his seat, uncomfortable with the way the conversation had turned. All that had been years ago. All three of them had moved on, and she had her own life now—one that didn't include him. Maybe he should have said something all those years ago, but he couldn't go back and change the past. It was behind them, where it should be.

"Even if what you're saying was true, it isn't anymore. It's way too late for anything to happen between me and Bree.

We're going to solve this case, then I'm heading back home, and she'll go back to Houston. End of story."

"Why does it have to be the end of the story?"

Really?

Jack tried to brush away his irritation from his brother's dogged line of questioning, wondering how he'd suddenly ended up on the receiving end of an interrogation. Just because Adam had found "the one" didn't mean Jack wasn't okay being single. He just hadn't found the person he wanted to spend the rest of his life with.

"It's the end of the story," Jack said, "because for starters, we're both different people than we were back then."

"I'm not sure things have changed that much. I see the same thing in your eyes when you look at her that I saw all those years ago, and I'm pretty sure I see the same thing in her eyes. You're both just too stubborn to admit it. And here's something else." Adam leaned forward and met his gaze. "Have you ever wondered why she didn't get married and move on? The only thing that makes sense is that she lost her heart to someone else, meaning you."

Jack stared out over the water. A cloud had covered half the moon, dimming its light and making him wonder if a storm was coming in. He knew Bree was glad to see him—that wasn't the issue—but the idea of her having romantic feelings for him was totally off base.

"Feel free to go ahead and ask her," Jack said. "But she isn't waiting for me. I can promise you that."

"What if you're getting a second chance to see if something could happen between you?"

Jack shook his head. "She never knew how I felt, and somehow telling her now would be—"

"Would be what? Think of it this way. What do you have to lose? Either she felt the way you did, or she didn't. Why not take a chance and find out?"

"Because I'm not in love with her anymore. That part of my life was good. She was my best friend, and I have a lot of good memories."

"And how did that friendship work out with you living a thousand miles away? You can't lose what you don't have now, and on the other hand, you have a lot to gain if I'm right."

Jack didn't answer, because his brother was right about one thing. He'd left to save their friendship, then watched as it slowly crumbled because of the miles between them. But none of that mattered. Not really. Because not only did he have no idea what she felt, he had no idea what he felt anymore.

"All I'm saying is that it looks to me like you're being given a second chance. Or more accurately, a chance to see what could happen. Like I said, what do you really have to lose?"

Jack's heart twisted inside his chest, but as far as he was concerned, it made much more sense to simply leave the past where it belonged. In the past. "If she felt something, she would have told me years ago."

"Like you told her?"

His brother's words stung.

Adam stood up. "I'm just giving you my two cents, but I still think she's good for you. I just want you to be happy. I'm heading home now. I'll call you if I hear anything."

Jack nodded, grateful for the reprieve. He was happy. And he didn't need someone in his life to complete him. Not even Bree. He watched his brother head back into the house. Part of him wanted to slug Adam square in the jaw. The man was infuriating. The other part wanted to believe everything he'd just told him.

He grabbed his computer and empty coffee cup and headed back into the house, locking the back door behind him. The house had a high-tech security system, and a couple of CCPD officers were parked outside. At least he didn't have to worry about Bree being safe tonight.

But did he have to worry about his heart?

She was standing in the kitchen, her hair down around her shoulders, wearing gray sweats and a pink T-shirt while fixing a cup of tea.

She looked up as he turned off the adjoining room light. "Jack? I didn't think anyone was up. Adam just left."

"I saw him."

She held up her mug. "I thought I might try some more of that chamomile tea."

"Having trouble sleeping?"

"Yes, but I think I'm just too tired to sleep."

He leaned against the counter while she waited for the tea to steep. "It's been a long day."

"With more questions than answers. What's next?"

"I've been working to see what we can get out of Hwang's phone contacts. Your father isn't the only person I'm looking for."

"I spoke with my boss and arranged to take a few more days off. He couldn't exactly argue when I told him I was going to be helping out the FBI."

He watched as she squeezed the tea bag into the mug before tossing it into the trash. "Do you ever regret not staying here?"

Her brow furrowed. "In Corpus?"

Jack nodded, not even sure himself where he was going with this conversation. Adam's suggestion that he tell her how he'd felt all those years ago was crazy.

"Why? Feeling sentimental about being back?"

"Not particularly. I was just talking to Adam, and he told me that I don't come down here near enough. Made me realize that I miss my family. That I always tend to get way too caught up with my work."

She took a sip of her tea, then set it down on the counter and caught his gaze. "You're good at what you do, and you have a job that makes a difference."

"Maybe, but I just can't help but wonder what might have happened if I had stayed here."

And if I'd told you how I felt all those years ago.

But he wasn't going there.

"Anyway," he said, steering the conversation back somewhere safe. "Do you have everything you need before I head up to bed?"

"All my stuff was already here, so I'm good. And you?"

"I had my things brought over, so I'm set up in one of the guest rooms."

She picked up her tea. "I'll see you in the morning then."

"Good night. And Bree . . ."

She stopped in the arch leading out of the kitchen. The soft glow of the light made a halo around her head. "Yeah?"

He swallowed hard. "It really is good to see you again."

CHAPTER FIFTEEN

AUBREY GOT UP WITH the sun the next day after a restless night with strange dreams, only to discover that Jack had gotten up even earlier. He was sitting at the bar in the kitchen, drinking coffee and already at work on the list of names they'd gotten off Hwang's phone.

"I've already found information on a number of them," Jack said as she poured herself a cup of coffee.

"What time did you get up?" she asked.

"Not too long ago," he said. "I couldn't sleep. But I was hoping you would. Yesterday was emotional for you."

She shook her head. "That probably accounts for my disturbing dreams. But I'm fine. How can I help?"

"I'm mainly just trying to see if any of Hwang's contacts' information matches up with anything I've got."

"And so far?" she asked.

"I think I hit the jackpot."

Between refills of coffee and leftover pastries someone had brought in the day before, they worked for the next hour in silence, grateful that the rest of the house was still asleep. She ended up following what she hoped wasn't a rabbit trail, and it paid off.

"Jack," she said, trying to stretch out the kinks in her back. "You need to see this."

"What have you got?"

"I had to do a lot of digging, but Cheng has a girlfriend."

"A girlfriend? I wonder why she wasn't in his file."

"Because I found her through his cell phone records. He's only been in contact with her recently. Her name is Mei Lien." She pulled up the file she'd started on the woman. "I'm not finding much on her, and only one photo of the two of them together, but it's recent. She doesn't have a criminal record, not even a parking ticket, but she is on Facebook. And she just accepted me as a friend from a bogus account."

"Seriously?"

"It's not that surprising, really. A lot of people accept invitations just to increase their friend count."

"Not bad. But how do you know she's his girlfriend?"

Aubrey showed him the photo she'd found of the two of them. "I'll admit I'm making assumptions, but I wouldn't put a photo up like this with just anyone."

"Point taken."

Aubrey smiled as she started flipping through the profile photos. "Looks like she's still in school right here in Corpus. She's a grad student, marine biology. They look pretty cozy and the photo is recent."

"But that's not the biggest news." She turned to him. "I dug a little deeper and discovered that her father works for a company that develops stealth technologies for the government. I think there's a good chance that Cheng's using her to get information or even more likely, trying to recruit her father."

"It would make sense. It happens all the time, and they definitely target the private sector as well as the government." Jack frowned. "If we could find a way to use her to find Cheng . . ."

Aubrey hesitated before throwing out her idea. "What if we turn the tables on them and use her as bait like they did with me?"

Jack sat down across from her. "What exactly are you suggesting?"

"They used me to try and get to my father. We need to find Cheng, and she can lead us to him."

"I suppose it's possible, but to do that, we'd have to turn her against him. Do you really think that's going to happen?"

"I learned something else interesting about her. During her undergrad work, she was a part of her school's ROTC program."

"That doesn't mean she's patriotic, or that she can be turned."

Aubrey frowned. "Don't all of you alphabet soup agencies know how to turn people?"

"Very funny."

"Well? I don't know about you, but I think it's worth a shot." She tapped her pencil against the table. "And I think I could do it."

That got his attention. "You? Seriously?"

"Yes."

"And you think you could use her to lead you to Cheng?"

"I do."

"What happens if she goes straight back to him and lets him know that the authorities are looking for him? We could lose him for good."

"It's not like we have him now. Besides, more than likely, he already has to know we're looking for him. I think it's worth the risk, and I want to be the one to talk to her. Because if you're right about the intel that's at stake, we don't have time to sit on this."

"Even if we did try to turn her—and that's a big if—I would send in a trained agent. Not you."

"I wasn't trained to flip assets at Quantico, but I know what it's like to be betrayed by someone you love. When she finds out the truth about Cheng, that's how she's going to feel."

He still didn't look convinced. "You're assuming she's going to disagree with what Cheng is involved in—if she doesn't already know—and will feel betrayed. We don't know that. The logical thing to do is surveillance."

Aubrey frowned. His resistance only made her all the more determined to convince him she was right. "Then let's do both. I'll talk to her, and then you follow her when she leaves. Think about it, Jack. I know what she's going to feel the moment she hears Cheng is using her. And I'll be right there to show her how she can make it right. I can do this, Jack."

"How?"

"By telling her the truth."

WALKING THROUGH THE ISLAND campus set on the edge of the water brought back memories of favorite professors, midnight food runs, and stunning ocean views.

"I don't know about you, but college seems like a lifetime ago," Aubrey said, matching Jack's long steps as they headed toward her rendezvous site with Mei.

"Yes, but I have no desire to be twentysomething again."

She laughed at the comment. "I have to agree."

She also had to wonder why he'd asked her last night if she regretted leaving Corpus. Maybe he was simply being nostalgic, but it wasn't something she'd thought much about. Her life was good. She loved her job, had good friends, was a part of a good church that challenged her spiritually. Just because she hadn't done what everyone had—gotten married—didn't mean she felt like she was missing something in her life or wanted to go back and do it over differently.

What she did miss was their friendship.

Aubrey stopped when she caught sight of Mei waiting for her on one of the shaded benches where they'd agreed to meet.

"I'll go ahead on my own now," she said.

"Yes, ma'am, but if anything goes wrong, I've got two agents out there helping me make sure you're safe."

"Just stay out of the way, Agent Shannon. I'll be fine."

She started walking down the brick pavement again, trying not to be irritated at his overprotectiveness. *That* was something about him that hadn't changed. Maybe the biggest surprise was that he hadn't protested more about her doing this on her own. Or maybe the reason he hadn't protested was because he'd gone overboard on security. His undercover agents—a student sitting on another bench listening to his headphones and a maintenance man cleaning up a spill—stood out like a sore thumb, as far as she was concerned.

"Mei Lien?" Aubrey sat down next to her on the bench and smiled. "I'm Aubrey Grayson. I appreciate your agreeing to meet with me."

"I'm happy to, although I realized after you hung up that I wasn't sure what you want from me. You said you're a former student here doing some research?"

"That's part of it. What I didn't tell you is that I'm a detective with the Houston police department, and I'm currently working with the FBI. I need to talk to you about your boyfriend, Peter Cheng."

Aubrey held up the photo of Mei and Cheng she'd found on Facebook.

"I don't understand." Mei's eyes narrowed. "What does the FBI want with Peter?"

Aubrey watched Mei drop the book she'd been reading into her backpack as if she were ready to run, but she couldn't let that happen. She needed to get the woman to see the seriousness of the situation before she bolted.

"I'm going to be honest with you," Aubrey said. "The FBI needs to talk to him. We have evidence that he's been recruiting spies and buying classified information for the Chinese government—"

"Peter?"

"I know it's hard to hear, but yes." Aubrey paused, giving her time to let what she was telling her sink in. "The FBI has evidence that he is responsible for the recent theft of military source codes that are used to control both US government and commercial satellite systems."

"Source codes . . . satellite systems . . . classified information . . ." Mei grabbed her backpack and stood up. "I don't know who you are, or why you're doing this, but what you're saying isn't possible. Peter isn't a . . . a spy."

"He's using you, Mei—"

"Using me? How? I'm just a grad student studying marine biology." Mei started walking away. "I don't have access to any classified government information."

Aubrey started after her. "Except you do. Or at least your father does."

Mei froze, then turned around. "Peter hasn't even met my father, and besides, you don't know him. He's not that kind of person."

"I know this is a lot to take in, but I asked to be the one to meet with you for one reason. I was just on the receiving end of this same conversation. The FBI has evidence that my father is one of the men Peter is working with, and that he's trying to get his hands on some specific classified information for him."

"I don't believe you."

"I know it sounds crazy, but the truth is that if Peter gets the information he's after, people are going to die."

Mei walked back to the bench, dropped her backpack beside her, and sat back down. "He loves me. I know he does, but now . . . now you're telling me I'm stupid and naïve to believe him."

"No. You're neither of those things. Peter knows exactly what he's doing and how to manipulate you."

Mei clasped her hands in front of her and stared at the ground. "I always knew I was out of his league. I'm a science geek and he's this rich, handsome, international businessman who's always traveling to interesting places. He promised to take me to Hong Kong next year." Mei shook her head. "I honestly thought he'd marry me and we'd have a family. I thought I could be a part of his world, but if you're right . . ."

"I'm sorry. I truly am."

Mei looked up at Aubrey. "You said your father was one of the people he hired."

"Yes. We're still trying to find him."

"You don't know where your father is?"

"I've been estranged from him for years, but it still hurts."

"And now you're trying to bring him in?"

Aubrey nodded. "I have to, because what he's doing affects more than just me. The consequences are far-reaching. We need your help."

She waited for Mei to respond, the conflict clear in her eyes. They were asking a lot from her, Aubrey understood that. But the consequences of doing nothing were far worse. That was what she had to make her understand.

"Mei. I need you to answer some questions for me. Would you do that?"

She nodded, but hadn't lost the dazed look in her eyes.

"Has Peter ever asked you to write anything for him, or do anything for him that made you wonder why he was asking?"

She'd done her research on how people were targeted. And even though she was convinced Cheng was after Mei's father, they couldn't rule out the possibility that Mei herself had been compromised. Educational exchanges weren't uncommon, nor was the recruitment of students.

"No," Mei said.

"How often does he go to China?"

"Several times a year for business. I don't know much about his company, but he seems to be doing well. But if he's passing along classified information, what's going to happen to him?"

"The FBI will question him and then go from there."

"We both grew up proud of our heritage. Both Chinese and American. In doing this, he's denying who we are. Betraying the country he lives in, his home, his family . . ." She stared out across the courtyard, silent a moment before continuing. "Will he know I'm the one who betrayed him?"

"I promise I'll do everything I can to keep your name out of this, but I can't make any promises."

"Do you still feel guilty about betraying your father?"

"Very." Aubrey nodded, wondering if she'd ever be able to get past it. "There is one more thing, Mei. We need to find him. And we need you to help us."

She hesitated before answering. "What do you want me to do?"

"We need a way to get ahold of him."

"He's been talking about buying a house and settling down, but with all his traveling, he lives out of a suitcase in hotels."

Which explained why the FBI was struggling to track him down.

"When are you going to see him again?" Aubrey asked.

"He just flew into town last night. I'm meeting him later today for lunch. I was going to talk to him about meeting my father for the first time."

"Good. I'll need to know when and where."

"What if he finds out what I've done?"

"The FBI will take care of that. There will be agents with you until Peter is taken into custody. In the meantime, confirm with him that you're still on for lunch, but I don't want you to show up. We will instead."

Mei nodded. "Okay."

"Thank you. I know it doesn't seem like it, but you're doing the right thing."

A minute later, Aubrey walked away with the rendezvous information hoping she'd done the right thing. She'd seen the look on Mei's face. The one of betrayal and shame, along with fear. There might have been another way to get to Cheng, one that didn't involve Mei, but either way the woman had lost.

"Bree."

She looked up. Jack was walking toward her. "I'm fine. I have an address and time where we can find him."

"Do you think she played you?" he asked.

"I can't be a hundred percent sure, but I don't think so."

"You don't look happy. What are you thinking?"

"I was just thinking about how life changes because of the decisions we make. How life can change in an instant because of the decisions another person makes."

"It happens far too often, but right now just think about all the men and women whose lives will be saved if we stop him."

"I know." Aubrey put her hand on Jack's arm. "You've still got a team surveilling her like you planned?"

"We do."

"Promise me you'll keep her safe. I'm not sure why, but I have a bad feeling about all of this. I'm worried that if Cheng finds out she was involved in his arrest, he'll go after her."

"He won't know she talked to us, and I've got a protection team on her."

Aubrey nodded. She trusted him, but there were things even Jack couldn't control.

CHAPTER SIXTEEN

JACK SAT IN THE BACK of the van while he worked with his team of agents on last-minute details of their plan before going inside the restaurant. Personally, he would have preferred a pre-dawn raid at a private location for the arrest, but their investigation had led them here. They'd spent the short amount of time they had planning the arrest, knowing this might be their only chance of bringing Cheng in. If they spooked him, he would disappear. And Mei's life—and that of her father—could also be put in danger. They had to do it right the first time.

"You're sure he's in there alone?" Jack asked Agent Brewster, who was in charge of the logistics.

"Yes, sir. He's sitting at a table on the east side of the restaurant."

"What about waiting for him to leave?" Agent Pepper asked.

"That would open up too many variables for him to get away. Going in quietly is our best option. The restaurant isn't very busy. We'll be in and out before he can protest."

"We have four agents set up outside the building, and two

more will go with you inside, Agent Shannon," Brewster said. "I want you in and out. Clean and fast."

"And I want a tracker on his car in case he does manage to escape," Jack said.

"Already done."

"Good."

Jack felt good about their plan, but from the profile they'd compiled on the man, he also knew Peter Cheng not only seemed to have nine lives, he was fearless. But Cheng wasn't the only one determined to win this battle. Jack glanced up at the video screen capturing all three exits of the restaurant. They were ready. There was no way this guy could get past them.

Five minutes later, he stepped out into the sunshine, thankful Bree had agreed to stay out of the action. He could see the hood of the car she was sitting in along with Agent Baker, guarding the side exit. Mei was at a safe house two miles away with agents, ensuring no one got to her before or during the arrest.

They'd worked to see that they covered every angle that had come up in the short time they had. He knew all too well the gamble he was taking, but it was time to bring Cheng in.

They'd bring in Cheng, and Cheng would lead them to the rest of his minions, as well as Bree's father, who hopefully would in turn lead them to the Chinese involved as well.

Their house of cards was about to collapse.

Cheng sat alone at a window table like Jack had been told. Apparently, he hadn't waited for Mei to order. He already had a plate full of food and a glass of wine in front of him.

Jack crossed the wood flooring, taking in the positions of

everyone else in the room. As he walked in, the manager, who was working with them, escorted the remaining customers out. If things did go wrong, they didn't want anyone caught in the crossfire.

"Peter Cheng . . . I'm Special Agent Jack Shannon." Jack stopped on the other side of the table across from the man and pulled back his suit jacket, revealing his badge. "I'd like to keep this as quiet as possible, but I need you to walk out of here with me. I have a warrant for your arrest for the recruitment of American citizens as assets for your government."

"Special Agent Jack Shannon." Cheng picked up his napkin and wiped his mouth. "I was wondering who they'd send in here. I've been waiting for you."

Jack forced himself to maintain an outward calm, wondering what he'd missed. He knew their plan was solid, but he also had no desire to underestimate the man. The FBI had been searching for him far too long to do that.

Cheng took a bite of his meal, as if they were chatting at a garden party. "Have you ever tried these? They're braised whole abalones."

Jack's irritation rose. "No, I haven't."

"Abalone is a mollusk that eats seaweed. It's expensive and tastes something like scallops. It's also very healthy and worth every bite."

"I don't know what kind of game you think you're playing, but you need to come with me now."

Jack felt the muscles of his jaw twitch. The man seemed far too . . . composed. There was no way he could have known they were coming unless Mei told him, and she was with his men, so that was impossible. She'd been monitored by agents ever since agreeing to help them take Cheng down.

"Don't worry. Mei didn't tell me, if that's what you're thinking," Cheng said, answering Jack's question without him having to voice it. "She thought my life sounded exciting, and thought she could be a part of it. But she's far too naïve. And so are you, if you think you can use Mei to corner me. But I'm being rude. Why don't you sit down and join me? I could call the waiter and order you something. If you don't like the abalone, I recommend the sautéed prawns. They're delicious."

Jack pulled out his firearm and pointed it at the man. The two agents behind him followed his lead.

"That isn't happening," Jack said. "You're going to put down your fork, stand up, and come with me."

"Here's the problem. Like it or not, this isn't exactly going to end the way you were hoping." Cheng looked up at him. "Because if you attempt to arrest me, Mei dies."

Jack's heart thudded in his throat. "What?"

"You heard what I said. Now sit down."

Jack hesitated—still unsure if he was bluffing—then sat down, signaling for the two agents behind him to stay where they were. Cheng had been one step ahead of them the entire investigation, and Jack needed to find out how.

Cheng slid his phone across the table. "Does this convince you I'm telling the truth?"

A photo of Mei stared back at Jack, hands bound in front of her and a gag around her mouth.

No.

No . . . This was impossible. They'd covered their bases and gone over every possible scenario they could think of. They'd taken Mei to a safe location and had a team watching her to make sure nothing like this could happen.

"When was this taken?" Jack asked.

"Just a few minutes ago. Your agents who were guarding her will live, but they will have bad headaches." Cheng grabbed his napkin and wiped his hands. "Which means that the trump card has just switched from you to me, giving me the pleasure of deciding what happens next. Which is this. As soon as we're done chatting here, I'm going to walk out that door, and you—and your entire entourage—are going to watch me walk away."

"No we're not. I have agents surrounding this place, and backup available immediately at Mei's location."

"Good for you, but here's what's about to happen. There is a camera on my shirt showing what is happening here. If I don't walk out of here in the next five minutes, Mei dies. If anything happens to me on my way out, Mei will die. It's as simple as that. A guarantee, shall we say, that you behave and do what you're told."

Anger swept through him, but Jack knew he couldn't gamble Mei's life. And something told him Cheng wouldn't hesitate to follow through with his threat.

"Why meet with me if you knew I was coming?" Jack asked. "Why not simply disappear?"

Cheng laughed at the question. "It's a part of the game. You had the advantage of knowing who you were after. Now I know who you are. Who is after me." He scooted his chair back. "Now tell your agents to stand down, Shannon."

Jack hesitated again, jaw tensed as he looked for a back door out of the situation. One that put Cheng behind bars and kept Mei safe. But it was already too late, it seemed. At least for the moment.

"You think I'm bluffing." Cheng picked up his phone and ran his finger across Mei's photo. "She's a beautiful girl, isn't she? Smart. Talented. But not smart enough, obviously, because she fell for me. Though it wasn't hard to charm her. She's also extremely naïve and innocent. Actually, a perfect mark. And she was getting me exactly what I wanted."

"This is far from over."

"That is where you are once again wrong. Last chance to call off your boys, Shannon. And I better not discover I'm being followed."

Jack hesitated, then spoke through his com. "Stand down, I repeat stand down and let Cheng through. Do not follow."

Cheng slapped a hundred-dollar bill on the table and walked out of the restaurant.

Ten seconds later, Jack stepped inside the back of the surveillance van with the other agents and slammed the door behind him. "You're tracking his car?"

Agent Brewster stared at the computer in front of him. "He had someone pick him up. We can put a BOLO out on the description of the car, but likely it's stolen, and they'll ditch it before we have a chance to find it."

"I don't care what the odds are. We need to find this man," Jack said, addressing the team. "I need to know how Cheng got a jump on us, and how he knew where Mei was. I want backup sent to her location to help the agents, along with an ambulance. And if Mei really is gone . . . I want to know where she is."

Jack reined in his tongue and managed to bite the rest of the words he wanted to throw at the men. Yelling wasn't going to get him the answers he needed, but neither was sitting here doing nothing. If Mei died because they fouled up . . .

"We had him." Jack's voice rose to a frustrated shout. "But now we just lost what was probably our best chance to bring Cheng in. And on top of that, we have an innocent woman's life on the line."

"I don't know what to say, sir, except I am trying to trace the signal from his phone."

"Trying isn't good enough." Jack loosened his tie and pulled it off. On top of everything else, it felt like a heat wave in the middle of November. "I need to know where he is. Now."

"Jack . . ." Bree stepped into the back of the van, her face pale. "What just happened?"

"He outplayed us."

"How?" She shook her head. "That's impossible."

"That's what I thought, but he did. He's gone, and he has Mei and possibly two of our agents."

"Do you think she told him?" Bree asked.

"He said she didn't, and I don't know how she could have, but it's possible."

"No . . . She wouldn't have told him. I saw the fear in her eyes when I told her what he'd done. She wouldn't have told him. But either way, we have to find her. Because whether she told him or not, he's going to kill her. She knows too much now."

"We will find her, Bree."

He could see her chest heaving as she tried to catch her breath. If they didn't find Mei—alive—she was going to blame herself for involving the innocent woman.

"What are we doing to find her?" she asked.

"Backup is on its way to the safe house now in case she's still there. We also have someone working to track the signal from Cheng's phone."

"How?" Bree turned to Brewster.

"It's a long shot at this point, but thanks to the information we got off Hwang's phone, we're trying to access Cheng's cell phone signal and become a middle man between him and the cell tower. If we can locate his phone, then we can tap into his text messages and phone calls and even his GPS."

"What about tracking Mei?"

"That's where it gets trickier," Brewster said. "If Cheng calls or texts the men who have her, we can try and tap into their signal as well. Then we might have a chance of finding her, but it won't be easy."

"Keep trying," Jack said to his team, then turned back to Bree. "Let's go outside and let them work."

She stepped outside the truck, her arms wrapped around her waist. "Why did he agree to meet with you if he knew it was a setup?"

"He told me it's a game."

"What kind of game?"

"His own twisted one. He's a spy who handles assets for a living. He loves what he does, and the risks he takes—that and the money—fuels him to stay in 'the game.'"

She leaned against the back of the van while the wind whipped her hair around her shoulders. "That's crazy."

"Yes, but it also makes sense. He does this for the adrenaline rush. At least partly. You know how it is. You love curling up with a good book, but I have a feeling that after a week, you wouldn't be able to stand the quiet. Why?"

She stared beyond him. "Because I want to be out there. Doing what I know makes a difference in the world."

"Exactly."

She blinked back the tears. "He's not going to let her go. He's going to kill her, Jack."

"Then we better find a way to get to her before he does."

CHAPTER SEVENTEEN

THE BACK DOOR of the van opened, and Agent Pepper stuck his head out. "You need to come in here and see this—both of you."

"You found Cheng?" Aubrey asked, pulse racing as she ducked inside. Just because they'd been played didn't mean this was over.

"So far we haven't been able to trace his cell phone—"

"But you have something," Jack said.

Brewster nodded. "We just screened an anonymous 911 call that was made in the same block where Mei was being kept across the bay."

"And . . ."

"A neighbor saw two men force a woman into the trunk of a car. We have the license plate of the car."

"What about a location of the car, or description of whoever took her . . . anything?" Jack asked, shutting the van door behind them.

"We're trying to get more information now, but a BOLO was just put out on the plate."

Aubrey glanced at Jack. "What about the witness?"

"Officers are on their way there now."

"Jack . . ." Aubrey turned to him. "We're only fifteen minutes away at the most. I want to talk to the witness."

"I agree." Jack turned to Brewster. "What about a GPS locator on the car?"

"We're working on it. If the vehicle's equipped with security like OnStar we should be able to use GPS to locate it. It even might be possible to remotely slow down the vehicle."

"We'll need the address of the witness," Aubrey said, heading back outside in front of Jack.

Brewster called out, "I've already sent it to both your phones."

Three minutes later, they were heading across the Harbor Bridge toward Portland, located across the Nueces Bay from Corpus Christi, past the Texas State Aquarium and the USS *Lexington*. Crime was typically lower in Portland, partly because of a higher police presence, making it the perfect place— she assumed—for an FBI safe house. But something in their plan had gone very wrong.

A sick feeling had started spreading through her the moment she'd heard Cheng had Mei. She'd been the one to convince the girl to trust her—that they needed her to bring in Cheng—and that she'd be protected. Instead Cheng had found a way to get to her. And if she wasn't already dead, she would be soon.

Guilt bored through Aubrey as she stared out at the water. If anything happened to Mei, she was to blame.

"I know what you're thinking," Jack said as they sped across the bridge.

"I'm thinking how sad it'll be when they replace this beautiful bridge with the new one," she said. She knew that wasn't what he'd been looking for, but she wasn't ready to talk about what they were facing.

"Okay . . ."

"I read that the new bridge will be the tallest point in South Texas." She picked at a broken nail as she stared out the window. "It will also be the longest cable-stayed bridge in the US."

"Bree—"

She sucked in a lungful of air, but it only seemed to feed her apprehension. Time was running out and they needed to drive faster. To find that vehicle before they took Mei to Cheng.

"This wasn't supposed to happen," Aubrey said. "I told her she'd be okay. That we'd protect her. How did he get to her?"

"I don't know, but we'll find out. We'll find her."

"What if we find her and it's too late?"

What if she's already dead?

Aubrey wiped away a tear she couldn't blink back, hating how weak and vulnerable the situation made her feel. But the bottom line was they'd underestimated Cheng, and now Mei was going to pay the price with her life.

"This isn't over," Jack said.

Biting back her frustration, she continued the prayer she'd started for Mei the moment she'd discovered what had happened. She prayed that Jack was somehow right and they would find Mei safe. That Cheng wouldn't be able to hurt her no matter what his intentions. And that they'd find a way to end this entire nightmare.

Because that was why she did what she did. To serve and protect.

They rode the rest of the way in silence. Ten minutes later, Jack pulled in front of the address they'd been given. The one-story, brick-faced house was located across the street and one down from the safe house.

He glanced at the text message Brewster had sent as they walked up to the safe house, where a yellow crime scene tape had been hung up. "Sergeant Fernandez?"

"Yes."

Jack held up his badge and introduced the two of them to the officer standing on the front porch.

"We were just informed that you were on your way here," the sergeant said. "Do you want to see inside the safe house?"

"Not right now," Aubrey said. "We'd like to speak to the witness first."

"I sent her back to her house. She was pretty shaken, but she's aware there will be more questions."

"Good."

"And the agents who were guarding Mei?" Aubrey asked.

"They've been taken to the hospital. The paramedics who responded believe they should fully recover."

"What do you know about the witness?" Aubrey asked as the three of them started walking toward the sidewalk.

"Name's Jacqueline Waters. She works at the post office here in town. Normally she'd be working, but she happened to be taking a sick day."

They nodded their thanks, then headed across the street. Aubrey stepped onto the front porch and rang the doorbell. A few seconds later, a woman opened the door, leaving the screen shut.

"Jacqueline Waters?" Jack asked.

The fortysomething-year-old woman, wearing sweats and a hoodie, nodded.

"I'm FBI Special Agent Jack Shannon and this is Detective Aubrey Grayson. I know you've already spoken to an officer, but we'd like to hear what happened from you."

The woman nodded again, then sneezed into a tissue. "Of course. And I'm sorry . . . I would invite you in, but I've got this horrible cold, which is why I was home in the first place."

"This is fine," Aubrey said. "If you'd just tell us exactly what you saw across the street, we'd appreciate it."

"I'd come into my living room to get my book"—she sneezed again—"when I heard a noise outside. I'm not even sure why I bothered to come look, but two men were carrying a woman to my neighbor's car parked in her driveway across the street. I was trying to see if it was my neighbor, thinking she must be sick, but then they dumped the woman into the trunk."

"Could you see the woman?"

"I didn't get a good look, but she seemed smaller than my neighbor and her hair was darker. Which is what confused me. I don't know who else it would be. My neighbor lives alone."

"But you recognized the car?"

"It was definitely my neighbor's car—her name's Bridget— and she has a blue Honda CR-V."

"And did they come from your neighbor Bridget's house?"

The woman paused at the question. "That's what I assumed, but to be honest, I can't be sure."

"Did you see them get into the car with the woman before they drove away?"

She shook her head, sneezing again. "As soon as I saw them pop the trunk and put her inside, I ran to get my phone. I got 911 on the line, and by the time I got back to the window,

Bridget's car was driving away. I was able to catch the license plate, which I gave to the officer I spoke with earlier."

"Were there any other cars in the area? Maybe a car you didn't recognize?"

The woman paused to think. "The house next door to Bridget has been empty for a while, but now that you mention it, there was another car there I'd never seen before. A dark sedan that was parked along the curb in front of the house. When I came back, it was gone."

Aubrey glanced up at Jack. "So there's a woman in the trunk of a car, and two cars that drove away about the same time."

It didn't make sense.

"Have you seen your neighbor?" Jack asked.

Jacqueline shook her head. "No, and I'm worried. The officer was going to check. She's seventy-two years old and lives alone in that house. I've tried calling several times, but she isn't answering."

"Thank you, Jacqueline," Aubrey said. "We'll be back if we have any other questions."

She started across the street with Jack, who signaled to two officers standing in front of the safe house to join them.

"The neighbor has to fit into this scenario somehow," she said, still trying to put the pieces together. "Where is she?"

"I don't know, but I'm calling Agent Brewster for an update."

"The license plate is registered to a Bridget Sanders," Brewster said once he'd answered. "But she has no online security, so there's no way we can track the car except through an old-fashioned BOLO."

"Our witness told us she was worried about her neighbor,

who's also the owner of the car. She's not answering her phone," Aubrey said.

"From what I heard, officers knocked but didn't go inside," Brewster said. "If we're looking at a possible second abduction, you need to go inside."

"Are we thinking they took both of them?" Aubrey asked as Jack hung up the call. "It doesn't make sense. If they had their own car, why use the neighbor's?"

"I can't answer that," Jack said.

Officer Fernandez and a second officer, Lawrence, joined them in front of Bridget Sanders's home.

"Did you search the house?" Aubrey asked.

"We just knocked on the door. No one answered," Officer Lawrence said.

"The owner's car was stolen, a woman was kidnapped, and then no one answers the door. You don't think that's suspicious?" Aubrey asked.

"We were responding to a 911 kidnapping," Fernandez said, "then we were told there were two FBI agents down next door." She looked distressed. "We didn't know anything about an elderly woman who might be in trouble."

Jack held up his hand. "Let's just make sure no one is inside."

It took them thirty seconds to breach the front door after their persistent knocks went unanswered.

"Bridget Sanders . . . this is the FBI," Jack called, stepping into the house first with his gun raised. "We're checking to make sure you're okay."

They spread out and started clearing the house, room by room, looking for any clue that could explain where the woman was. Aubrey started down the hallway toward the master bedroom, checking each room as she went.

"Clear."

"Clear."

"Clear."

She stopped inside what must be the woman's bedroom. She had seen no signs of struggle anywhere in the house. Here the bed had been made, the closet and dresser drawers were neatly shut, and perfume bottles and jewelry still sat neatly aligned on the dresser.

Aubrey checked the bathroom, then headed to the front of the house.

"Her cell phone is here in the kitchen," Jack said, picking it up.

"So she left in a hurry and forgot it," Officer Fernandez said.

"Or she was taken by force," Aubrey said. "But I didn't see any signs of a struggle."

"I didn't either," Jack said.

"We have officers canvassing the rest of the neighborhood in case someone else saw something," Fernandez said. "We might get lucky."

Jack nodded. "Good."

But they were back to square one.

Two agents down.

And now two women were missing.

Aubrey started for the front door of the house. A car was pulling into the driveway. A blue CR-V.

"Jack . . ."

A woman matching the description of Bridget Sanders got

out of the car with a package in her hand, stopping in the driveway when she saw the officers exiting her house.

"Ma'am—"

"What's going on?"

Aubrey held up her badge. "I'm Detective Aubrey Grayson. I need you to stay where you are."

The older woman took a step backward, clearly panicked. "I don't understand!"

Aubrey signaled for Officer Fernandez to stand with her while Jack opened the trunk. "Just stay where you are, ma'am."

Aubrey headed toward the back of the car, heart racing at what they might find. Their witness could have made a mistake. Identified the wrong car or misinterpreted what she saw. But until they looked inside that trunk, there was no way to know.

She heard the click of the trunk release as Jack pulled the latch and stopped for a few seconds before lifting it open. Her lungs gasped for air.

"Jack . . ." Mei's body lay in front of her, blood running down her head into a pool beneath her cheek. Nausea swept through Aubrey. Cheng had ordered her killed, and now they were too late.

Jack stepped beside her.

Mei's hands had been bound in front of her and a gag placed in her mouth. Aubrey pulled out the gag, then stopped. There was something else inside her mouth. Aubrey forced herself to pull out the crumpled-up piece of paper and felt a wave of terror slice through her as she read the note.

GAME ON, AGENT SHANNON

CHAPTER EIGHTEEN

AUBREY TOOK A STEP back from the trunk. "Wait a minute . . . she's still breathing."

Mei gasped for air and tried to sit up.

"Mei." Aubrey grabbed the young woman's shoulders. "Mei. You're safe now. Take a deep breath."

"We need to get her out of here, now," Jack said.

"There's a chair on the front porch."

Jack lifted the young woman out of the trunk and headed for the house with Aubrey right behind him.

"Fernandez," she shouted. "Call 911. We need to see where this blood is coming from."

"Already on it."

"I'll grab the first-aid kit and a blanket," Lawrence said, running toward their patrol car.

"What's going on?" Bridget Sanders stood at the edge of the driveway with a dazed look in her eyes. "I had no idea there was anyone in my car. I don't understand."

Aubrey brushed past the woman. "Ma'am . . . I need you to stay out of the way for the moment."

On the porch, Jack sat Mei gently in the wicker chair, then

pulled out his knife and cut the cord around her wrists. Aubrey stepped forward with the blanket from Officer Lawrence and wrapped it around Mei's shoulders.

"See what you can find out from her," Jack said. "I'm going to talk to Bridget Sanders."

Aubrey nodded and knelt down in front of the young woman.

"Mei . . . Mei, you're safe now. Can you tell me where you're hurt?"

She pressed her hand against the side of her head. It came back covered in blood. "My head. My head hurts."

"You're going to be okay. We're going to find out why."

Aubrey grabbed some hand sanitizer from the first-aid kit Officer Lawrence set down beside her, pulled on a pair of latex gloves, then started gently parting Mei's hair, searching for the source of the blood.

After a few moments, she said, "Looks like you've got a cut just above your hairline on the side of your head."

"I . . . I remember hitting it on something."

"It's not near as bad as it looks. The gauze will help stop the bleeding. You're going to be fine."

Mei nodded, but she was still shaking.

"Mei . . . I know you're scared, but do you think you can answer a few questions for me?"

"I think so."

"Can you tell me what happened?"

"I don't know. It all happened so fast. Two men broke into the house. They took out the agents, then dragged me outside and put me into the trunk."

"Did you see the men who took you?" Aubrey asked.

"No . . . I don't know . . . I was so scared."

"It's okay. Right now, I just want you to take some deep breaths and try to relax."

Aubrey finished cleaning up Mei's wound, then attached a sterile gauze over the cut. A siren whirred in the distance as the ambulance grew closer. A couple neighbors were standing in their yards now, including their witness, who'd been held back by an officer from coming to check on her neighbor. Cheng might have won this round, but at least both Mei and Bridget Sanders were going to be okay.

"Peter was behind this, wasn't he?" Mei asked.

Aubrey hesitated.

Mei moaned. "I know he was, but I didn't tell him you were coming. I promise."

"We're not sure how he found out, but he used you as leverage to get away."

"What about my father? If that's who he's really after, and he finds him . . ."

"Agents are already at his house to make sure he's okay. They're going to bring your father to the hospital so he can see you."

Mei shook her head as Aubrey closed the first-aid kit and stood up.

"I should have seen it," Mei said. "He was after my father all this time. He never cared about me."

"I don't want you to think about that right now. Right now, I just want to make sure we do everything we need to ensure you're okay."

"But he's still out there?"

Aubrey nodded.

"And if this happens again?"

"I promise we're going to do everything we can to make sure it doesn't happen again."

Mei closed her eyes and swayed forward.

"Mei . . ." Aubrey caught her, placing both hands on her shoulders.

She opened her eyes. "I'm okay. Just . . . dizzy."

The ambulance arrived and two uniformed paramedics stepped onto the porch. "What have we got?"

"There's a large cut on the side of her head. Plus, possible shock or even a concussion. She's dizzy." Aubrey started to move out of the way. "We're going to follow you to the hospital, Mei."

The young woman grabbed Aubrey's arm. "Please . . . please don't leave me. He got to me once, and he can get to me again."

One of the paramedics nodded at Aubrey. "You're free to ride with her if you'd like."

"Thank you."

Aubrey found Jack while she waited for the paramedics to get Mei into the ambulance, unable to shake the guilt and anger that had taken hold of her.

"Her purse was in the trunk," Jack said, handing it to her. "If he wanted to kill her, he could have. Instead, he let her go."

"I know, but I want to know why. I want to know what his endgame is, because to him, this is clearly not over."

"Maybe, but I have a feeling that he's long gone by now. His job is securing government secrets, and unfortunately, there are plenty of people out there who are willing to sell him what he wants."

"I hope you're right," she said. "And Mei won't have to worry about him anymore."

He brushed his hand down her arm and squeezed her hand. "I'm going to talk to Bridget Sanders and see if we can figure out how Mei ended up in her trunk, then I'll be right behind you."

Aubrey climbed into the ambulance as soon as they had Mei's gurney loaded inside. Fifteen minutes later, they were ushering her into an exam room and waiting for a doctor to see her. There had been no sign of Cheng or his men, but Jack had arranged for two officers to stand outside Mei's room, just in case they did show up.

She sat next to Mei, who'd fallen asleep on the bed, while they waited for the doctor. Memories of the last time she'd been in the hospital rushed through her. It had only been a few days since she'd driven here, excited about a time of rest with Papps and his family. It seemed like forever ago.

Jack stepped into the doorway, noticed Mei was sleeping, then signaled Bree to join him in the hallway.

"This is Mei's father, Samuel Lien," Jack said, introducing the two of them. "And this is Detective Aubrey Grayson."

"How is she?" her father asked.

"They've done an initial assessment," Aubrey said, "but we're still waiting for the doctor."

"I know you have a lot of questions," Jack said. "And I promise you can see her in a minute, but first I need to ask you a couple of questions."

"Okay, but I need to know what's going on. All I was told is that her life is in danger because of Peter Cheng, the man she's been dating."

"That is true," Aubrey said. "We understand you work in intelligence?"

"Yes."

"We have evidence that Cheng was using your daughter in order to get to you."

"Why would he do that?"

"Did you ever meet him?" Jack asked.

The older man shook his head. "No. Mei was planning to bring him over this weekend so we could go out to brunch together. She seemed nervous about introducing me, but apparently he wanted to meet me. From everything she told me he was a nice young man. I just can't believe he'd do this to her."

Aubrey frowned. "Unfortunately, Peter Cheng is anything but nice."

"We believe that the two of you were targeted in connection to your job and the classified information you work with," Jack said. "Have you ever had anyone approach you and offer you money or goods? Either in person or through social media?"

"Once I was contacted through a professional site, but I realized what was going on and ended up deleting my entire account. But this . . . I never imagined them going through my daughter." Mr. Lien let out a heavy sigh. "Can I see her now?"

Aubrey nodded, then opened the door and let him in.

"What did Mrs. Sanders say?" she asked Jack when they were alone in the hallway again.

"Apparently, she's been having some memory issues. She was getting ready to leave for the store when she realized she'd forgotten her purse in the house. She left her car running and went to get it."

"So she didn't see anything," Aubrey said.

"No, and while I'm not sure of Cheng's motivation, he must have told his men to keep Mei alive, but dump her somewhere.

They noticed an empty car running and decided to pop the trunk and leave her there. I looked inside the trunk again. There was blood on a metal toolbox where I believe she hit her head."

Aubrey frowned. There were still so many things that simply didn't add up. "Why go to all the trouble of getting her out of the safe house, only to let her go?"

Jack shook his head. "I think it's Cheng's way of letting us know he's in control."

Mr. Lien stepped back out into the hallway. "I'll double-check with the nurse, but she asked me to get her some Sprite for her stomach. And Detective Grayson . . . Mei wants to know if she could talk with you for a moment."

Aubrey glanced at Jack, then nodded. "Of course."

Mei was sitting up in bed when Aubrey went back into the room. She kept her head down, avoiding Aubrey's gaze. "I just wanted to say I'm sorry."

Aubrey sat down on the bed beside her. "You have nothing to be sorry about."

"Yes, I do. I was so stupid. I planned to introduce Peter to my father this weekend. We were going to drive out to the beach and have brunch at this little restaurant along the coast. I was so excited." She drew in a ragged breath. "I can't believe it now, but I actually thought he was the one I was going to marry. I trusted him, and instead, now I've put not just my life in danger, but yours, that nice old lady's, and more than likely my father's. I just . . . I should have seen that he wasn't the man I thought he was."

Aubrey shook her head, searching for the right words. "You're not the first person to believe someone's lies. He knows how to manipulate people. It's his job, and he's good at getting them to do what he wants. What you can't do is let this situation stop you from trusting other people in the future. Not everyone is like him."

Aubrey hesitated. She knew what it was like to feel betrayed. It made it hard to trust the next person. She knew the road back to trusting people wasn't easy.

"Is he your boyfriend? The FBI agent. He's super cute."

"Jack?" Mei's question took her off guard. "No."

"I'm sorry if it's too personal. There was just something— this spark—between the two of you. He seemed worried about you. Protective. Like he really cares."

"We've been friends for a long time. Since junior high, actually. But there's never been anything romantic between us. He's more like a . . . brother."

"I'm always playing matchmaker for my friends, but apparently I don't know how to pick them for myself."

"I'm sorry. I know this hurts. But you can't let someone like Peter control you. Give yourself time, and when you're ready, there are men out there who will treat you the way you deserve to be treated. You'll have to look, but they are out there. I promise."

"I just feel so stupid. And my father . . . I know he's angry with me."

"He's just worried about you. But we're going to find Peter and make sure he can't do this to anyone else. I promise."

She nodded. "I didn't tell him I spoke with you. I don't know how he knew where I was, but I never told him."

"He, or one of his men, had to have been following you."

Or he'd overheard their conversation on the university campus earlier that day.

Aubrey felt her heart pound. It was the only thing that made sense.

She pressed her finger against her lips, motioning for Mei to be silent, then glanced around the room. The young woman's purse had been set next to her on a small metal table.

Aubrey grabbed the purse and started pulling things out and laying them on the bed. "You know, let's not talk about this anymore. I understand you're studying marine biology."

Mei nodded as she watched Aubrey work, but the spark of fear was back. "My parents have never been thrilled about my choice. They'd much rather I study to become a doctor, but the ocean has always fascinated me."

Aubrey kept looking through the bag. She knew the agents had checked Mei's phone and made sure she couldn't be traced with it, which meant it had to be something else. "What do you want to do when you finish school?"

"Right now, I'm planning on going into research. This summer I've been accepted to be a part of an internship in Alaska, focusing on sea lion research."

"I bet that will be fascinating."

Aubrey paused. She felt something in the lining. She tore the seam and pulled out a small metal button, just barely bigger than a quarter. She quickly popped out the battery and laid it on the bed. Maybe the reason he'd let her go was that he knew he could always find her again.

"What is it?" Mei asked.

"A tracking device."

"So he was tracking me."

Aubrey paused before continuing. "I'm pretty sure this tracker was also monitoring your conversations."

"So he heard everything I said to you."

A chill ran up Aubrey's spine. She nodded.

"Don't tell my father."

"Our priority right now is simply to keep you safe. And that means we will have to move you—"

"Because he knows where I am."

Aubrey scooped up the tracker as Mei's father came into the room with a Sprite and a cup.

"I'll leave you two alone," she said, nodding at Mei before slipping out of the room.

Aubrey held up the tracking device in front of Jack. "I've disabled it, but he's been monitoring her. We can have an IT person confirm, but I've seen these before, and they can monitor conversations."

Her mind raced through her conversation with Mei on the campus bench. "He heard everything, allowing us to play right into his hands. And it could have gotten her killed."

Jack nodded. "There's no way to know how long he's been doing this, but he was monitoring to keep tabs on where she was and contact with her father, hoping to pick up information. There was also a larger tracker found on her car."

"Do we have any idea where he is now?"

"He's gone under for the moment, but I don't think that's the last we'll hear from him. Like we talked about earlier, he sees this as a game. He won't walk away until he gets what he wants."

"So, what do we do?" she asked.

Jack frowned. "We find a way to give him what he wants."

CHAPTER NINETEEN

AFTER TOSSING AND TURNING for an hour and a half, Jack finally headed downstairs to the kitchen, hoping to find something to eat without waking anyone up. A light was on in the family room that looked out over the pool. Maybe he wasn't the only one with insomnia.

He stopped in the doorway, the lamp casting a yellow glow across the corner of the room. Bree sat in one of the comfy chairs, snuggled up with a blanket and an e-reader. But instead of reading, she was staring out at the blue lights dancing across the swimming pool.

He started across the room. "Hey."

She looked up and smiled back at him. "Hey."

He sat down on the ottoman next to her feet. "Can't sleep?"

"No."

"Looks to me like this running into each other after hours is becoming a habit." He nodded at the half a piece of chocolate cake and empty milk glass on the end table next to her. "But of course, I also couldn't get that cake out of my head either."

She laughed. "Can I get you a slice?"

"I'll get some in a minute."

She set the e-reader on the arm of the chair. "I thought some cake and milk and maybe a chapter of the book I'm reading would finally make me sleepy, but three chapters in and I'm still wide awake."

"What are you reading?"

"A suspense novel."

He shook his head. "That's the problem. You shouldn't be reading something intense before bed."

"Maybe I should have chosen something a bit more—I don't know—low-key and dull."

He reached out and felt the muscles on her shoulders and frowned. "You are tense."

"I wonder why?"

"Touché." He stood up. "Scoot down on the floor, and I'll rub your shoulders."

"Really?"

He pushed the ottoman aside. "Why do you sound so surprised?"

She scooted onto the floor in front of the chair, he took her place in the chair, and she settled down in front of him, her head down. "How many years have I known you?" she said.

"Fifteen . . . maybe sixteen? Why?"

"This is the first time you've ever offered to give me a massage. So now I'm thinking of all the back rubs I could have had."

"Don't be surprised. I might not have offered before, but I am a man of many talents."

"Or a con man." She looked back at him and frowned, but there was a sparkle in her eye.

"A con man?"

"Somehow you've got my chair, and I'm on the floor."

"Very funny. Turn back around." He moved her hair out of the way, then started working out the knots in her shoulders. "You're going to regret you ever said that."

She lowered her head. "Okay, I just might have to take that back. Your fingers are magic."

"I'm also a good listener. Do you want to talk about anything? Today was a hard day."

She hesitated before answering. "Sometimes I think there are too many days like this. Days when we take two steps forward and then three steps back."

"I guess it's part of the job. But Mei's going to be okay. That has to count for something."

She shook her head. "She wouldn't have been in that situation if we hadn't dragged her into it."

"I'm not sure that's true." He started working slowly down her spine. "She was already involved with Cheng, and even if we hadn't gotten involved, you know it wasn't going to end well for her."

"Maybe, but it's still hard not to take at least some of the blame for what she went through."

He let the comfortable silence settle between them as he continued to work out the knots in her back and shoulders. This was what he'd once imagined happening between the two of them but he'd let any chance of that slip away years ago.

"Why do you do what you do?" she asked, breaking into his thoughts.

"You mean my job?"

She nodded.

"Lots of reasons. It's a chance to save lives. A hope to make the world a better place while I serve my country." He paused. "Somehow that came out like an idealistic rookie was talking, but I've never completely shed my desire for a better world. What about you?"

"To see justice done in the world. At least my part. Though I was sharing my frustration with Papps on how we take one perp off the street and another one takes his place. He reminded me that my job isn't to take them all down. All I have to do is the job I'm assigned to. I know he's right, but that doesn't always make it easier."

"He is right. Because while we work for justice, I think it's easy to forget that God never intended this world to be free from suffering or that justice would be served for every crime committed." He moved slowly down her spine again, working out the knotted muscles. "Remember Job?"

"Of course."

"He had a long conversation with his friends who pretty much said he must have sinned because of what happened to him. And yet God's response was completely different. He showed Job what an amazing and intricate world we live in, but it wasn't created—at this point anyway—to alleviate all suffering. Even though the Creator is good and what he created is good. Job saw God as unjust in his situation, but God reminded him that he wasn't big enough to see the whole picture. Just like we aren't."

"It's still hard not to get angry when people—like my father and Cheng—get away with what they're doing. When people are hurt, I want to see justice in the end. I hate it when it's not there."

"Sometimes, all we can do is trust him."

"I know you're right. It's just hard when it's my own father involved in this. It makes me question why my mother suffered so much. Why Mei had to be caught up in this today. And basically, why life just seems so . . . unfair sometimes."

"It is unfair. It's not fair that what your father and Cheng are doing could in the end cost lives if they're not stopped. It's not fair when someone's bad choices affect another's life."

Bree scooted around and looked up at him. "And when I doubt God for not stepping in?"

"I don't have all the answers, but I don't believe God gets frustrated at our trying to get to know him better. Even when it involves questioning what he allows to happen."

"You're right. Job did that. David did that in the Psalms." She laid her arm on his knee and looked up at him. "Thank you."

"You're not the only one who needs the reminder."

"I just wish I could let go of the anger I have toward my father right now."

"You have to remember that you can't change him, nor are you responsible for him. You can't make his decisions. All you can really do at this point is pray that God will move in him. To show him what real redemption is."

"And forgiveness?" she asked. "How do I do that?"

"I believe God can help you do that as well, even if it's only for you. You've got to find a way to let go of it, because if you don't, it will eat you up." He pushed back a lock of hair from her eyes. "I've missed this. Us. Sometimes it seems like yesterday that the two of us were back here training for a marathon."

"You could have called."

But then you fell for my brother, and I did what I never should have—let that relationship put a wedge between us.

Her e-reader fell off the chair arm and onto the floor, and something fell out of the inside cover. She picked it up.

"What's that?"

She held it up. "You're probably going to think this is silly, but I always carry this with me."

"A postcard?"

"From Italy." She got up and nestled in beside him with his arm around her on the extra-wide lounge chair, then laid the worn card on her lap and ran her fingers across the handwriting. "I was nine years old. My father had gone on a business trip to Frankfurt. When it was over, he took a train south through Switzerland to Milan and then to Rome where he spent a week as a tourist."

She turned it over to show him the photo of a gondola floating down one of Venice's waterways. "I remember the day it came in the mail. My mom almost didn't give it to me, but I was so excited, she finally did. I carried it around for weeks, waiting till he came back. I didn't know much about Italy, so I checked out a book in the library, then spent my summer dreaming I was floating down the Grand Canal or standing in the middle of the Piazza San Marco eating gelato."

"I don't think it's silly that you carry it around."

"Somehow it seems . . . juvenile."

"Why? Because as a child you wanted your father to be a

part of your life? Because you loved him even though he didn't deserve it? I don't think it matters if you're nine or ninety. It makes sense that you wanted to have him in your life."

She tapped her fingers against the postcard. "When I was nine, it was the only connection I really had to him. A worn postcard of a beautiful place I could only dream of visiting one day. As the years passed, I just kept it. Wishing he'd take me and my mom on one of his trips. Wishing he'd finally come back home so we could be a family."

"But he didn't."

She shook her head. "Eventually, I realized he wasn't coming, and we'd never be a family again, but something made me hold on to it. There were times when I was so angry with him, I decided even if he did come back, I didn't want him. But I still kept it. I guess it was a reminder of what could have been. That maybe my father would remember he loved me and come home. And now all these years later, I still have it."

Jack felt the pain in her voice, knowing Charles Ramsey had never become the father she always wanted so badly. That she never went on any trips with him, or knew he was waiting up for her when she'd gone out. And the thought broke his heart.

"As much as he hurt my mom and me," she said, "I'll always be grateful that God put Papps in my life. He was the one who taught me what a real father should be like. Made me realize that not all fathers walk out of their children's lives. Helped me understand what a loving father was. He helped me understand that I had a heavenly Father who loved me unconditionally."

"I'm sorry. I know you lost a lot growing up."

She shook her head. "It doesn't matter anymore. Not really. And you didn't need to hear all of that."

"But I wanted to."

He pulled her against him, letting her head rest against his shoulder. "You used to tell me everything. Or at least most things. I miss that. I've missed you."

He wished he could bury his feelings for her again, but he knew he couldn't. They'd somehow managed to resurface in the past couple days, something he wasn't prepared for. He knew where she lived and had considered showing up more than once so they could catch up, but this . . . he'd never expected this.

But neither was this the time or the place to go *there*. The conversation about them—if it ever came—would have to be later.

"I've missed you too." She pulled away and looked up at him. "You always knew exactly what to say, and never made me feel like I was crazy."

"You did the same for me."

"So what happened?"

"I don't know." He wanted to ignore her question because it reminded him of how he'd walked out of her life. He never meant to hurt her, but then neither did her father, probably. He always told himself he left because he wanted her to be happy, but the truth was his reasons were far more selfish. He didn't want to see his brother marry the girl he was in love with. So he ran.

"I didn't plan to stay away. But life has this crazy way of pulling you, and then you realize that a year's passed, then two . . ."

"I guess life never turns out the way we think it will when

186

we're eighteen. But maybe that's good. I'm happy with my life and have so much to be thankful for. Even with all of this coming up with my father again."

"You always were resilient," he said. "And this situation . . . You'll get through it."

"All I know is that I'm glad you're here with me."

For a moment he was twenty again, sitting across from her in the cafeteria, wondering what life would look like if he told her how he felt. But life wasn't like the movie *It's a Wonderful Life*. It didn't let you see what might have happened if you chose a different path. All you had was the consequences of your decisions.

She started to yawn and pressed her hand against her mouth.

He fought the sudden urge to kiss her. Wondered what she'd think if he did.

"You think you can sleep now?" he asked instead.

She nodded. "Thank you."

"You're welcome."

"I don't just mean the back massage. For being here through all of this."

She leaned forward and kissed him on the cheek before grabbing her e-reader and standing up. "I can still get you some cake."

"I think I'll turn in as well."

"Okay. Good night."

He watched her walk across the room and head up the stairs, wondering what he was supposed to do with his heart now.

CHAPTER TWENTY

THE SHRILL RING of her cell phone jolted Aubrey out of her dark dreams. She opened her eyes, then took the next few seconds to remember where she was.

And to remember that reality was just as dark as her dreams had been.

She fumbled for her phone on the bedside table. "Hello?"

"Miss Grayson?"

"Yes." Aubrey worked to clear her mind. "Who is this?"

"It's Wendy Masters, from River Oaks. I'm sorry to call you so early, but I'm getting ready to get off my shift in a few minutes and just found out that your grandmother had a visitor last night."

Last night?

Aubrey glanced at the clock and frowned. It was ten minutes to seven. If her father had stopped by River Oaks last night, he'd be long gone by now.

She pulled her knees toward her chest and squeezed her eyes shut. "Was it my father?"

"Yes. He didn't sign in, but one of the orderlies spoke briefly to him. I'm sorry I didn't catch it last night, but we had a patient code, and I was busy most of the evening."

"That's fine, Wendy. It's not your fault. I appreciate your taking the time to call me."

She hung up the phone, then quickly pulled on a pair of jeans and a T-shirt before slipping down the hallway to the guest room where Jack was sleeping.

She knocked on the door once, then again a few seconds later, waiting impatiently for him to answer.

He opened the door, yawning. "Bree . . . is everything okay?"

"I'm sorry to wake you up, but I just got a call from River Oaks, where my grandmother lives. My father was there last night, visiting her."

"Okay." He ran his fingers through his mussed-up hair. "Meet me downstairs in ten minutes."

Fifteen minutes later they were in the car, headed up I–37 toward San Antonio.

Aubrey gnawed on one of her fingernails, a nasty habit she'd picked up in college. "What if this is nothing more than a wild-goose chase, or even worse, some kind of trap?"

"We'll know before we get there. I'm sending in a colleague of mine to check the security camera footage there to see if we can find out what car he's driving. With law enforcement looking for him, he won't get far."

She hoped he was right. Needed him to be right. Because all she could think about was that Papps was still in ICU, and now there was a chance her father had put her grandmother in danger.

Jack reached out and squeezed her hand. "I'm going to make sure your grandma's safe."

She nodded, appreciative of his presence.

"Tell me more about her," he said.

Aubrey smiled. "She was always my favorite grandmother. Nana taught dancing classes until she was in her early seventies, and never backed away from an argument."

Jack laughed. "I bet she had a colorful life."

"She did. Her mother named her Mary, after silent-film star Mary Pickford. Nana said that when she was a little girl, she was really shy. She got good grades in school but was terrified to speak up in class. Her mother took her to the movies to see actors like Clark Gable, Katharine Hepburn, Bette Davis, all those guys, but Fred Astaire and Ginger Rogers were her favorites. She wanted to dance just like Ginger. My great-grandmother enrolled her in a dance studio, and she found her passion. After World War II she opened up a small dance studio in the suburbs of Dallas where she taught until she started having children. Once all her kids were grown, she went back to work, teaching dance."

"Quite a woman."

"She always had time for me. Even taught me the Charleston when I was in junior high. It was amazing how she was able to boost my confidence."

Jack's phone rang, interrupting their conversation. "Mark. Thanks for calling me back."

"Sure thing."

"I've got you on speaker. I'm in the car with Detective Aubrey Grayson right now, headed your way."

"I wish I had more for you. We went through the security tape. Ramsey did come by River Oaks last night. Video footage has him walking in the front door at a few minutes past seven and leaving thirty minutes later. He spoke to one of the orderlies here, Jerry Hart, who stopped Ramsey and spoke briefly to him."

"What about a license plate or make of the car he was driving?"

"We didn't get that, but we've started going through the footage from a restaurant across the street, hoping something might pop up."

"Thanks, Mark. Let me know if you find anything else."

Aubrey frowned. So they had nothing other than a verification that he had been there. That wasn't enough. She checked her text messages in case she'd missed his response to her message that she needed to see him. No reply. She couldn't even be sure if he'd read it.

It was ten o'clock by the time they walked into the memory care facility. Familiar feelings of sadness swept through her. Half a dozen patients sat in their wheelchairs in the lobby, staring out the windows or at the floor as another day drifted by. They were in a constant state of waiting. Waiting for medicine. Waiting for meals. And hoping for the off chance that someone might remember them and stop by for a visit.

Her conversation with Jack had brought good memories but also the familiar feelings of loss, knowing she'd never watch her grandmother dance the Charleston again. She'd never again receive an encouraging card from Nana. The resulting loss felt like a physical ache. It always struck her how easy it was for society to forget that these were men and women who had once led productive lives. They'd started families and businesses and fought in wars to protect their country. They'd watched grandchildren and great-grandchildren come into this world, only to now sit wrapped in a shroud of the past.

They stopped at the front desk to sign in and were greeted by a familiar face. "Aubrey . . . it's good to see you. Your grandmother will be happy to see you."

Aubrey held up the sack she was carrying. "Or at least she'll be happy to have her favorite pudding. How is she, Tammy?"

"About the same, but she's always smiling. Always happy. She keeps asking where Gillian is."

"Gillian was her sister," she told Jack. "She died about ten years ago, but she doesn't always remember that." Aubrey tapped her fingers on the desk. "I understand my father visited last night?"

"He did. Wendy told me you might be stopping by. The local FBI's been here as well." Tammy's smile vanished. "Is there a problem I need to know about?"

Aubrey glanced at Jack, then gestured for him to explain.

"I'm Special Agent Jack Shannon. I'm an old friend of Aubrey's, but I'm also with the FBI. We're needing to talk to Mr. Ramsey as soon as possible. I know that the FBI has already been here looking at video footage, but we'd like to look at it as well."

"Of course."

"I'd appreciate that. Thank you."

"It will take a few minutes for me to get it set up again. If you'd like to see your grandmother while you wait, I'll come get you when it's ready."

Aubrey looked up at Jack. "You don't mind, do you?"

"Of course not."

"She enjoys the sunroom in the mornings," Tammy said.

"That's a great idea. Thank you."

Aubrey recognized the familiar scent of Nana's rose lotion as they walked into her room. When they had moved Nana into the nursing home, Aubrey had spent an afternoon making the space personal and familiar by framing and hanging family photos on the walls.

There was a nurse in the room, standing over Nana in her chair.

"Hi . . . I'm sorry to interrupt . . . We're here to visit Mary. I'm her granddaughter."

The nurse took a step back and smiled. "It's nice to meet you. I just came in to give her her morning meds." He had a pleasant English accent.

Nana took the pills and handed the empty cup back to the nurse.

"I'll leave the three of you to visit," he said. "Is there anything you need?"

"We're fine. I think we're going to take her out to the sunroom for a few minutes."

"I know she'll enjoy that. She's been watching birds from her window."

Aubrey knelt beside her grandmother. "How are you doing today, Nana?"

Nana smiled at the window where Aubrey had put up a bird feeder last spring, but there was no sense of recognition.

Aubrey pulled the pudding cups out of the sack. "I brought you a present. Tapioca pudding."

Nana's face lit up.

"Just don't eat them all at once." Aubrey laughed. "You don't want to ruin your beautiful figure."

Nana's smile broadened. "I was a dancer."

"You remember?"

"I remember dancing in the attic with Gilly."

Aubrey set the pudding on the bedside table. "Gilly was your sister, and the two of you used to dance."

"I remember Gilly. I want to see her."

"I know you miss her, Nana."

"Where is she?"

Aubrey hesitated. "She's not here right now, but I brought someone with me I'd like you to meet. His name is Jack."

Her grandmother looked up at Jack and smiled. "'Jack Sprat could eat no fat . . .'"

"'His wife could eat no lean.'" Jack finished the sentence for her with a big grin on his face.

Nana looked surprised. "You know the nursery rhyme?"

"Of course I do. Kids used to tease me growing up."

"They used to always tell me, 'Mary, Mary, quite contrary, how does your garden grow?'"

"'With silver bells and cockle-shells, and pretty maids all in a row.'"

"I like you," Nana said. "Though I'm really not contrary."

"I'm sure you're not at all."

Nana turned back to Aubrey. "I like this young man. Are you going to marry him?"

"Marry him?" Aubrey laughed. "No, Nana. He's just an old friend of mine who wanted to come visit you with me. Would you like to go out to the sunroom and look at the garden?"

"Yes, but I'm tired today. Too tired to dance. Too tired to play."

"Maybe some sunshine will help. It's supposed to be a beautiful day."

Nana yawned. "Gilly loves the sunshine too. Maybe she can come with us."

"I'll come with you, if you tell me about your sister," Jack said, pushing her wheelchair toward the door.

"She lives near here. In a big yellow house. She's my oldest sister, but she hasn't visited me for a long time. I don't know why. Why doesn't she come see me?"

"She would if she could, Nana."

"Do you remember the house? There was a . . ." Nana searched for the word.

"A swing?" Aubrey offered as they started down the hallway.

"Yes, a swing. Can Gilly come with us? I haven't seen her in such a long time."

Their conversations always went in circles. The same questions asked over and over.

The sunroom had large windows overlooking well-kept lawns.

"Nana, do you remember Charles?" Aubrey asked.

"Do I know him?"

Aubrey sat down next to her and pulled out her phone. "He's your son. Remember? Here's a photo of him."

"Charlie. Yes . . . I know Charlie. He sends me postcards when he goes on trips."

"Yes, he does."

Nana pulled out a handful of postcards from the flowered

pouch attached to the side of the wheelchair. "I keep them with me."

Aubrey glanced through the stack of cards dating back several years. Paris . . . Berlin . . . Beijing . . . They were an itinerary of where her father had been.

"Can I look at them?"

Nana nodded. "He likes to travel."

"Yes, he does."

"I went to Paris with my mother when I was sixteen."

It always seemed strange how the memories of decades long ago were clearer than what she'd had for breakfast this morning. It was all a part of slowly sliding out of this life and into the next, but the difficult process made Aubrey realize that the woman she'd known growing up was gone forever. And asking her questions about her father's visit was more than likely going to be futile.

"Nana . . ."

But her grandmother had fallen asleep.

One of the nurses walked into the room wearing dark blue scrubs and pushing her medicine cart.

"There you are, Mary," she said before noticing Nana was asleep.

"She seems extra tired this morning," Aubrey said.

"I just need to give her her pills, then you can let her go back to sleep."

"Her morning pills?" Aubrey felt panic bubbling as she glanced at Jack. "One of the nurses already gave them to her a few minutes ago when we first arrived."

"Are you sure?" The nurse headed back to the computer on

her cart. "There must be some mistake. I take care of her wing every morning and came looking for her here when she wasn't in her room. What did the other nurse look like?"

Aubrey's heart pounded as she looked back at her grandmother. Something was very wrong.

"He was about five ten, blond hair pulled back," Aubrey said. "I'd never seen him before."

"We have several male nurses, but none that match that description."

Aubrey looked at Jack. "We need to call 911 and get her to the hospital."

Jack already had his phone out.

Aubrey knelt down next to her grandmother. "Nana . . . Nana, I need you to wake up."

Nana opened her eyes. "I'm too tired."

"I think she's been drugged," Aubrey said. "I have no idea what he gave her, but he gave her something."

The nurse started checking Nana's vitals while Aubrey told her exactly what had happened.

"Until we do a tox screen, I won't be able to tell you what he gave her, but from her symptoms, it looks like it was some sort of sedative. Her blood pressure has dropped a little and her breathing is shallow. If that's all it was, she should be okay once it wears off."

But if that wasn't all it was?

"There's an ambulance on the way now," Jack said.

Aubrey stood up. "This is insane, Jack. They came after my grandmother. What were they planning to do with her? If we hadn't shown up when we did . . ."

He glanced at her. "I don't know what they're planning, but now there's a second problem as well. Now they know where you are."

"That's the least of our worries. We've got to help Nana."

"I'll put in a call and get a couple agents to guard her room, both in the hospital and then when she returns here. We'll track down whoever is behind this. But I'm also going to do whatever it takes to keep you safe."

Aubrey felt the room begin to spin. She grabbed on to a chair to steady herself, anger raging inside her, quickly taking the place of fear. Whoever was after her had somehow managed to hurt the two people in the world she loved the most, and she didn't know how to stop them.

CHAPTER TWENTY-ONE

THEY NEEDED TO FIND out who had drugged Bree's grandmother. Jack watched as the manager typed in the time stamp on the nursing home's surveillance system, starting thirty minutes ago, in the hallway outside her room.

"Fast-forward slowly," Jack said, describing the man they were looking for.

At the fifteen-minute mark, Jack motioned for her to stop. "There he is. Entering her room with the pills."

He watched it play out. Thirty seconds later he and Bree entered the room. The man talked with them for thirty seconds, then he left, managing to avoid any clear shots of his face. But unfortunately for him, they didn't need the footage to be able to identify him.

"Do you have any cameras outside?" Bree asked. "Any of the parking lot? We need to see what he's driving."

"Give me a second . . ." The manager switched to another camera, then pulled up footage of the parking lot after the guy left Mary's room.

They waited for him to emerge from the building. "There he is."

"I think his goal was to enter without anyone seeing him and take her," Bree said. "He was hoping by the time someone discovered she was missing, he'd be long gone."

Jack could hear the panic in her voice. Two of the staff plus a security guard were with her grandmother right now, ten feet away from them, waiting for the ambulance that had been called. He'd encouraged Bree to stay with her, but Bree had said there was nothing she could do right now. She'd insisted on helping him find whoever was behind this.

"Here we go," the manager said. "Looks like he got into a white van."

"What about the license plate?" Bree asked.

"I can try to zoom in, though I'm not sure our system is good enough to pick it up."

Jack drummed his fingers on the desk while he waited. The camera zoomed forward.

Bingo.

The license plate number came into view.

He picked up his phone and called his contact at the local FBI headquarters in the city. "Kate, this is Special Agent Jack Shannon again. I need you to put out a BOLO for this vehicle, and I want you to also try and track it down for me using city surveillance cameras."

Jack gave her the model and license plate number of the white van that had left the facility.

"I'm on it, sir."

"What's the ETA on my backup?" Jack asked.

There was a slight pause on the line. "I'm estimating another minute, sir."

"Give them directions to escort the ambulance to the hospital and stay with our victim until I get there."

"Yes, sir."

"And call me the minute you locate the vehicle."

He hung up and heard the wail of a siren getting louder outside. "There's the ambulance now. Kate said our backup should be here in a minute."

Bree went to say goodbye to her grandmother.

His cell phone rang.

"Kate, what have you got?"

"The van's stolen, but I'm working with OnStar to track it. Right now they're heading south toward the Riverwalk."

Jack signaled at Bree while Kate gave him the location. "We're on our way. Keep us updated."

Backup arrived as he and Bree reached the parking lot. Jack quickly made sure they knew what to do, then unlocked his car. Bree slid into the seat next to him and he started the engine.

"They'll keep her safe."

She stared out the window as he backed up. "I know."

"I'm sorry," he said.

"Me too."

They rode in silence for a few minutes, headed toward the location where the van had last been spotted. Thankfully, Jack was relatively familiar with the city, having spent three months in San Antonio working on a joint task force between local PD and the FBI.

"Seeing Nana always brings back so many memories. Like how much she loved to bake," Bree said, breaking the silence between them. "She always made the best cherry pie with cherries from the trees in her backyard. I remember standing on a chair watching her rolling out piecrust when I couldn't have been more than four or five. There was always homemade fudge and caramels for Christmas dinner along with all the trimmings. And she also made the best homemade jams. She was a stay-at-home mom who kept the books for my grandfather's gas station. She wore hats on Sunday to church, and never went out without her stockings." Her voice broke. "I'm sorry . . ."

"You have nothing to be sorry about."

"Do you remember coming with me to visit her that one summer?"

"Of course. She eyed me up and down until you assured her—in private—that the two of us were simply friends. Then I remember her telling stories about the Depression."

Bree laughed. "I'd forgotten about that. She was always so protective of me until her memory started to fade. Now . . . now she doesn't even know who I am half the time."

He reached out and squeezed her hand. She'd already experienced so much loss. Her father had deserted her family. Her mother had died. And now, not only was the senator involved in all of this, her grandmother had just gotten dragged into it as well.

His phone rang and he pushed the button on the steering wheel to answer it. "What have you got, Kate?"

"I'm not sure where he's heading, but we've got him close to the Riverwalk on Alamo Street. I'm working with OnStar to remotely slow down the vehicle."

Jack made a right-hand turn, still scanning the street for the van. It had to be here somewhere.

"Jack," Bree said, "stop the car."

He glanced to the right where she was looking. A white van had just pulled into one of the side streets in front of them.

"Do you see the driver?" he asked.

"He just got out of the van and is heading east."

"Bree, wait . . ."

But she was already out of the car. She slammed the door shut and started running after him toward the Riverwalk as Jack pulled up next to the curb.

Bree shouted at the man. "Stop! Police!"

Jack parked the van and headed after them. Dozens of people were dining along the famous Riverwalk in the middle of San Antonio that was lined by shops and restaurants. Bree was already twenty yards ahead of him, and their suspect another ten in front of her.

Jack groaned. Did the guy really think running was going to make things easier? They came to where the sidewalk split and continued on both sides of the river. Bree had taken the left side, in pursuit of the suspect. Jack took the right, crossing the narrow river. He sprinted down the sidewalk, running parallel to Bree and the man. A boat filled with tourists floated down the river between them. Pedestrians window-shopped and ate an early lunch at outside tables. Dozens of tourists hurriedly stepped out of his way as he dodged between and around them.

He was gaining on the man. If he could get ahead of him and cross over . . .

A woman pushing a stroller was in front of him, oblivious to what was going on. Jack shouted again, trying to get her attention as he barely managed to squeeze by her without knocking her over.

He kept running, watching out of the corner of his eye. He was ahead of the man now. Ten feet . . . fifteen . . . Jack ran up the steps and crossed a short bridge back over the river, then turned toward their suspect. With Bree seconds behind him, their suspect was trapped. Realizing his options had just run out, the man tried to dodge past Jack. Instead, he lost his balance and fell into the waist-deep water.

The man staggered to his feet, then started to wade toward the other side.

"Really?"

Jack jogged back across the bridge, his irritation growing. The man hesitated again, then held up his hands in surrender. A moment later, Jack pulled him out of the water and forced him facedown on the sidewalk, ignoring the crowd of people forming around him capturing everything on their cell phones.

"You okay?" Bree asked, coming around behind him.

"Better now, considering we caught this lowlife."

Bree handcuffed the suspect, then turned him over. "What did you give her?"

He turned away and spit out a mouthful of water. "Who?"

"Don't play games. We were there. At the nursing home."

"Nothing, I—"

"We saw you give her medicine. What did you give her?"

The man's British accent that she'd noticed back at the nursing home was gone, replaced by a thicker Russian accent.

"It won't hurt her. Just a mild sedative."

"Why?"

He still refused to look at her.

"Answer my question."

"I was supposed to deliver her to a certain location. That was it. The pill was just to make sure she didn't freak out on me. I know how difficult old people can be."

"Do you?" Bree asked him. "Do you really know how terrifying that would have been for her? Your plan was to push her out of there in her wheelchair and kidnap her."

"No one would have noticed, if you hadn't shown up. And I'm sure they would have returned her. She probably never would have known."

"None of that matters. You're facing charges of attempted kidnapping and assault at a minimum."

The man just looked away, ignoring her glare.

"One more question," Bree said, helping him to his feet. "Where were you taking her?"

"I'm done talking."

"That's not a problem," Jack said. "We'll take you down to our local field office and see if you can come up with the rest of the story. Because if you don't, you'll take the fall for whoever hired you."

CHAPTER TWENTY-TWO

AUBREY WAITED FOR JACK in the atrium at the FBI's division head-quarters, trying to suppress her uneasiness. Sunlight shone down from the top of the atrium, casting muted shadows on the floor. Their suspect had planned to take Nana somewhere. They needed to know where.

"They've got our suspect set up in an interrogation room," Jack said, coming back from security. "We can head up there now."

"Good," she said, and they started for the elevators.

"Have you heard anything about your grandmother?"

"I just got off the phone with the hospital. They're still monitoring her closely until they can confirm exactly what was given to her, but they're pretty sure our guy was telling the truth and it was just a sedative. Pulse is stable. Oxygen and blood pressure are low, but there don't seem to be any complications other than the fact that she's confused."

He pressed the file he was holding against his chest. "I know you want to be with her. And it's okay if you are."

She punched the button for the elevator, feeling torn between wanting to be with Papps and her grandmother and her need to find a way to end this. "One of the staff from the nursing home is there with her now, and besides, I don't think she'd know if I was there or not. At least I know she's safe, and for now, that's what's most important. I'll have time to see her when this is all over."

"She's lucky to have you in her life," he said as the elevator doors slid open.

"I just hate the fact that she was dragged into this. I don't know how my father lives with himself knowing he's endangered both me and his mother." The familiar anger surged through her toward a man she barely knew and yet who'd managed to control so much of her emotions her entire life.

"People can usually find reasons to justify what they do."

"It's just sad when greed trumps love and relationships."

"It is at that."

"At least we were able to catch this guy." She shot Jack a smile. "Though for a minute, I thought I was going to get to watch you go swimming in the river."

"I must admit, I was worried about that for a moment too."

"I'd like to know where he thought he was going."

"I don't know, but I'm pretty sure where he'll be going after a judge and jury get their say."

The elevator doors slid open again, and he led her down a hallway, pausing outside a closed door. "Joking aside, I know this is personal for you—"

"I'll be fine, Jack."

She followed him into the interrogation room, and they sat down across from their suspect.

"Sasha Yakovich." Jack dropped the file onto the table and frowned. "Your file says you are here on a student visa, but I'm going to assume that's not all you do."

The man just stared at the table.

"There's no question right now what you did at the nursing home, so let's not even take the time to argue that point." Jack slid photos across the table of shots of him from the security camera. "What we want to know is where you were going to take her and who hired you?"

"Who says someone hired me?"

"You said it yourself earlier," Aubrey said. "Are you saying now that you're alone in this escapade?"

"Yes."

Jack started writing on his notepad. "That will mean your list of charges is pretty long. Attempted kidnapping, consumption by fraudulent means, second-degree assault, resisting arrest, and, oh yeah . . . Depending on what you really drugged her with, attempted murder—"

"Whoa . . . hold on." The man leaned forward. "All I was supposed to do was give her a pill to make her sleepy. I didn't hurt her. He told me he wouldn't hurt her."

"What else did he tell you?" Aubrey asked.

Sasha's frown deepened. "He told me no one would notice me."

Jack tapped his pen on the table. "So . . . who is 'he'?"

Sasha shrugged. "I don't know. He didn't give me a name or anything. Just said he'd give me five grand to deliver this old lady to him. I don't ask too many questions when someone wants to give me five grand."

"Where were you supposed to take her?"

"He texted me an address. The medicine was to make sure she didn't cause a ruckus while I was taking her out."

Jack rubbed his temples. "I'm assuming whoever it is needs her for leverage. Leverage for what?"

"I don't know the details. I just did what I was told."

"What time were you supposed to be at the address?" Aubrey asked.

"Thirty minutes ago or so, which means I'm already late. He'll know something's wrong."

A cell phone rang. Jack pulled it out of his pocket. "This is your phone. Is that him?"

Sasha glanced at the number, then nodded.

"Here's what you're going to do. You're going to tell him there was a delay—I don't care what you come up with, as long as you convince him that you were delayed. But everything is fine now, and you're on your way. You'll be there in thirty minutes."

"And if I don't?"

"Do you want me to go over the list of charges again?" Jack asked. "If we add them all together, you're looking at some serious prison time. You might want to think about cooperating with us."

"Fine."

Jack swiped the screen and put the phone on speaker after shooting the man another warning look.

"Where are you? I've been trying to call you."

"I had to wait until she was alone," Sasha said, "but I'll be there in another . . . thirty minutes."

"You better. There's a lot riding on this."

"I told you I'll be there."

The caller hung up abruptly.

"Give me the address," Jack said.

Sasha frowned again, then picked up the phone and scrolled to the text message with the address.

Jack nodded at Aubrey and headed for the door. "We need to go."

"Wait a minute . . ." Sasha stood up. "What about me?"

"What about you?" Jack smiled. "The two agents who've been watching from behind that window will be in here in a minute to continue the questioning. You better sit back down. You're in for a long day."

TWENTY MINUTES LATER, Jack hung up the call he was on, then took the bulletproof vest from Bree, praying they wouldn't need it. The address they'd been given was just another house in the suburbs. An older neighborhood with tree-lined streets and brick-faced houses. No one would ever question someone bringing their grandmother home for a few hours. But the thought that they'd gone as far as planning to use Bree's grandmother for leverage had him alarmed.

"Was that more information on who we're going in for?" Bree asked, sliding her vest over her head.

"Yes. The house belongs to a John Bryant. He teaches engineering at a local university," Jack said, adjusting the side straps on his vest. "IT analysts just connected him to the call Sasha took, and they told me that he's been under investigation the past eight months for stealing US technological secrets."

"That has to be the tie to my father," Aubrey said.

He nodded, trying to gauge her expression as she finished adjusting her vest straps. Despite what had happened with her grandmother, it was clear that her determination to catch the bad guys hadn't diminished. And he knew what she was thinking. What they both were thinking. Was it possible that John Bryant had somehow been involved in recruiting her father as an asset? Charles Ramsey had portrayed himself as a man who had no qualms about selling out his country in order to enrich himself.

Agent Kendrick signaled his team, then walked up to Jack and Bree. "I want the two of you to wait outside until our tactical team clears the house. At the moment, we believe he's a flight risk. We don't want him leaving with evidence inside we can't afford to lose."

Jack nodded, checked his vest again, then pulled his weapon from his holster as a precaution. With confirmation that Bryant was in the house, they'd set up squad cars blocking the road as the team prepared to go in. He and Bree waited on the front porch for the all clear signal.

Someone shouted from inside the house. "He's running!"

Their suspect came flying out of the side gate from the backyard and was headed across the neighbor's yard toward the street. Knowing they were the closest, Jack and Bree sprinted down the street after him. There was no way to know if the man was armed, but for the moment, they were going to have to assume he was.

Jack pulled a couple feet ahead of Bree, with their suspect heading toward the intersection. He felt his lungs burn and groaned inwardly at the thought of two pursuits in one day.

With half a dozen agents and local PD at the scene, where did the man think he was going?

Jack slowed at the squeal of brakes, and a car smashed into their suspect in front of him. The man's body flipped up onto the hood, first cracking the windshield and then bouncing back and landing on the ground. Stopping a second too late beside Jack, Bree slammed into the side of the car.

Someone started shouting orders behind them. "Get the medics over here now. We can't lose this guy."

An officer started CPR on Bryant. Another directed traffic. How had this happened?

Jack steadied Bree as she pushed off the car. He backed her away from the scene. "Bree . . . are you okay?"

She nodded as she fought to catch her breath. "I'm fine. I just had the wind knocked out of me."

She pressed her palms against her knees as he looked for signs she was hurt. There was no blood. No obvious injuries.

"Did he say anything?" she asked. "We need to talk to him."

He led her to a grassy spot on the side of the road. "I want you to sit here until the paramedics can check you over. I'll see what I can find out."

She nodded, and he was thankful she didn't argue with him.

Jack ran up to the sergeant, who was shouting orders. A moment later, he turned around to Jack. "Is she okay?"

"I want to have her checked out, but I think so. She ran into the side of the car while in pursuit."

Saying the words out loud sent a chill through Jack. She could have easily been the one lying on the pavement fighting for her life.

"What about our suspect?" he asked.

"He's gone."

Jack looked back at Bree, not wanting to tell her that they'd failed. That they were back to square one. They'd continue questioning Sasha, search the house, and follow any connections they might find there, but they weren't going to get answers out of John Bryant.

He walked back over to where she still sat on the side of the road staring at the scene. "He didn't make it, Bree."

"We needed him," she said.

"I know." He reached out and squeezed her hand. "But we'll find out the truth another way."

"What if we can't? Too many people are getting hurt, and there are too many unanswered questions."

"Right now, we're going to get you checked out at the hospital, and then we'll go check in on your grandmother."

It took over an hour and a half to see a doctor and another thirty minutes for Bree to be told that other than bruising from hitting the car, she would be fine. All Jack could think of was how thankful he was that she wasn't the one lying in the morgue right now.

He shook off the thought as he walked with her to Nana's room, three floors up, where they stopped at the nurses' station for an update before going to see her. A nurse they'd seen at River Oaks was talking to one of the hospital nurses.

"Jennifer?" Bree asked, walking up to the older woman. "I was told someone from River Oaks was here, but I didn't know who it was. Thank you so much for staying with her."

"Of course." The older woman smiled back. "I couldn't stand the thought of her being here alone."

"I should have been here."

"That's where you're wrong." Jennifer shook her head. "I've heard a little of what's going on, and trust me, you're exactly where you need to be. Out there putting an end to this so we can know she's safe."

"I hope you're right." Bree introduced Jack, then asked how Nana was doing.

"Her blood pressure and oxygen levels are still running low, but overall she seems fine," Jennifer said. "The authorities found midazolam in the van. They're still waiting for the bloodwork results, and because older people metabolize this drug slower, they'll want to keep her overnight for observation."

"But no long-term effects?" Bree asked anxiously as they started for the room.

"She'll be fine. I promise."

Jack hesitated outside the door, feeling the need to give Bree her privacy with her grandmother if that was what she wanted. "I'll wait here—"

"No," Bree said, turning to him. "I want you to come in too. Besides . . . she likes you."

"Aubrey . . ." Mary Ramsey's eyes lit up when her granddaughter walked into the room. "You've come to visit me. It's been so long. I miss you."

"I've missed you too, Nana. I didn't bring any pudding this time, but I did bring Jack. Do you remember him?"

Nana motioned for him to come closer, then reached up and felt the stubble on his face. "Jack."

He took her hand. "You remember me."

Her smile brightened.

"Jack Sprat . . . you're handsome."

"Thank you, Mary."

"Are you going to marry my granddaughter?"

"Your granddaughter?" Jack let out an uncomfortable laugh.

"Aubrey Jean. She was born on a . . . Wednesday, I think. It was spring. Just after Easter." Confusion flickered in the elderly woman's eyes. "Where is your mother, Aubrey?"

"She's not here, Nana. It's just Jack and I."

"I'm glad you're here, but you didn't answer the question, young man. Are you going to marry my granddaughter?"

"Bree and I are just . . . friends. We've been friends for a long time."

"She needs to get married. Have a family. Someone to take care of her when she's old like me. I have a son. His name is . . ." A tear fell down Nana's face. "Why can't I remember his name, Aubrey?"

"It's Charlie, Nana."

"That's right. Charlie. He came to see me."

"You remember?" Bree glanced at Jack, then turned back to her grandmother. "What did you talk about?"

"He brought me flowers."

"I saw them in your room. They're beautiful."

"And he gave me something else."

"What's that, Nana?" Aubrey asked.

Her grandmother pulled a postcard from the pocket of the red housedress with white flowers she'd been wearing this morning and handed it to Bree.

"He gave you another postcard?"

"He told me he was going to take me on a trip with him. I

told him I wanted to go to Australia. I always wanted to go to Australia and see a koala bear. He promised to take me. Said we could go on a boat."

Bree flipped over the travel postcard and shook her head. "There's writing on the back and an old postmark. It's one he sent her a few years ago. She's just confused."

"He always sends me postcards," Nana continued. "For my birthday. When he goes on a trip. I like to keep them in my pocket."

Bree squeezed her grandmother's hand. "I need to go now, Nana. But I'll be back. I promise."

"Will you bring Jack?"

Bree blinked back the tears, not wanting to leave her. "Of course I will, Nana. Of course I will."

CHAPTER TWENTY-THREE

THE FBI ALREADY HAD a search warrant secured and had started combing through John Bryant's house by the time Aubrey and Jack returned. Jack had insisted she needed to eat something, so they grabbed barbeque on the way. She managed to finish half a sandwich and some potato salad. But her stomach was still queasy over the day's events. She was trying not to think about what might have happened to her grandmother if they hadn't shown up in time, but that was proving impossible.

She could feel the tendrils of fear closing in around her and threatening to drag her down. But as much as she wanted to stay with Nana at the hospital, there was too much that needed to be done. Too many things that needed to be resolved. Until they found her father and ended this, there was no way to guarantee her grandmother's safety. Yet the more they searched for answers, the more tangled the web around them seemed to become. And John Bryant had managed to spin it even tighter.

Agent Kendrick ushered them inside the house where they'd first attempted to arrest Bryant. It looked just like the interior of the typical suburban ranch-style home—except for the dozens of stacks of documents lining the walls.

"What is all this?" Jack asked.

"We found them all throughout the house. In the dining room, office, a spare room down the hallway . . . We've found schematics of US Navy aircraft carriers, destroyers, and mine countermeasure ships. There are also detailed plans of Air Force fighter planes, jets, and other warplanes . . . and that's just the tip of the iceberg. We've found everything from printouts on biological attack plans to classified US intelligence on defense systems against nuclear and chemical attacks."

Aubrey stared at the stacks of documents. Classified documents . . . US intelligence . . . This had to be connected to her father.

"The problem is that going through this much information is going to take weeks," Jack said. "We don't have that kind of time."

"My agents have already started boxing everything up, but you're right. It's going to take time. I've also got IT going through Bryant's phones and computers."

"What about his wife?" Aubrey asked. "She had to know about this."

"I'm counting on it," Kendrick said. "She was picked up fifteen minutes ago and is on her way now to be questioned. In the meantime, I'm going to suggest you start looking through Bryant's office. Hopefully you'll get lucky."

While agents continued boxing up the stacks of documents, Aubrey and Jack spent the next hour searching Bryant's office, hoping to find something that directly connected him to her father. A motivation as to why he'd arranged for someone to kidnap her grandmother. Floor-to-ceiling bookshelves lined one wall and were filled with hundreds of dusty books that were interspersed with a few photos and knickknacks. Four metal file cabinets stood against another wall, jam-packed with more files and documents. Finding that needle in a haystack was going to take a miracle. But the connection to her father had to be here somewhere. They just had to find it.

"Bree."

Aubrey looked up at Jack. The muscles in her lower back had tightened into knots from kneeling on the floor and going through the bottom drawer of one of the file cabinets. "Did you find something?"

"Maybe." He stepped back from some books he'd been riffling through and walked over to her. "What did Rachel do for a living when she was with your father?"

"Rachel?" His question took her by surprise.

Jack nodded.

"I don't know . . . I think she was a secretary for some big corporation."

"For AKL International?"

"Maybe . . . why?"

"I found this photo on one of the shelves behind the books." He flipped around the frame and held it up so she could see the photo. "Her hair's blonder, and she's ten pounds or so heavier, but if I'm not mistaken, this is her with our dead suspect."

Aubrey felt her stomach churn as Jack handed her the photo. Three people stood smiling in what looked like a lobby in front of a sign that said AKL International. The one in the middle was definitely Rachel.

"It's her, though this had to be taken at least twenty years ago. Maybe right out of college."

"This could be a coincidence, Bree," Jack said.

She shook her head. "This is a photo of my father's second wife with our dead suspect, and both men are linked to the selling and buying of classified information. I'd say we just found our connection."

The unsettled feeling she'd carried with her all week seemed to multiply in her stomach. She'd been told her father was a traitor. That he'd sold out his country and had been passing on classified information to foreign governments. Had Rachel been involved somehow in her father's treason?

Jack stepped into the hallway and asked Agent Kendrick to join them.

"Ever heard of AKL International?" Jack asked, once the three of them were back in the office.

Kendrick nodded. "It's a government-contracted company here in San Antonio that works extensively for the National Security Agency and the CIA. Why?"

"What kind of contracts?" Jack asked.

"Mainly ones that provide intelligence. For example, military contracts to our forces in the Middle East."

"The government contracts out that kind of work?" Aubrey asked.

"Military contractors have become the norm now, for everything from managing satellites, to manning listening posts, to supplying interrogators for US prisoners. What's going on?"

Aubrey's mind battled to put the pieces together as Jack explained to the fellow agent what he'd found.

"It definitely sounds as if she's involved in this somehow," Kendrick said.

Jack caught Aubrey's gaze. "Rachel needs to be picked up, and we need to head back to Corpus now and talk to her."

They spent most of the three-hour trip in silence. A call to the hospital had assured her that her grandmother would be fine. Aubrey's job was simply to find out why someone had attempted to grab her, but she was tired of the continued ripple effect of his actions.

Thirty minutes outside of Corpus, Jack received a call from Kate at the local FBI headquarters back in San Antonio reporting that Rachel had been picked up by local law enforcement and was waiting to be questioned upon their arrival. He put her on speakerphone.

"But that's not all," Kate said. "I did some digging into Rachel Porter's background."

"And . . . ," Jack said.

"Rachel immigrated to the US in 1999 from St. Petersburg. Six months later, she got a job at AKL International. Her real name is Lidia Tyurina." Kate paused, as if she realized they needed time to let things sink in. "From what I've managed to uncover, it looks as if even though the Russians sent her here, she wasn't guaranteed diplomatic protection from their government if anything went wrong."

"So this is looking like she was brought to the US and put into this company for a very specific reason," Jack said.

"With what I know about the situation, I would guess she

was probably a spotter, trained to identify American assets for Russia."

Aubrey's nails bit into her palms as she clenched her fists. Her father had married a spy. Not an immigrant who'd come to this country for a better life, but a Russian spy.

"Thanks, Kate, and let me know if you find out anything else." Jack ended the call.

"Explain exactly how that works," Aubrey said.

"To put it simply, before a foreign government can recruit an asset, they have to know who to target. So they often place a person in universities or corporations whose job it is to identify targets. They do an extensive background report on the potential recruit, then hand the information over to an intelligence officer, who will make the final assessment and make contact."

"So she wouldn't have been the one to approach my father?"

"Probably not. As a spotter, she would have observed your father, and then passed her information on to the contact person. That way, if your father refused to become an asset, he would never connect her with the contact person, and she could keep her job as a spotter."

But then they'd become romantically involved. Her father, working for the Russians and eventually marrying a Russian spy. The odds of all of this just being a coincidence were now clearly impossible.

Jack's phone went off again as they were getting out of the car in Corpus. He glanced at the message, then turned back to Aubrey. "It's Kate again. She just found us the leverage we need."

Fifteen minutes later, they were sitting in another interrogation room, this time with the woman Aubrey had always known as her father's second wife. She sat across from them, fear clearly reflected in her eyes as she picked at a chipped fingernail.

"You've been told already the reason why we brought you in?" Jack asked.

"Yes, but I don't know what evidence you think you have, because whatever it is, you're wrong." Rachel leaned forward. "Four agents showed up at my door and accused me of treason. Of being a spy. I don't understand."

"Is it true your real name isn't Rachel Brook?" Jack asked.

"Yes. I moved to the US a lifetime ago, and yes, I changed my name. But there isn't anything illegal about either of those things."

"And is it true that you were employed by a company that was contracted by the NSA and the CIA?"

"Yes, but just because they handled classified government contracts doesn't mean I knew anything about that. Do you actually think they would have given me—a low-level secretary—access to government secrets?"

"Your access to government secrets isn't the issue at the moment," Aubrey said. "Let's start with what you really talked to my father about when he came to you a few days ago. What did he want from you?"

"I already told you about our conversation. He came to me and asked for money. I told him I couldn't help him. And that was it. I didn't pass on any secret documents, or spy gadgets, or whatever it is you think I did."

"That's not exactly true, is it?" Jack said. "I don't have time to beat around the bush, so here's what's going to happen if you refuse to cooperate." He set a photo on the table. "Do you recognize this little girl?"

Aubrey watched Rachel's face pale as she stared at the photo, unable to hide her emotions.

Jack continued. "I was told her name is Marianna. She's eight years old and adorable. You share custody with the girl's father, a man in Woodsboro who you had a relationship with before your current husband."

"Marianna has nothing to do with this."

"Oh, but she does. Because there are requirements that go along with the issuing of a green card. Requirements that even I can't control. One of them is that the card can be taken away if you are suspected of espionage. You would then be repatriated back to Russia."

"No . . . Her father is an American citizen, and he has partial custody. If I have to leave the country, I'll never see her again."

"Then you need to think about cooperating with me now, if you want a chance that the courts will cooperate with you and allow you to stay in the country."

Rachel's jaw tensed. She hesitated. "What do you want?"

"What was the meeting with my father really about?" Aubrey asked.

She turned the photo of her daughter over before answering the question. "He told me he was in trouble. He had been selling government intel for years—which I knew—primarily to the Russians and the Chinese. Once he retired from his government job, and his security clearance was gone, new intel became harder for him to get. He told me he'd been selling carefully chosen declassified intel off the internet to both countries, but when his handlers found out, they threatened to kill him for double-crossing them."

"So he needed to get away," Aubrey said.

"Yes, but that requires money, and the only way he could get enough money to disappear was one more sale. So he promised both the Russians and the Chinese a list of names that included the real names and aliases of dozens of US intelligence officers posted overseas."

"The Chameleon List," Jack said.

Rachel nodded. "But when he couldn't make good on what he promised, both governments believed he was holding out on them—especially when he wouldn't meet with his handlers—so they tried to draw him out."

"The Chinese tried to use me as leverage," Aubrey said. "And the Russians tried to use my grandmother."

"Yes. Your father came to me, needing a name. Someone who has access to that list. Someone he could blackmail into giving it to him."

"What name did you give him?" Jack asked.

"I didn't want to help him. You have to believe me."

"What name did you give him?" Jack repeated.

"Sean Christiansen."

"Who is he?"

Rachel's jaw clenched.

Jack held up the photo of her daughter. "Who is he?"

Rachel turned her head. "I told you. Someone who has access to the list. Someone who could be blackmailed."

"And as a low-level secretary, how did you know that?" Aubrey asked.

Rachel stared down at the table, avoiding their eyes. "There were a lot of things I saw working at my old job that I had to keep confidential. And I did."

"Things you thought you might be able to use one day?"

"No—"

"You weren't just a low-level secretary," Aubrey said. "You were a personal assistant, weren't you? To Sean Christiansen. You had access to classified and confidential information on a daily basis. And now, you know about his new government job with the CIA and how to blackmail him."

Now Rachel looked up at her. "I knew I shouldn't have told him, but he threatened me. He said he would tell the authorities that I was a spy, even though that's not true. He told me I could lose Marianna. I guess that's going to happen anyway."

"That list could get people killed," Aubrey said.

"I didn't give him the list—"

"No, but you're involved in him accessing it, Rachel."

"What about my little girl?"

"That's out of my hands," Jack said.

"Please . . . You told me if I cooperated—"

"He told you that if you wanted any chance of staying in the country, you needed to cooperate, but the final decision isn't ours," Aubrey said. "What you did has the potential of sealing the fates of dozens of American operatives. The men and women on that list are on your conscience just as much as my father's."

Rachel stared right through Aubrey. "You don't know your

father, not like I do. He always knew what to say to convince me he was right."

"Then you just played into his hands," Jack said.

She shook her head. "I never meant to hurt anyone. You have to believe me. I didn't know what to do. When I found out your father was involved in selling secrets, I left him. I never wanted to be a part of it then, and I certainly don't want to be a part of it now."

"Then maybe you should have said something a long time ago," Jack said. "Because I have a feeling it's too late."

He stood up, motioning for Aubrey to leave the room with him, then shut the door behind them. "We need to go find Sean Christiansen."

Bree nodded. "I know, but . . ."

Jack hesitated. "What's wrong?"

"So just because we're for the greater good—the country's greater good—does that make it right for us to blackmail Rachel into telling the truth, and what about Marianna? If she loses her mother—"

"You're making this too personal, Bree. It's a part of the job, to get people to tell the truth. There's a lot at stake here."

She knew he was right, but that didn't make it any easier. "It just doesn't seem fair when adults mess up and the kids have to pay the price."

"No. None of this is fair, just like none of this was fair for you when you were a little girl and your father was never there. But God brought people into your life, like the senator's family, and we can pray that the same thing happens for Marianna."

"You're right." She drew in a deep breath, allowing him to

help pull her out of the dark place she'd been headed. There was no time to let the past color the situation they were in. If she couldn't be objective, she would have to walk away.

"Don't let her get to you, Bree. We know she's lied, and from what I've seen, there's a good chance she's not as innocent as she wants us to think she is."

CHAPTER TWENTY-FOUR

AUBREY SLID INTO THE passenger seat of Jack's car, frustrated at her reaction to the interview with Rachel. Jack had warned her about suppressing the trauma she'd gone through, and she kept telling herself she'd be fine. She fought to keep out her personal feelings and simply work the case objectively, but what if she wasn't able to do that? Their interview with Rachel had aggravated those feelings. She was clearly no longer able to separate the case from her relationship with her father.

But neither could she just walk away. Which meant she was going to have to work harder to shove back her personal feelings and just focus on the case.

Jack started the engine, then placed a call to his liaison in the Corpus FBI office. "This is Special Agent Jack Shannon. I need an address for a Sean Christiansen here in Corpus Christi."

"Give me a moment, Agent Shannon."

After a moment, Kate came back on the line and gave them the address.

"You should know that there was also a 911 call that went

out to that address about twenty minutes ago. Local police were called in on a potential robbery."

"Do you have any details of what happened?" Aubrey asked.

"Just that law enforcement is currently at the scene."

"We're on our way."

"Ask for a Detective Mayweather when you get there," Kate said. "I'll let him know you're coming."

Fifteen minutes later, Jack pulled in front of the address they'd been given. Four squad cars sat in front of the house, along with a fire truck and an ambulance.

"This is supposed to be a robbery?" Aubrey asked as they headed toward the porch to find the detective in charge. An uneasy feeling spread through her gut, not for the first time over the past few days. Did this have something to do with her father? Everywhere he went, trouble seemed to follow. According to Rachel, he'd planned to come here, so whatever happened inside that house had to somehow be connected to him.

She was just afraid to find out what he'd done.

They walked up to a uniformed officer who'd just stepped out the front door.

Jack held up his badge. "I'm looking for Detective Mayweather."

"That's me."

"I'm FBI Special Agent Jack Shannon and this is Detective Aubrey Grayson. We're here following up on a lead for an FBI case and looking to speak with Sean Christiansen. We heard that a 911 call came through from this address."

The older man nodded. "I was told you were on your way

here. I'm sorry to say that we found Christiansen's body inside, in his office."

"Any suspects?" Aubrey said, dreading the answer to her question.

"I'm afraid not. Single gunshot wound to the head. It looks like suicide, but there are also signs of a robbery. We're going to have to wait for the coroner's report until we know for sure."

"Any witnesses?" Jack asked.

"We haven't found any yet. A neighbor called in a couple minutes before the wife to report a gunshot." Mayweather hesitated. "His wife came home, found the front door partially open, then found him lying on the floor in his office. He was already dead."

"We're going to want to see the crime scene, then speak with the wife," Jack said.

"The coroner is on his way here now, but I was told to let you in on our investigation."

Aubrey headed inside toward the office with Jack, then stopped short halfway into the room. Sean Christiansen's body lay on the bloodstained carpet with a handgun still clutched in his hand. She tried to visualize what had taken place. Her father had come demanding information. Harsh words had been exchanged, then eventually he'd blackmailed the man, demanding the information he wanted.

And Sean had ended up dead.

Which meant either he'd killed himself, or her father had tried to stage his death. Neither option sat well with her.

"My father was here," she said.

"We don't know that for certain, Bree. Not yet."

"I think it's a good deduction. Treason to murder isn't a far step, especially if you are desperate to save yourself. My father needed money, needed intelligence to sell to his contacts, and is running for his life. We know Rachel gave him Christiansen's name. How else do you expect me to connect the dots?"

Aubrey took a step back, irritated at her sharp reaction. Her father was desperate, and as much as she didn't want to believe her scenario, desperate people did desperate things. But that didn't give her the right to take it out on Jack.

"I'm sorry," she said, catching his gaze.

Jack stepped in front of her. "You don't have anything to be sorry for."

"Yes I do. I shouldn't have snapped at you."

"Bree—"

"Nothing that's happened is an excuse."

"It's a pretty good one, if you ask me, and trust me, I can handle your irritation. What you need to remember is that you are not responsible for your father's actions. Okay?"

She nodded. "Okay."

Still, she was going to have to find a way to handle the situation. Jack of all people deserved better. And he was right. She'd carried her father's bad decisions with her, feeling somehow responsible for what he did. But they were his decisions. Not hers.

She turned away from him, focusing her attention on the room and what had gone on in it. A manila envelope lay on the carpet three feet from Christiansen's head. She reached down and picked it up with her gloved hand, then opened it up and felt her stomach clench as she looked through the black-and-white photos.

"Jack . . . look at this."

She handed him the photos of two people coming out of a hotel. Holding hands. Huddled beneath an umbrella in the rain. All very personal and intimate.

"Rachel mentioned blackmail," Jack said. "And something tells me this isn't Sean Christiansen's wife he's with in this picture."

He turned the picture over and held it up. "Jeanette" was written on the back of one.

"So my father arrives to talk with Christiansen, he has blackmail photos, an argument ensues, with him demanding the intel that the Chinese and Russians want. Christiansen refuses, argues with him, and my father shoots him and stages the death to look like suicide."

"There is another possibility," Jack said.

She nodded. "Christiansen realizes he's been exposed, can't face his wife for what he's done, and he kills himself."

Either scenario could have easily played out.

"The other question is, did my father get what he came for?" Aubrey asked.

"I don't know. The list could have been in a file, a briefcase, on a flash drive . . ."

"I think it's time we speak with his wife."

Violet Christiansen looked to be in her early fifties and was dressed like she'd just come back from church or lunch at a nice restaurant. But wherever she'd been, she clearly hadn't expected to come home to this. She sat on the couch, arms clasped around a pillow, her face red from crying.

"Mrs. Christiansen . . ." Aubrey sat down on the chair closest to the woman. "I'm Detective Aubrey Grayson. I want you to know that I'm truly sorry for your loss."

The woman nodded but didn't say anything.

"I'm here with FBI Special Agent Jack Shannon. I know this is difficult, but we need to ask you some questions."

"You don't understand," she said. "My husband would never kill himself. You didn't know him, but I do."

"So you believe he was murdered?" Jack asked.

She shrugged. "I just know he wouldn't kill himself."

"Can you tell me about the last time you saw your husband?" Aubrey asked. "Did he seem upset? Distant?"

"No. He came home for lunch and seemed fine. He planned to go back to the office, and I went to meet a friend. It was her birthday, and she wanted to go to this . . . this teahouse she likes. When I came home and noticed the front door was open, I called for Sean. His car was here, but there was no answer, which seemed odd. Neither of us ever leaves the door open." She pulled a tissue from the box next to her and blew her nose. "I . . . I found him in his office. He wasn't breathing, so I called 911, but I knew it was already too late."

"Did you see anyone enter or leave the house?" Jack asked.

"No."

"Did you notice anything missing from his office? His computer, files, a briefcase."

"I wouldn't know. I don't involve myself in his work. He was always pretty private about it. Much of what he does is classified."

"So you don't know what your husband was working on?"

"He doesn't—didn't—talk to me about his job. He was a

computer engineer and worked in digital forensics for the government. I learned to never ask questions. It made things easier between us. He kept his work out of the house, and we talked about other things when he got home."

Aubrey glanced at Jack. "I know this is difficult, but I need to ask you about something else. Do you know a woman named Jeanette?"

"She . . . she works with my husband. Or used to, at his old job. What does she have to do with this?"

"Were the two of them friends?" Aubrey asked.

"I know they worked on some projects together, but I haven't seen her for a long time. Why?"

"We're not sure at this point. But I do have one last question." Aubrey hesitated. "Did your husband ever mention anyone trying to recruit him to sell government classified information?"

"No, but I can't imagine him doing something like that. Sean was always incredibly cautious about the information he dealt with. Like I said, he wouldn't even talk to me about what he was working on." She drew in a deep breath. "Besides, he loved his job . . . loved his country . . . he wouldn't have betrayed it. That's not possible. Not who he is."

Did he love his country enough to give his life for it?

"We appreciate your time," Jack said, standing up. "Do you have family who can come stay with you?"

"I . . . yes . . . my sister lives here."

"Can I call her to come get you?"

"I already called her. She's on her way."

"Good."

"And again," Aubrey said, "we're very sorry for your loss."

235

A man in dress pants and a button-down shirt was heading up the front walk as they headed out of the house. Detective Mayweather and another officer were talking to one of the neighbors as CSI worked the crime scene.

"What's going on?" The man charged up the sidewalk, waving his arms as if that would get him the answers he wanted sooner. "I just got a call that Sean was shot, and now there's police everywhere and the coroner just pulled up."

Jack stopped him on the front porch. "And you are . . ."

"Bill Geiser. I work with Sean."

"I'm sorry to inform you that Sean was shot and didn't survive," Aubrey said.

"What happened? What about Violet?"

"We're not sure at the moment, but she's inside, and I'm sure she could use a friend." Jack introduced himself. "You said you worked with Sean?"

"Yes."

"We need to know if anything could have been stolen from Sean. Any files, specifically classified."

"I don't know. Sean worked in IT, primarily ensuring the integrity of all our classified data. So people couldn't steal it."

"But he had access to it?"

"Potentially. But Sean would never have compromised his job or his country, if that's what you're implying."

"What do you know about the Chameleon List?"

"The Chameleon List . . . enough to know that Sean didn't have direct access to information like that."

"But could he have accessed it?"

"It's possible, but I have no idea how he would."

Jack gave him his card. "We'll be in touch."

Detective Mayweather stepped away from the woman he was talking to and caught up to them at the car.

"We've got a possible description of our assailant from the neighbor across the street. We're sending her to a sketch artist now, but the man was late sixties, graying hair, thin . . ."

Aubrey's stomach dropped. The description matched her father.

"What about a car?" she asked, pushing her feelings aside for the moment.

"According to our witness, he was driving a black SUV. She didn't get the license plate, but we just put out a BOLO for him."

"I think you need to try your father again," Jack said, as the detective headed back into the house.

"Do you really think it will make a difference?"

"The situation has changed. His face will be all over the news. He's looking at being charged with murder. And on top of that, he still has both the Russians and the Chinese after him."

"You're assuming he didn't get the list from Christiansen." She took her phone from her pocket. "What do you want me to say?"

"That you can help. That if he's innocent of murder, the FBI is willing to make a deal with him if he comes in."

"Are you?"

"We've been investigating Cheng and the others for months, so if he can get them for us, then yes. I'm willing to make a deal with him."

She waited for him to pick up, but half a dozen rings later, it switched to voice mail. She hesitated, then decided to go ahead and leave a message.

"Hi . . . This is Aubrey. I know you're in trouble. I'm working with the FBI and I can help, but I need to see you. Call me back. Please."

She hung up the call, then blew out a sharp huff of air.

"You okay?"

"Yes, but I'm not expecting to hear back from him."

"He hasn't said no yet."

She smiled. "Funny, but you realize this is a long shot. If he's already made a trade with the Russians or the Chinese, then he's gotten his money, and he's long gone."

Aubrey's phone buzzed with a text message.

"Who is it?"

"It's him." She glanced up at him. "He said he's being set up, and he's willing to meet me tonight."

CHAPTER TWENTY-FIVE

JACK STOOD BY THE window of the senator's family room and watched Bree pace outside next to the pool. The fading sunlight brought out the red highlights in her hair, and if he were closer, he knew he'd see the flecks of gold in her eyes. He knew she could handle what was about to happen, but she'd been through so much emotionally these past couple days that he hated that she couldn't just walk away from it all. The past few days had been like ripping off an old scab and had left her in pain emotionally and feeling vulnerable.

He went outside and stepped in front of her before drawing her into a hug and letting her nestle her chin against his shoulder. "You okay?"

"Honestly . . . I don't know."

"Then talk to me." He stepped back, catching the emotion in her eyes before nodding toward a wooden bench overlooking the water. "We still have a few minutes before we have to leave."

"Okay."

They sat down on the bench and she leaned forward with her forearms on her legs. Growing up, she'd always been his sounding board, and he couldn't count the number of times she managed to keep him out of trouble with her advice. She'd always been that kind of friend. He always hoped he'd been the same to her. And now, she needed a friend more than ever.

"What are you thinking?" he asked.

"It might sound strange, because it's been almost three years since I last saw him, but I didn't think I'd feel so emotional over the thought of seeing him again. It just doesn't make sense. There's never really been a relationship between us, but somehow I still feel as if I'm betraying him." Her voice softened as she looked up at him. "I go through with this, and he will end up in prison."

"That's where you're wrong." He reached out and laced their fingers together. "The truth is, your father's going to prison whether or not you're involved in his arrest. You're just helping us speed up the process. All you have to do is say the word and you can walk away without anyone thinking less of you."

She shook her head. "I can't just walk away. My job is to bring people to justice, and it shouldn't matter who's on the other side. This is who I am, Jack. I can't simply walk away. I just didn't think it would be this hard."

He searched for the right words, knowing she needed a friend more than any advice. But he didn't agree with her. "Honestly, I think what you're feeling makes perfect sense. He's your father. That connection will never change, no matter what he's done."

She looked up at him with those wide eyes that always managed to make his heart melt. "What about this guilt I can't shake? That seems the craziest of all to me. He betrayed his country, and yet somehow I'm the one who feels guilty over planning to turn him in."

"The difference is, you're not betraying him. You're the one who's doing the right thing, and he has to know that at some point what he's done is going to catch up with him. When he goes to prison—and he will—he's going because of his own choices. Nothing you ever said or did."

"I know, but what my heart feels and what my head thinks aren't always the same thing. It's hard not to feel as if I crossed the line into betrayal, even though I know that's not true."

"You're doing the right thing. Just remember that."

She nodded. "I know. I think."

"And I meant what I said just now. You've already proven to be a tremendous asset on this case, but you don't have to go through with this—"

"Yes I do, and you know it. He might not talk to you, but he'll talk to me. And I know in the end, I won't regret deciding to do this, but right now . . . right now it hurts. And perhaps it always will."

He wrapped his arm around her, wanting to give her time to grieve. Because that was exactly what this was—a grieving process. A reminder of the loss of everything she'd hoped for growing up.

"Thank you for being here with me." She wiped away a tear with the back of her hand. "And for being so patient as I deal with the chinks in my armor."

"Everybody has chinks, Bree, but you're the strongest person I know."

"Hardly."

"And it's okay to be vulnerable."

She let out a soft laugh. "Good, because I feel like I've just been knocked off my horse in the middle of a battle, and my cracked armor isn't helping at all."

For a moment it was almost as if they were back in college. Two good friends, talking about life and their future. Jack couldn't help but wonder if it was too late to get that back. He brushed away the thought. She might have waltzed unexpectedly back into his life, but that didn't mean they were going to simply pick right back up where they'd been years ago. That wasn't how life worked. If they did manage to stay connected—and she managed to feel the same way he did—it was going to take time for them to bridge all the years that they had been apart. It wasn't going to happen overnight.

"I wish I could fix things for you. Make all of this go away. Erase the hurt that he caused when he left you."

But that was something he'd never been able to do.

"No one can fix it, and maybe that's what's still hard for me to accept." She stared across the yard toward the ocean in the distance. "I've wanted for so long to find a way to change him. To fix him. But I think I'm finally realizing that is never going to happen. No one can fix him. I sure can't. Which is why I can't put my ultimate hope in people or circumstances. I can only put it in God, because he's always faithful."

"As hard as it is, you're so right," Jack said. "My father always told me that God is about the long game. That he's more interested in who you become, even if the actual process is difficult. I'm not saying God doesn't care about the little things, but he's more interested in my reaching the finish line."

"I know that's true—refining us like silver through the fire. Constantly working on us and redeeming us. I've seen it in my own life, that despite my mistakes, he's right there waiting for me to stop and listen to him."

He pulled her tighter against him. "You've always been like your mom. You have this strength. Stubborn, I believe I used to call you, but that's what's gotten you to where you are right now. Brave and unashamed to step out there and take a chance."

She pulled away from him and walked to the railing. "I don't feel brave right now."

He got up to join her where she stood, palm trees swaying over her and the subtle crash of the waves in the background. "The profession we chose makes it easy to close our hearts, especially when we see so much brokenness around us. But Jesus prepared us to endure hard times. Told us we'd have them. Promised us we'd never be alone."

"I know." She smiled up at him. "And I've seen over and over how when I've felt at my lowest, he's brought people into my life who have reminded me that I'm not alone and who have helped. I'm just tired of this endless cycle. I feel like I'm never where I want to be. I try to forgive him and let go. Then I think it's over and can almost forget about him. But then he walks back into my life and I have to start the process all over again. It's just so hard."

He stood silent beside her. Wanting to simply listen and show her that he was here for her. No matter what happened to her father. No matter what happened between the two of them.

"Thank you. Just for being here. I don't know what I would

have done without having you here. I'll be fine. I promise. I just . . . I just needed someone to listen to me."

"I'm always available to do that. You know that, don't you?"

"I know." She hesitated before continuing. "It's something I've missed. Talking to you about things. Bouncing off ideas, no matter how crazy they are. More than anyone else, you always understood me."

"And I always felt the same way about you."

And crazy enough, I still do.

He savored her nearness and felt what it did to him. He wasn't sure how he could still feel such strong emotions for her after all these years. It hadn't lessened at all.

He tilted her chin so she had to look up at him.

"I meant what I said earlier. You really don't have to do this, Bree. If you want to walk away right now, all you have to do is say the word, and I'll back you up. So will Adam. There are other ways to bring him in that don't involve you—"

"We both know I have to do this. There are people's lives at stake here, and I'm not going to let my feelings determine my actions. He has to be held accountable for what he did no matter who he is."

"Okay."

He was close enough now that he was tempted to forget everything that was going on around them and tell her how he felt. How he admired her courage and her desire to push through even when he knew that inside she was hurting. That he regretted ever going away and not telling her the truth. That a part of him still wanted to find out what might happen if the two of them gave love a second chance.

244

"Bree—"

She slipped her hand into his and laced their fingers together, still standing close to him. "Don't try and change my mind. Please. I know you want to protect me, but I need to follow through with this."

"It's not that. It's—"

The door to the house opened behind them, and Adam stepped out. "Jack . . . Aubrey . . . it's time."

CHAPTER TWENTY-SIX

AUBREY SIPPED ON A COFFEE in the back of a van that looked more like a soccer mom's minivan than an FBI surveillance vehicle. At least on the outside. On the inside it was a whole different story. Instead of fast-food wrappers and sippy cups covering the floor, the back was filled with monitoring equipment, computer screens, and GPS trackers.

She took another sip of the coffee, then set it down, wishing she could stop her insides from churning. The anxiety that had spiked had yet to calm, though in reality, Jack seemed more anxious than she did.

And he'd been right. She had no reason to feel guilty about what she was going to do. Not over the man behind all of this, even if he was her father.

Her phone went off, and she pulled it out of her pocket.

"Is that him?" Jack asked.

"Yes. He . . ." She clicked on the message. "He said he's ten minutes out."

"That's a good sign. At least he's still planning to show up."

"He still has ten minutes to change his mind."

"Let's not go there," Jack said. "You have your earpiece so we can hear you, and here's the pendant so we can see everything you do. As soon as we have eyes on him, my agents are going to move in and arrest him."

She nodded.

"Bree? Are you going to be okay?"

"It's why I'm here. Jack . . . I'm not one of your confidential informants. I've done this before. I'll be fine."

"I just don't like the idea of not having you in my sights in case something goes wrong. Mei almost died because we miscalculated Cheng's motivation."

She smiled up at him. "I'm nervous about seeing him again, but not because I think he'll try to hurt me. And besides, in case you hadn't noticed over the past few days, I'm pretty capable of taking care of myself. I escaped a kidnapping, saved you from the entangled snares of someone's discarded fishing line—"

He held up his hands in defeat. "Trust me, I've never doubted your ability to work on this case, but there's a lot at stake here and already too many have gotten hurt. I just want—I need you to be okay."

She hesitated before putting on the necklace, trying to read into what he was saying—what was in his eyes as he looked at her.

"Jack?"

He stood up, shaking his head. "I'm coming with you into the hotel. I'll stay out of sight."

"No, you're not. We've already discussed that, Jack. If my father recognizes you, he could figure out what's going on and get spooked. We can't have that happen."

"Bree—"

"I'll be fine."

She knew he wasn't happy with the part of the plan that kept him in the communications van outside, but she also knew that she'd been right to insist he stay out of sight until they arrested her father. It had been a long time ago, but Jack had met the man several times. Her father recognizing Jack wasn't a chance they were going to take. She didn't mind the fact that Jack was being overprotective, but he had to realize that she could do the job. And despite the personal connection with the suspect, that's all this was. A job.

"Okay, but remember that we'll be able to hear your conversation with him, and—"

"Jack."

He frowned. "Just let me finish. Please."

She shot him a smile. "Go ahead."

"If you ever feel uncomfortable, just say the word, and the team will swoop in."

She reached out and squeezed his hands. "I'll be fine."

"I'm overreacting, aren't I?"

"Just a bit. It's a public place. He might have stolen state secrets, but he won't hurt me. I'm sure of that."

"And you're trained and completely capable of dealing with this situation."

"Yes, I am."

"Okay. I'm not worrying, but we've got four undercover agents in the lobby posing as hotel guests. I'll be in the van just outside the hotel, and once we have visual confirmation, our agents will move in and arrest him. You don't even have to talk to him if you don't want to."

She nodded. She'd always had a dozen questions she wanted to ask Charles Ramsey. Like why he walked out on her and her mother. Why he didn't come to her mother's funeral. But she no longer needed to ask them. She wasn't that lonely child who'd been abandoned by her father anymore. She'd moved on with her life. He wasn't a part of it, nor would he ever be again. But sometimes it was still hard to convince herself.

"I want you to know that the FBI appreciates what you're doing. And I'm . . . I'm only acting this way because I don't want anything to happen to you."

"It won't." She reached up and kissed him on the cheek. "Thanks for backing me up on this."

"Always."

There was something about his expression that made her want to stop and ask him what just passed between them. In college, he was the one she always went to when she was struggling. But something . . . something had changed in the way he looked at her. She shook off the feeling and instead stepped out of the van and headed toward the hotel where her father told her he would meet her.

Walk with me inside, God. I can't do this alone.

Her fingers felt for the necklace. There was no reason to be afraid. She wasn't alone.

She took in a deep breath as she approached the building. Darkness had long since settled over the city, but the hotel lit up the area around them. She walked through the glass doors and into the hotel lobby. To her left was a bar with dimmed lighting and music playing in the background. To her right were a dozen cushioned chairs that matched the hotel's green-and-blue color scheme and elegant décor. Straight ahead was the registration desk, with a polished counter and two fresh-faced employees.

She sat down on a chair in the far corner of the lobby where she could watch people coming and going through the front doors, and tried to relax. She identified the undercover agents immediately. The first one sat at the bar, looking bored—but not quite bored enough—and nursing a drink. An older woman sat three chairs over from her, reading a book. The third and fourth agents—one wearing a baseball cap—stood near the elevators talking about something in hushed tones.

She glanced at her watch. She was now six minutes early. She grabbed a magazine from the wooden table next to her and started flipping through the pages without really seeing them. One of the last times she'd seen her father while her mother was still alive had been at a school play where she had one of the lead roles. He showed up for the last act, apologizing that he was late because he'd been handling some government emergency. Excuses had become routine. He took her out, bought her dinner and a new dress, then apologized again before saying he had to catch a midnight flight to Hong Kong.

Hong Kong, Berlin, Morocco . . . It was always somewhere urgent and, to her, exciting. She'd carry around the postcards he sent her for weeks, memorizing everything she could about the places he was visiting, along with his promises that one day he'd take some time off from his work and take her on a trip around the world.

She glanced at the door as a family with three kids stepped into the lobby. She knew Jack was worried about her, but her father had never been prone to violence. Any abuse on his side was neglect. Always gone, missing birthdays, anniversaries, and school plays. She stopped expecting him to show up.

Her biggest concern at the moment was that he wouldn't show up tonight either.

A flat-screen television, playing the news in the corner of the room, caught her attention when her father's face filled the screen. She dropped the magazine onto the table and crossed the thick carpet, stopping in front of the TV. The broadcast switched to a female reporter, standing in front of the Christiansen home, where yellow crime-scene tape flapped in the wind in front of the house.

"Local authorities were called to the house of Sean Christiansen earlier today after a 911 call by a neighbor who claimed to have heard a gunshot at the house of the university professor. While details are still sketchy as to what happened inside the house, sources tell us that Christiansen was found dead in his home. A witness points to this man, Charles Ramsey, who is a person of interest and wanted by the authorities in connection to the case. This is a developing story, and we will bring you more details of the situation as the story unfolds."

"Jack . . . Christiansen's death has already hit the news cycle," Aubrey said out loud, her gaze glued to the screen.

"I'm surprised it took this long, to be honest." Jack's voice came over her earpiece.

"Have you heard anything from the coroner's office?"

"Not yet, but if your father sees this, there's a good chance he's going to run. He's already five minutes late."

"He's also out of options. He needs to know what the FBI is offering him."

"The FBI isn't going to be as willing to work with him if murder's on the table."

She checked her watch, her pulse pounding. Six minutes late and there was still no sign of him.

"Maybe you should call him," Jack said. "He could have spotted the agents and left."

She headed back to her chair, hesitating with her response. "How would he have known?"

"How did Cheng know we were coming after him?"

"Unlike Mei, I'm pretty sure he isn't tracking me, Jack."

"Just stay alert. Please."

This had turned into some kind of game of cloak-and-dagger. Stolen government secrets, rogue agents, and dead bodies. And she'd ended up smack-dab in the middle of it all.

When she'd been patrolling the streets in a squad car, she was on the front lines as a first responder. She had to learn to simply ignore the grief she felt over things she saw on the streets. It was a balance she still struggled with, because disregarding her feelings made it easier to close off her heart and not deal with uncomfortable situations. Like with her father.

And Jack.

She pushed away the unwanted thought, knowing she was going to have to deal with him at some point. Just like she was going to have to deal with the feelings of betrayal by her father that were impossible to strip away no matter how hard she'd tried over the years.

"Bree . . . any answer?"

Jack's voice resonated in her ear.

"Bree?"

She let out a sharp breath, decision made. "I'll call him now."

She placed the call and let it ring. No answer.

Thirty seconds later, her phone rang. She checked the caller ID. Unknown.

"Aubrey Grayson . . . I'm going to need you to listen to me very carefully. You're going to do exactly what I tell you, because I'm watching you." The distorted voice paused. "Leave your phone in your seat, then head for the side door, past the restrooms. There'll be a black sedan waiting outside for you. Don't give the agents in the lobby any signals, because one, I've jammed your earpiece and camera, and two, there is a bomb in the hotel that will go off if you do."

A bomb?

"There are women and children in that lobby. An older couple, and a family of five. You have exactly sixty seconds. Now . . . go."

The call dropped.

Aubrey glanced up from her phone and searched the room for the caller.

"You've got forty-five seconds." This time the voice came through her earpiece. "Find a way to get the agent standing by the elevator in the baseball cap out of the way, but remember I can hear everything you say—they can't—and I'm watching you. No signals. Or people will die."

"Do you have my father?" she asked, standing up and dropping her phone in the chair behind her.

"Yes."

"Is he okay?"

"He is for now. As long as you do what you're told."

She didn't miss the irony in the situation. She was being asked to risk her life to save her father? The man who'd never truly loved her. But whoever was behind this didn't know that. They wanted to use her for leverage, and now not only was her life at stake, but also the lives of everyone in this lobby.

Aubrey felt a surge of adrenaline as she looked around the lobby. She walked slowly toward the bathrooms. Past them was a set of doors leading outside. There had to be a way to let Jack and his team know what was going on, but there was that family, standing at the counter checking in. No. She couldn't risk it.

Aubrey held the gaze of the agent in the baseball cap for a moment. "I need to go to the restroom, but Special Agent Shannon asked that you meet him at the check in counter."

"Of course."

She continued down the short hall, pushed open the exit door, and stepped outside without looking back.

CHAPTER TWENTY-SEVEN

JACK GLANCED AT HIS watch again, wishing he was sitting inside the lobby with his eyes on Bree instead of in a van parked near the front entrance of the hotel. Even though he knew it was the right decision to stay out here, it was still hard not to question its validity when he couldn't get rid of the worry.

But maybe it didn't matter. He wouldn't be surprised if Bree's father didn't show up. The man had a bad habit of breaking his promises. Especially to his daughter. Not showing up would simply fit his character. He'd never been reliable or engaged in her life, so what was going to make this any different? Probably nothing. But he was still praying that the man would show up. It was their last real option at the moment to bring him in.

Jack forced himself to wait another full minute before contacting her again.

"Bree . . . any sign of him?"

Silence.

"Bree, I need an update."

Still nothing.

His heart stilled for a moment. Why wasn't she responding? "Who's got their eyes on her? Baker . . . Ortiz . . ."

There were four agents inside the hotel, and none of them were answering.

"Simon." He turned to his IT man who was running the communications from the van. "What's going on?"

"I don't know, sir, but it looks as if our communications have been jammed. Not just with her, but with the entire team."

No . . . No . . . No . . . This wasn't possible.

"Then unjam them," Jack said. "I need you to reestablish communication with her now."

He jumped out of the van and sprinted toward the hotel lobby, his heart racing as he shoved open the glass door. Their plan was supposed to have been foolproof. Simple. She was to ask her father for a meeting in a public place. When he showed up, they were going to grab him. It couldn't get any more straightforward than that. The only issue that might come into play was if he didn't show up, but all that would do was leave them back at square one. And as for Bree . . . Using her was the safest way to get him to come out into the open.

His thoughts flashed back to Cheng, who'd ended up eluding arrest.

But this was different.

Wasn't it?

"Bree . . . Agent Baker . . . I need an answer . . ."

Still nothing.

What's going on?

Inside, he quickly located Agent Baker, who was standing near the elevators. "Where is she?"

"She went into the bathroom. Our target still hasn't arrived."

"One of you was supposed to have eyes on her at all times," Jack said.

"I couldn't go in the bathroom with her, could I?"

Jack ran down the narrow hallway toward the restrooms. Maybe he was overreacting, but his gut told him that wasn't the case. Something was wrong. He knocked on the women's restroom door, announced his presence, and walked in.

"Bree?"

He kicked open the stalls one at a time, but they were all empty. She wasn't there. A flood of anxiety and anger rushed through him as he ran back toward the lobby. With communications down, he signaled to Baker and the other agents to join him.

"Detective Grayson is missing, and at this point we can assume she's with her father, Charles Ramsey. He's never been violent with her, but he is a person of interest in a murder investigation, so don't assume anything. On top of that, we know he's desperate, so don't take any unnecessary risks. The three of you"—he pointed at them—"split up and do a thorough search of the premises. Ortiz, check the hotel security footage and try to find out where she went and who she's with. I'll check the parking lot near the bathroom exit."

Jack ran out the side door of the lobby, needing to determine where she could have gone. One distraction, and someone could have grabbed her. But why would her father do something like that?

The answer was obvious. The man was a traitor, involved in spying on his own government, and because of it, had both the Russians and the Chinese after him. On top of that, he'd added murder suspect to his résumé over the past twenty-four hours. Not only was the man desperate, he'd worked in intelligence and had the tools to pull off something like this. Charles Ramsey would do whatever it took to get what he wanted, even if it entailed using his daughter to get it.

But he also knew that Ramsey wasn't the only one who could use Bree as leverage. The Chinese had already attempted it once. If they'd decided to try it again . . .

"Jack—" Simon's voice came through Jack's earpiece.

"What have you got?"

"I was able to change the frequencies, and we're back on now, though I don't know how long it's going to last. He could jam them again."

"Do everything you can to keep them open."

If he could hear Simon, then Bree could hear him if she still had her earpiece in. "Bree, can you hear me?"

Jack waited for her response, but there was none.

He kept walking, then stopped midstride. Charles Ramsey stood at the end of a row of cars, holding a young woman in front of him with a gun pointed at her head. Bree stood twenty feet in front of her father, her own weapon pointing at him.

"We've got a hostage situation developing in the parking lot," Jack said to his team. "Ramsey's armed with one hostage. Detective Grayson is trying to defuse the situation. I need backup out here now, but keep the perimeter clear for the moment. He's already spooked."

Jack took another step forward.

"Don't come any closer," Ramsey said. "You and your team need to stay back if you want these women to live."

"Are you okay, Bree?" Jack lowered his voice so only she and his team could hear him.

"Yes, but do as he says, Jack. Stay back."

"Ramsey, Aubrey wanted to meet with you because she believed she could help you. You want the Russians and the Chinese off your back—"

"Shut up or I'll shoot her. I'll shoot both of them. You weren't supposed to get involved in this. It was only supposed to be Aubrey and me."

The young woman Ramsey was holding sobbed quietly. "Please don't hurt me. Please . . ."

"I said—"

"Ramsey, wait. Please." Jack held up his hand. "Just tell me what you want."

"What I want? I came to meet with my daughter, but when I show up, there's an entire FBI team waiting to arrest me."

"We're simply here to make sure Aubrey is safe."

"No." Ramsey shook his head. "If I'd walked in there, you would have arrested me before I even saw her."

"Here's the bottom line," Jack said. "We know you're in trouble. She was telling you the truth when she said the FBI wants to work with you. We can help get you out of this mess. All you have to do is put your weapon down and let the women go, then we'll talk. Just the two of us. I promise. And I'll listen. Just like we're doing now."

"It's too late for that." Ramsey shook his head.

"It's not too late. I want to hear your side. Let the woman go. She has nothing to do with this."

"Enough." Ramsey turned back to Bree. "I decided to meet

you because you're my daughter. I hoped you wouldn't betray me, but I know you're a detective, so I needed to be prepared. And I was right. You never intended to meet with me. You led me straight into a setup. If I can't trust you, I certainly can't trust him."

Bree's voice was pleading. "I need to talk to you. That's the truth."

"And then what happens after we 'talk'? You know as well as I do that no one is going to let me walk away."

"But this . . . ," she said. "You're only making things worse—"

"Worse? You have no idea what's really going on here. How far they will go to get what they want."

"Who? The man who shot Grant McKenna? The men who tried to execute one of their own to keep him from talking? I've seen what they're capable of doing."

"Here's what's going to happen." Sweat shone on Ramsey's brow as he came to a decision. "The three of us are going to leave together. Once I know we're not being followed, I'll drop the woman off somewhere safe."

"Think about what you're doing, Ramsey," Jack said. "False imprisonment . . . aggravated kidnapping—"

"If she does what I say, she'll be fine." Ramsey's gaze momentarily locked onto Jack's. "I recognize you."

"Jack's an old friend," Bree said.

If you'd been around back then, you'd have known that.

Jack stuffed down the thought.

"I'll go with you. Just you and me. But let her go." Bree held up her weapon then set it on the ground in front of her.

"Bree, don't—"

"I have to do this, Jack."

"Okay." Ramsey hesitated, then tossed her a pair of handcuffs. "Handcuff yourself behind your back."

"Bree, don't—"

She turned to face him. "It's alright, Jack."

"You and your fellow agents are going to wait at the back entrance of the hotel without following us," Ramsey said.

Jack weighed his options. He wanted to believe Ramsey wouldn't hurt anyone, but he could hear the desperation in the man's voice. No, he couldn't take any chances. Getting a sniper and negotiator in place would take longer than they had, but letting Bree leave with him . . . How could that be his only option?

"Walk in front of me to the vehicle . . . both of you. I've got nothing to lose at this point, so if your men do anything to make me uncomfortable, she pays."

Bree caught his gaze. "Do what he says, Jack. I'll be fine." She turned and walked to her father.

He wanted to argue with her. Did she really expect him to walk away and do nothing? No. He couldn't let anything happen to her.

Ramsey shoved the woman away and told her to walk toward the hotel before he grabbed Bree's arm. "Tell your men to back off and go back inside. Now."

Jack hesitated. "Stand down, I repeat . . . stand down."

"Now drop your earpiece on the ground."

Jack did what he was told. Ramsey ushered Bree to a black SUV and forced her inside. As soon as Ramsey pulled out, Jack reinserted his earpiece and pulled out his phone. This was far from over.

"Simon," he said, once the call he made had been picked up.

"Yes, sir."

"There's a black SUV with no visible license plate coming out of the parking lot in the next few seconds. I want you to follow it in the van, but do not engage. I want you to let me know his every move. And establish communications again."

"Yes, sir, I'm on it."

Jack ran back into the lobby. "Ortiz, get a statement from the hostage. The rest of us will split up into the other two cars and follow Ramsey. Simon is already on his tail in the van."

"Yes, sir."

Thirty seconds later they were pulling out of the hotel parking lot and headed in the direction Simon told them Ramsey had gone. Jack drummed his fingers against the steering wheel. Every second that passed meant Bree was another second in danger.

"We're going to find her," Baker said from the passenger seat. "You did everything you could."

"No, I didn't. My job is to anticipate what the bad guy is going to do. It's my job to keep something like this from happening. It's my job to keep her safe."

"It's all of our jobs."

Jack heard Simon's voice in his ear. "I've lost him. He blasted through a red light and then I got caught in traffic."

"Any idea where he's taking her?" he asked.

"At this point, no. There are boat harbors and marinas nearby, but he could also be heading for Houston, for all we know."

"We need a plate number so we can track the vehicle."

"The plate is gone."

Jack banged his hands against the steering wheel. Bree was gone, and they had no way to track her.

CHAPTER TWENTY-EIGHT

AUBREY OPENED HER EYES and stared up at the ceiling, trying to figure out where she was. She started to sit up, but quickly lay back down when the room started spinning. She squeezed her eyes shut. Snippets of memory fluttered to the surface. She'd gone to meet her father, and he'd been late. Someone called her, told her there was a bomb in the hotel that would go off if she didn't do what she was told. That something would happen to her father. And she tried to save him.

But there had never been a bomb. The distorted voice on the phone belonged to her father. When she found him in the parking lot, his anger was evident as he accused her of deceiving him—they'd agreed to meet alone, and instead, the place was swarming with FBI. Her response was automatic. She pulled out her weapon, intent on ending the standoff and handing him over to the authorities herself. But from that point, things quickly spiraled out of control. He grabbed a woman walking to her car and took her hostage. And in an effort to save the woman, Aubrey ended up here.

Light peeked through the window to her left. She scooted

off the bed and looked out, suddenly understanding why the room seemed to be moving. In the distance was an oil rig. She was on a boat, surrounded by water.

He had to have drugged her. She had no memory of last night, and her body felt as if she had slept for days. She had no idea how much time had passed—except that the sun was up, which meant it had to be the next day.

She tried the door handle, expecting it to be locked, but it wasn't. She stepped into the adjoining cabin, unsure of what to expect. Her father stood in front of a small stove, flipping pancakes like he used to on Saturday mornings before he left. She studied his familiar figure, surprised like she had been last night when she first saw him. His hair was completely gray now, and he'd lost at least ten pounds.

"How long have I been asleep?" She didn't even attempt to keep the anger out of her voice.

He glanced at the clock on the wall. "It's just after seven. I thought you might be hungry. I made blueberry pancakes, remembering they were one of your favorites."

She glanced around the cabin, somehow feeling vulnerable that he would remember something like that. Irritated that he seemed to expect her to think this was all normal.

She looked at him, incredulous. "You kidnap me, drug me, and now somehow think that offering me pancakes for breakfast is going to make everything okay?"

"Of course not." He started scooting the pancakes onto a plate. "And I'm sorry. I just needed time to figure out what to do."

She took a step forward. "And this was your answer? Blueberry pancakes?"

He set the plate on the table. "Why don't you eat them while they're hot."

She ignored the offer. "Why don't you tell me what's going on? You've put my life and Nana's life at risk. Senator McKenna's lying in the hospital with a gunshot wound, and Sean Christiansen is dead."

"It's more complicated than you've been led to believe."

"Really?" She bit back the heated response on the tip of her tongue. "Because it seems pretty simple to me."

"What do you think you know so far?"

"Basically, that both the Chinese and the Russians recruited you as an asset, and you've been selling government secrets to them for years."

"Sounds like one version of the truth."

One version? Really?

She struggled to stop herself from lashing back. Of course, she was about to hear his set of excuses. He'd always had them.

He poured two glasses of orange juice and put them on the table while another batch of pancakes bubbled on the stove. As much as she didn't want to play into his hand, she'd missed dinner last night and was hungry. And there was no telling when this was going to be over.

She sat down at the table, poured the syrup, and took a bite. "Then tell me your version."

"When Peter Cheng first approached me, I didn't even realize what he was doing. I admit, I was tempted by the money they offered me, but one day you're doing a professional favor for someone, and then before you know it, they're asking you to steal classified documents for cash."

He paused to flip the pancakes.

"I apologize for the theatrics," he continued, "but I needed to talk with you. I've got two foreign governments plus my own after me."

"The FBI is planning to charge you with treason."

"But none of it's true, Aubrey. And once I realized the feds were there at the hotel, I panicked. I figured the only way to talk to you was to get you out of there without getting arrested myself."

"You took another woman hostage, then kidnapped me."

"I never would have hurt either of you." He dropped the spatula onto the counter. "Just like I didn't kill Christiansen. I just went to talk with him. He was alive when I left."

"Why go talk with him?"

"He had something I needed."

"So you tried to blackmail him."

Her father looked away. "You still don't get it. I was out of options, but I am sorry. None of this was my original plan."

She frowned at his excuses. "Sorry doesn't go very far when over the past week I've been shot at and kidnapped all because of your actions. Even if you didn't pull the trigger, you tried to force Christiansen to give you classified information—"

"No. This is why I wanted to talk to you and prove to you that I'm innocent, and the feds are wrong. I'm trying to figure out a way to stop this. I know I wasn't the best husband and father, but I'm not a traitor to my country. Surely you wouldn't think that of me, Aubrey."

The knots in her stomach tightened. Aubrey frowned at the familiar technique. First the excuses, then the guilt . . . He'd always been a smooth talker. Trying to fix everything he'd broken with snake oil and empty promises. But she wasn't ten anymore, and his lies weren't going to work.

"So you weren't planning to use me to get what you want?" she asked.

"You were okay with using me to get what you want."

She pushed a bite around with her fork. He had a comeback for everything.

"I served my country for thirty-five years." He flipped over the bubbly pancakes. "Do you think I'd suddenly become a traitor? I'm not plotting against this country. I'm working to take down the very same people the FBI is."

Aubrey shoved her plate away, trying to swallow the nausea. He couldn't be serious. How in the world was he able to rationalize that selling secrets to China and Russia made him a hero? On the other hand, she couldn't miss the sincerity in his expression. Surely he didn't really believe what he was doing was the right thing. Or maybe he'd lived with the lies for so long he'd started to believe them.

What she did know was that she wasn't ready to believe him.

"The FBI has evidence that you're involved in selling secrets," she said. "Secrets that compromise national security. If you're innocent, then why not simply go to them and tell them the truth?"

"Because secrets *were* sold." He pressed his lips together, hesitating. "I just wasn't the one who sold them."

She looked up and caught his gaze. "What are you talking about?"

"Rachel and I had been married about two years when I first

realized that someone had hacked into my computer. I spoke with Rachel about it, but she denied it. Of course I wanted to believe her, but she was the only one that had access to it. That's when I started digging into her past." He turned off the burner and rested his hands on the counter. "I found out that she was born in Russia and eventually, I found out that she was put here in the US to help identify potential targets that could be used as assets for her government. That she was a Russian spy. And she was stealing classified information from me."

The news took Aubrey by surprise. Not that she'd ever liked or trusted Rachel, but she'd always seemed more like the victim. If what her father was saying was true, she'd managed to play them all.

"From the look on your face, it's clear that's not what she told you." He stared out the window at the ocean. "By the time I figured out what was going on, she told me that there was plenty of evidence stacked up against me, that the feds would arrest me if I tried to turn her in. I decided at that point I didn't want to just take down Rachel, but the entire ring."

"You can see how it looks to the feds."

"Yes, but I had to have solid evidence before I turned her and her cohorts in."

"And the Chinese?"

He leaned forward. "I figured I could take them down at the same time. Don't you see?"

"If you didn't feel that you could go to the FBI, why didn't you go to one of your bosses and tell them what was going on?"

"Because I didn't have enough evidence to prove my innocence. And I knew that the Russians and the Chinese were watching me. I had to gain their trust. Going to someone in the CIA would have destroyed everything. Don't you understand? If anything, I'm a hero, Aubrey. All I need is a little more time. I've sold them a few bits of intel, nothing that really compromises anything, and in the end, I'll have enough to bring them down. What they're accusing me of is exactly what I'm trying to stop. And why I can't take a chance that the FBI and your Agent Shannon will ever believe me."

"His name is Jack," Aubrey said.

"Whose?"

"Agent Shannon." She looked up at him. "His name is Jack. He was my best friend growing up."

"I thought he looked familiar." Her father grabbed a fork and sat down across from her with his plate of pancakes. "I remember going to one of his basketball games, then out for pizza. You guys seemed inseparable."

"Jack would listen to you. And if what you are saying proves to be true, he'll help you."

"I don't know if I can take a chance, especially now that Christiansen is dead. I'm sure they're looking for a way to pin his death on me as well." He pushed a bite around with his fork. "You might not believe this, but despite everything that's happened, I only have one regret. And that's you and your mother."

She waited for him to continue.

"I honestly never meant for things to end this way between us. Or between your mother and me. I loved her, you know. In fact, she was the first woman I ever loved, and probably the last as well."

She heard his words, trying to read his face. Could she really believe he regretted what happened? Regretted leaving his family and trying to find happiness somewhere else? She still wasn't sure.

She glanced at the packed bags sitting on the floor. "Why did you really bring me here? Why did you need to talk to me?"

"Because I need your help, Aubrey." He looked up and met her gaze. "I need you to help me put an end to all of this."

CHAPTER TWENTY-NINE

JACK PACED INSIDE THE FBI OFFICE at One Shoreline Plaza, located less than a hundred yards from the Corpus Christi Bay, trying to stop himself from going into a full-blown panic. He was starting to question his decisions. Taking risks was one thing, but everything they'd done so far had seemed to backfire.

And now, because of last night's decision, Bree was missing.

Ramsey's black SUV had been found ditched in a parking lot early this morning. If her father had fled—taking Bree with him as a hostage—they could already be hundreds of miles in any direction. North through San Antonio and Dallas, northeast through Houston, west through El Paso and Tucson, or even south across the border into Mexico. And those routes didn't even include a water getaway.

Further questioning of Ramsey's ex-wife, Rachel, had convinced him she didn't know where he'd gone. He also wanted to know who had leaked Ramsey's possible involvement in Sean Christiansen's death to the media, something that might have sparked the man's erratic reaction. But so far, he had no idea what had motivated last night's behavior.

271

Jack stared out of the large window at the bay, trying to come up with a next move. They'd canvassed the hotel, interviewing staff and guests, scoured security footage across the city, and sent in forensic technicians to process the SUV, but every lead had simply led to yet another dead end.

"You doing okay? I'm sure you didn't sleep at all last night."

Jack turned around at the sound of his brother's voice.

"I didn't, but I'll be fine." He pointed to a large cup of coffee on the desk where he'd been sitting. "My third cup this morning and it's not even nine."

Adam had arrived at the local offices early this morning in order to help the roomful of agents sift through data as they searched for answers. But they'd lost Ramsey's trail. They had no license plate number, no make and model of a car . . . nothing. Which meant Bree could be anywhere.

"What does he need her for, Adam?" Jack asked. "Some kind of leverage? What's his motivation?"

Adam shook his head. "From everything I've read about the case, I think his priority right now is to get the money he needs so he can disappear. As for Aubrey's involvement . . . I'm still not sure why he needs her."

"He's using her for something."

Adam put his hand on Jack's shoulder. "We're going to find her, but in the meantime, why don't you go back to the senator's house? Take a shower and sleep for a couple hours—"

"I can't."

"He's right, Jack." Agent Brewster walked up to him with a file folder. "Though you might want to hear what the coroner's office just sent us first."

"Does he have a cause of death yet?"

Brewster nodded. "Sean Christiansen committed suicide."

"So, Ramsey didn't kill him," Adam said.

"We know he didn't pull the trigger," Jack said. "He still might have been the motivating factor. Brewster, I want you to keep trying to track down the reporter that leaked the story last night and get them up here."

"Yes, sir."

Jack jumped as his phone rang. He quickly pulled it out of his pocket, praying it was Bree. Caller ID said Unknown Caller.

"Jack?"

"Bree." He felt a flood of relief at the sound of her voice. He put the call on speaker. "Where are you?"

"I'm safe. He had someone drop me off at the Bar & Grill next to the pier where we used to go."

"Okay . . . Where's your father?"

"He's not with me, but we need to talk."

"Okay, but are you sure you're safe?"

"I'm fine. I promise. I'm in a public place. I decided I'd rather have you come get me than call 911 and end up with half the city's law enforcement picking me up."

"Stay where you are, I'm coming to get you now."

"Brewster and I will come with you," Adam said after Jack hung up. "We can't take any chances at this point."

A minute later, Jack was heading toward the pier, praying she really was fine. She'd sounded okay, but until he saw her—until he knew what her father's endgame was—he wasn't going to assume anything.

He stopped at a red light, drumming his fingers against the

steering wheel, regretting—not for the first time—ever letting her get involved. He knew she was completely capable of running an investigation, but this situation had become far too personal.

He started praying as he waited for the light to change. Praying for wisdom and discernment, and peace for Bree as she lived with the consequences of her father's actions. He wanted to pull her from the case, but knew she'd never walk away from this. And he knew he'd never make her. He sighed as the light turned green and he sped through the intersection. It had been a long time since he'd worried this much about someone.

A long time since he'd loved someone as deeply as he loved her. But it was true.

He'd loved her for as long as he could remember, and somehow, he let her get away. Then after last night, he was so afraid he'd never see her again. Terrified that just when he finally got her back into his life, he'd lose her because of someone else's greed.

How was he supposed to tell her that he'd always loved her but never told her? That he could do his job and risk his life to save others, but when it came to his heart, he was a fumbling mess. He should have told her years ago how he felt, but instead, he'd been a fool and walked away instead of facing the truth.

The ocean spread out to his right as he sped down the road. Bree stole his heart from the first time he met her years ago, and he was just now admitting to himself that nothing had changed about that.

"Jack."

He nodded at his brother riding shotgun. "I'm fine."

She was fine.

She had to be.

Five minutes later, he pulled in front of the restaurant and parked in the sand. "Let me go alone."

"We're right here if you need us," Adam said.

She was standing on the pier on the other side of the restaurant, leaning against the wooden railing and looking out over the water as a storm brewed in the distance. The wind tugged against her hair where wisps had come out of her ponytail. She was beautiful. He'd always known that, but it had been more than her appearance that had drawn him to her. Even before he'd known he loved her.

For whatever reason, they'd always clicked. She was the person he could laugh with, and still tell her anything. She loved fingernail polish and lipstick, but also baseball, soccer, and video games. He told himself he hung out with her because he wanted to protect her from a couple of the boys in her neighborhood who bullied her. It never mattered to him that she came from a single-parent home with no money.

And as crazy as it sounded, he wanted to fill that place in her life again.

"Bree?"

"Jack." She started running toward him as soon as she saw him.

"I'm so . . . so sorry." He gathered her into his arms and pulled her tight against him. She buried her head in his shoulder. "Are you sure you're okay?"

"I'm fine." She nodded. "He didn't hurt me. I promise."

"Did he say what he wanted?"

"Yes . . ." She took a step back. "He has a rendezvous scheduled with his handlers—both the Chinese and the Russian. He wants the FBI there."

Jack shook his head, not understanding what she was saying. "What does that have to do with you?"

"I know this sounds crazy, but he told me Rachel was the one stealing intel. He said he's been working to gather evidence that would take down both the Russian and Chinese spy rings."

"Bree, you of all people know your father's a charlatan."

"But we also know Rachel's not innocent in all of this. She's Russian and connected to a known Russian operative."

"Don't tell me you believe him?"

Her gaze dropped. "Honestly, I don't know . . . but at this point, he's offering to hand both Cheng and his Russian handler to you on a silver platter. I don't think we can just ignore it."

"And what does he want in return?"

"I didn't make him any promises."

"Good, because I wouldn't give him any. As far as the FBI is concerned, he's guilty, Bree."

"I know. He wants to be able to disappear without having to always watch his back."

"Sounds rather convenient, if you ask me. Especially asking the FBI to do it for him."

"What if he's telling the truth?"

"You can't be serious, Bree. I don't know what he said to you, but last night he took a woman hostage and kidnapped you. He's lying. There's just too much evidence against him."

"I know. But what if Rachel framed him, Jack? He was working for the government and had access to classified information.

She was his wife. How hard would it be for her to steal that information? She was a Russian operative. We know that." Bree looked up at him. "He gave me evidence."

"What kind of evidence?"

She pulled a flash drive out of her pocket. "He told me to give this to you. According to him, it contains evidence that exonerates him. It also has details about the deal he wants to make with the FBI."

"I'm supposed to make a deal with your father?"

He took her hand and laced their fingers together as they started back to the car. Surely, she didn't believe him. There was no way in his mind that Charles Ramsey was innocent.

"I'm sorry. I'm just glad you're okay. If anything happened to you . . ."

She nudged him with her shoulder. "Getting sentimental in your old age?"

"Very funny."

"I'm kidding. What I should be saying is thank you. For coming to get me. For helping me through this. I know you don't believe he could be innocent. Maybe I just want him to be."

"Bree . . ."

"I didn't think it would hurt this bad." She stopped and looked up at him, her eyelashes wet. "I shouldn't care what he says or does. I should be able to keep my emotions out of this, but I can't help it. Maybe in some warped way I really do want to believe him. No matter how many times I tell myself I never should trust him, the fact remains that he is my father. And no matter how much I harden my heart against him . . . I'm always that little girl again, begging for his approval."

"Everything you're feeling is normal, Bree. Don't be so hard on yourself."

She started walking again. "I know what you're thinking."

"What?"

"That you want me to walk away from all of this."

"Would you?" he asked.

She shook her head. "No. I can't."

"I know. Even though it's been a long time since I've seen you, I think I still know you pretty well. You'd never just walk away. No matter how personal it is."

She shot him a smile. "I thought we'd end up in a big fight over this."

"I just want you safe. To keep you safe."

They approached his car, and he resisted the intense urge to pull her into his arms and kiss her. To tell her that he hadn't been able to shake the feelings he thought were long buried.

But there would be a time for that conversation later.

"So, what happens now?" she asked, stopping at the edge of the pier.

"We'll go back to the office and see exactly what kind of deal your father is wanting to make."

FORTY-FIVE MINUTES LATER, there were six officers sitting in the FBI conference room while Bree gave her statement. Someone had brought in a box of donuts, but it was still at the end of the table, unopened. They were all too intent on her story. As far as Jack could tell, none of the agents sitting around the long table were convinced that Charles Ramsey was an innocent victim who instead of being a traitor was really a patriot. The idea was ridiculous.

"Do you know where he was holding you?" Adam asked.

"On a boat. I could see the oil rig to the east, but it doesn't matter. He's not there anymore."

"So you have no idea where he is at this time?"

"No," Bree said.

Agent Brewster leaned forward. "I'm not convinced of his innocence, but his story is worth looking into. I spoke to the reporter who leaked Christiansen's death. Ramsey's name was given to him by an anonymous source, not the authorities."

"Your father didn't kill him," Jack said. "We received the coroner's report. He's ruling the death a suicide."

"You think it could have been Rachel who leaked to the press?" Bree asked.

"If she's trying to frame your father, it would make sense."

"The bottom line is that he wants the FBI to raid an exchange between him and his handlers," Brewster said. "What does he want for that?"

"He wants to get the Chinese and the Russians off his back. For them to think he's going to prison for treason while he disappears."

"That's not going to happen." Jack held up his hands and leaned back in his chair. "At this point, we've yet to prove he's innocent. We have no idea what we'd be walking into."

"Maybe, but I'm not sure I agree." Agent Brewster shook his head. "Once we arrest his handlers, we'll be able to take down two spy rings with one raid. Sounds like a no-brainer to me."

"What does he get out of this?" Adam asked.

"Protection," Bree said.

Jack frowned. "He's got this all worked out. Which is why I don't believe him. We've been investigating him for months and have evidence that he's been selling government secrets. I can't ignore that. On top of that, he took a woman hostage last night and kidnapped his own daughter. And now we're just supposed to trust him."

"The FBI would step in and arrest them during the exchange," Bree said.

Jack shook his head. "We're going to need time to investigate his claims."

"We don't have much time." Bree leaned forward. "He's already arranged a meeting with both his handlers early tomorrow morning."

"He'll have to postpone it."

"He's lucky they agreed to meet him. Both sides have already made it quite clear they believe he's betrayed them."

"Where is he meeting them?" Brewster asked.

"Near the port," Bree said.

Jack leaned forward and caught her gaze. "You were with him, Bree . . . Do you think he's playing us?"

She hesitated before answering. "I think it's a good possibility."

"So you want us to do this, but you don't even believe your own father."

"I'm convinced if we intend to end this, we don't have a choice."

CHAPTER THIRTY

JACK HEADED OUT of the guest room where he'd been staying, in search of Bree. She'd been extra quiet all evening, though he couldn't blame her. For the first time in years she'd had to confront her past face-to-face with her father. He knew that even as strong as she was, it wasn't easy for her. And almost losing her again shook him to the core. It was a reminder—not for the first time—how much he needed her in his life.

Two of the senator's grandchildren ran past him, screaming and chasing each other with Nerf guns, their father following a few yards behind. Ryan grabbed the youngest and disarmed him before doing the same to his brother. "It's bath time for our crew, though if you ask them, you'd think they were about to walk the plank."

Jack laughed as Ryan set the boys down.

"You've got exactly two minutes to get undressed and meet me in the bathroom," Ryan said.

More squeals followed as they ran into the bedroom.

"You definitely have your hands full," Jack said.

Ryan shook his head and laughed. "Yes, and I'm not sure how I always get volunteered for bath duty."

"They seem like good kids."

"Energetic, but you're right. I wouldn't trade fatherhood for anything."

"Any updates on your father?" Jack asked.

"The doctors are still pleased with his progress, though understandably he's already feeling restless and ready to come home. It'll be a few more days."

"I'm glad he's doing better."

"Me too." Ryan started into the bedroom, then turned back around. "There's pizza out by the pool, by the way, if you're hungry."

"Thanks," Jack said. "I was just going to look for Bree. Maybe I can get her to eat something."

"Last time I saw her she was heading into the formal dining room with a stack of files and her computer—"

"Dad!" One of the boys hollered from inside the bedroom. "Lucas hit me."

Ryan shook his head. "Gotta run."

Jack headed downstairs, chuckling under his breath. Fatherhood had always been something he wanted to experience. In fact, he'd always assumed he'd have a wife and two or three kids with a dog in the suburbs by now.

But for whatever reason, that had never happened.

The formal dining room at the senator's house held a solid oak dining set long enough for twelve people, and a large buffet table. A glass chandelier hung from a wooden ceiling beam. The room was far too ornate for Jack's tastes, but the decor was the last thing on his mind at the moment. Bree sat at the large table with piles of papers surrounding her and her laptop.

"I was told you might be in here," Jack said.

"I needed a quiet place to go back through all the intel collected so far on my father. See if I can find something we've missed."

"I've still got a dozen agents trying to prove what he told us, and we have a solid plan in place for tomorrow."

"And if he's lying? If this is another scheme of his?"

"The bottom line is we're going to have to let this play out. And in the meantime, there's pizza if you're hungry."

She glanced up, still looking preoccupied. "Maybe later, but thanks."

"Bree . . ." He sat down next to her and shut the laptop. "I want you to forget about all of this for tonight. Stop and go take a bath or read a book. You need a break."

"I know you're right. I need to . . . decompress a bit, but it's hard to just put all of this aside."

"This is not how you decompress after a hard day." He reached out and squeezed her hand. "Besides, hopefully tomorrow this time, all of this will be over."

"I know." She smiled. "You're right."

He hesitated. Maybe it was simply seeing Ryan and his boys that had triggered the feelings, but he couldn't help but wonder if he should push the conversation a step further.

"I know this question is personal, but I noticed that you haven't mentioned anyone special," he said.

"That's one way to change the subject." She shot him a smile. "You mean like a boyfriend?"

He nodded, wondering why he suddenly felt so awkward. "That's what I was thinking."

She pushed back the computer and rested her hands on the table. "No boyfriend. I date some, but nothing serious. Not for a long time, actually."

He sat back in his chair. "I'm surprised. You're smart, beautiful, funny . . . I always thought my brother was a fool to let you slip out of his hands."

Actually, I was the fool for never telling you how I felt.

"What about you? You're a pretty good catch yourself. A bit rough around the edges, but—"

"Rough around the edges?" he asked. "Really?"

"I'm kidding."

"I'm not so sure about that. Sarcasm always holds a measure of truth."

She laughed. "Very funny. Though you haven't answered my question."

"There isn't anyone."

How was he supposed to tell her that the reason he'd never found someone was because no one measured up to her in his eyes? All the others seemed to come up short when compared to her.

"Have you ever wondered what would have happened if we had gotten together?" he asked. "Romantically involved, I mean."

She dropped her hands into her lap as if taken aback by the question. "You and me?"

"You make it sound . . . improbable."

"Not improbable, I suppose." She hesitated. "Your question just took me by surprise."

What would happen if he took things a step further and told her what he felt right now?

"If you really want to know—"

"I do," he said.

She started gathering up the files she had spread out on the table. "If you had asked me out back then, I probably would have said no."

"You wouldn't have even considered it?" he asked, half teasing, half serious.

"I guess we'll never know," she said. "Because you never asked."

He felt a sliver of guilt raise its head.

"What did happen to us, Jack?" She sat back in the upholstered chair. "You were my best friend, and then one day you were gone. I've always wondered if I did something to push you away. But I never heard from you, and eventually . . . eventually life went on, and you weren't a part of it."

Jack shook his head. "You didn't do anything. Trust me."

"But there has to be a reason."

The implications of her statement struck hard. In a way, he'd done exactly what her father had done. Walked out because, for some stupid reason, he thought it was the best thing.

He'd clearly been wrong.

"I know."

"I remember being surprised when you left—I guess I saw your ties to Texas and your family and assumed you'd always be a part of my life. Plus, I wanted what was best for you, and knew how much you wanted to join the FBI. I guess I hoped you would find what you were looking for close by, so I could be a part of your life."

He swallowed hard, wondering why it took so much courage to tell her the truth. "My decision to leave was partly because of you, but not for what you think."

"Me?" She shook her head. "I don't understand."

"I don't want this to sound like an excuse, but you'd started dating Adam, and I . . . I didn't know where I fit into your life anymore."

"Why not? We talked about it. You said you were okay about my dating him, and I believed you, because losing our friendship . . . that was something I didn't want. And if I recall, you were dating—what was her name—"

"Courtney. That ended up being a royal mess."

She picked up the pen she'd been using and tapped it against the table. "I remember."

She was right. Their timing had always been off. They kept missing each other. But he'd also never been completely honest with her.

"What if I told you that I was young and stupid, and I really was in love with you."

She looked up at him, surprised. "In love with me?"

He frowned. So she really hadn't known. He suddenly regretted all the missed opportunities that now seemed to stare him in the face. How could he have been so stupid?

"We were friends," he said. "I was afraid it would ruin things between us if a relationship didn't work out. I didn't want that to happen, and then you settled for my brother."

She let out an awkward laugh. "I wouldn't exactly say settled. Your brother's a great guy."

"I have to agree. He is."

"But in the end, he wasn't the right one for me." Bree dropped the pen back onto the table. "Kristy's perfect for him. Far more than I'd ever be."

"I agree with that as well." He laughed, trying to lighten the moment. But the reality was, he lost her because he'd never said anything.

She shook her head. "Seriously. I don't understand, Jack. I never got the impression that you wanted to change our relationship to something romantic. Why didn't you just tell me?"

"I don't know. I was sure you'd have shot down the idea of you and me."

He tried to read her expression, but all he saw was confusion in her eyes. Maybe he'd made things worse by saying anything. Just like what he'd been afraid would happen all those years ago.

But now . . . now he wanted to take this second chance he'd somehow just been offered. Though maybe it was nothing more than the emotion of the moment that was dragging him back to those feelings. A lot of time had passed since they'd spent any time together.

"And this is probably going to sound crazy," he said, forcing himself to continue, "but those feelings I had for you all those years ago have never completely gone away."

"What are you saying, Jack?" She looked at him and tilted her head. "That you're still in love with me?"

He nodded. "I know these past few days have been hard and emotional, particularly for you, but I can't ignore the connection that's still between us. And I can't help wondering what might happen if we stop and explore not just a friendship, but something more."

He tried to read her expression but couldn't tell beyond the fatigue in her eyes what she was thinking. What he did know was that he'd pushed her too far. He should have simply enjoyed seeing her again and the few moments they had alone together catching up on old times. Because of course it wasn't going to last, and he never should have expected it to. The years had changed both of them, and there were no do-overs in life in situations like this. He'd made his decision to leave, and now he had to live with the consequences.

"Why didn't you ever tell me any of this?" she asked.

"Would it have made a difference? You'd fallen for Adam. It seemed like the right time to make my exit."

"So you just walked out of my life. And what about after Adam and I broke up? You could have told me then. Instead you pushed me out of your life. I missed you, Jack. You were my best friend, and I felt as if I lost you, and I didn't even know why."

"I know, and I'm sorry."

She sighed. "If I'm honest, there was a time when I thought about what could happen if we decided to turn our friendship into something more."

He sat quiet, waiting for her to continue.

"But I worried about some of the same things. That it would mess up our friendship. And I guess after watching my parents, relationships in general have always made me run in the opposite direction. But with you, I was always afraid that would have been the end of our friendship. That if things didn't work out, I'd lose you. The sad thing is, I feel like I lost you anyway."

"You never lost me, Bree."

"Didn't I?" She shook her head. "When you left, I felt like

my safe place disappeared. You'd always been there for me, and I assumed you always would be. I felt like I lost the one person who was supposed to be there for me."

"I never meant to hurt you."

"You stopped communicating. I called, and you never called back."

Just like her father had. "I know I can't justify this, but Bree, I've discovered that my feelings for you haven't changed. And if I'm honest, I was thinking—when this is all over—that we could see what might happen between us. If I'm interpreting things wrong, I'm sorry, but this time . . . this time I'm not willing to walk away again."

"I don't know, Jack—"

He turned around as someone stepped into the room. "Agent Brewster."

"Sorry . . . am I interrupting something? They told me I'd find you in here."

He glanced at Bree, then shook his head. "No. You're fine."

"I know it's late, but I was just given a few last-minute questions we still need to go over for tomorrow."

Jack grabbed her hand as she stood up. "Can we continue this conversation later?"

She nodded silently, then followed the other agent. Jack hesitated, wondering what he'd just done. He'd walked out on her all those years ago because it had been the easy way to avoid dealing with how he felt.

And to her, he was no different from her father.

CHAPTER THIRTY-ONE

AUBREY HELD UP A PAIR of binoculars and studied the scene from her concealed position in a warehouse not far from the port. The adjacent abandoned building her father had chosen for the exchange—approved by the FBI—was located at the end of a dirt road that dead-ended into a field. One side of the fence was lined with old car parts and sheets of metal that desperately needed to be cleaned up.

The countdown to the exchange was still five minutes away, but their team—made up of FBI agents, SWAT, and local law enforcement—had been in place for over an hour. Snipers were hidden on the roof of an adjacent building where she and Jack, along with part of the team, waited in their strategic position for the meet to take place. More agents had surrounded the rest of the property out of sight and were also waiting for the command to move. On top of that, two helicopters were on standby a few hundred yards away.

She shifted in her spot near the dusty window where she and Jack had taken cover. Even on a mild winter day like today, the bulletproof vest was miserably hot. Perspiration ran down the middle of her back, trying to pull her focus away from her assignment. But she barely noticed. Her attention was fixed on her father, who'd just driven up in an old Jeep, parked in front of the empty building, and was now making his way toward one of four large industrial doors that at one time would have been used for offloading supplies.

"You doing okay?" Jack asked.

"I'm grateful he actually decided to show up, though I keep waiting for something to deviate from the plan."

"Hopefully we've already considered all the variables that could happen."

"I don't know. These guys are smart and have their own agendas. If they didn't want this information so badly, they wouldn't be here." Her thoughts shifted to a worst-case scenario. "Or there's always the chance they're planning to simply take the information, then eliminate him. He hasn't exactly made friends in this business."

As much as her father had hurt her, she didn't want to see him killed in cold blood. And they still needed him to help them take down the two spy rings.

The sound of a vehicle shifted her attention to the far side of the abandoned building, where a dark sedan drove up.

"Someone's here."

She heard Commander Sinclair's voice in her earpiece. "Hold your positions."

She felt the familiar rush of adrenaline. Their last encounter with Cheng had ended in losing him. They wouldn't have another chance if they lost him this time.

"Second vehicle arriving on the property," the commander said. "Hold your position until I give the signal."

Three men got out of the first vehicle, including Cheng. The men with him, both armed and one carrying a duffel bag, stayed a few steps behind while Cheng approached her father.

Aubrey forced herself to keep breathing, wishing she could hear the conversation, but they'd decided not to put a wire on him, fearing the consequences if it was discovered.

Another vehicle pulled around the corner of the warehouse, and three men, presumably Russian agents, got out with their own weapons and duffel bag. For a second, all six suspects' focus was caught on each other, and the two groups pulled their weapons. A second later the commander's voice blasted over a bullhorn for the six suspects to drop their weapons and get on the ground.

"Move in now." The commander's order came through her earpiece. "Go . . . go . . . go."

Agents and local LEOs hit the ground running, following the plan to converge on the suspects. Clearly taken off guard by the show of force, the six men started to drop their weapons.

An explosion rocked the ground beside Aubrey as she ran toward the suspects, throwing her to the ground. Smoke filled the air as a second explosion went off, followed by a third. Her hand scraped against gravel as she got up and struggled to find her balance. She could hear the commander shouting over their com system, but she couldn't understand what he was saying over the ringing of her ears.

Debris fluttered to the ground beside her. One of the large doors of the abandoned building had been blown away in a blast. An agent sat on the ground, holding his arm. A second agent looked as if he'd been hit on the side of his head.

And they still had no idea where the attack was coming from. "Stay down."

She could hear someone's voice but couldn't see anyone because of the smoke. Someone else shouted behind her. Another explosion rang out, or was it gunfire? She couldn't tell. Her eyes burned as the smoke settled around her. Someone grabbed her hand and pulled her toward the building, where the smoke was dissipating. Agents were swarming the area, but those who had moved in first toward the suspects—like her and Jack—had caught the brunt of the blast.

"Take them down now." The commander spouted the order again.

She turned back to where agents had managed to handcuff their suspects. Six men lay on the ground in a row, facedown.

Where was her father?

Jack grabbed her arm. "Are you okay?"

"Yes, but he's not here, Jack. He was standing right over there when the explosion went off."

Or was he?

She replayed in her mind what had happened. The commander had ordered the suspects to get onto the ground, before he ordered the agents to advance. Six men had been standing there, plus her father.

No.

He hadn't been there. But if not, then where had he gone? Her lungs burned, still breathing in the smoke, as she ran to where his Jeep was still parked. If he'd known about the explosions—if he was responsible for them—he had an escape plan.

He'd played all of them, never intending to take the Feds' offer of protection.

Charles Ramsey was gone.

WHILE AGENTS TOOK CHENG and the rest of the suspects into custody, Aubrey stood with Jack, Agent Brewster, and Commander Sinclair fifty feet away from what remained of the side of the warehouse. The Corpus Christi bomb squad had already arrived to start investigating the explosives and to ensure the area around the abandoned building was clear of any more, and an ambulance had taken two of the agents to the closest hospital for non-life-threatening injuries.

But they still had no idea where her father was.

What they did know was that there was no sign of him or the three hundred thousand dollars—times two—in cash that had been brought for the information he'd promised his handlers.

"He never intended to let the FBI protect him," Aubrey said.

"Then where is he?" Jack asked. "He has to know it's going to be almost impossible to leave the city. We've got the entire state looking for him. Airports, train stations, and bus stations will be impossible to get through."

"He might have a second passport," Brewster said.

"Maybe," Jack said, "but we'll get his face up on every news station, and every officer will be looking for him. It's not going to be easy, and he has to know that."

Aubrey took a step back, still hearing a slight ringing in her ears from the explosion. What would her father do in this situation? He'd clearly planted the explosives as a distraction—not caring if anyone got hurt—so he could escape in the confusion. And that part of his plan had worked. But how did he think he was going to escape?

Unless . . .

"She mentioned they were going by boat," Aubrey said.

"Who?" Brewster asked.

"My grandmother," Aubrey said. "She said that my father promised to take her on a boat to Australia. But she gets confused. What if what he really told her was that *he* was leaving on a boat?"

That had to be it. It was the only thing that made sense.

"What kind of boat?" Jack asked.

Her mind ran through the options. "It would be easier to slip out of the country on a freighter as opposed to anything commercial."

"On a cargo boat?" Brewster asked.

She nodded. "Many take on a handful of passengers all the time."

"Is there any way to check the ships' manifests?" Jack asked.

The commander pulled out his phone. "There has to be. I'll find out."

"It's already been close to an hour," she said. "There's a good chance that if he's on one of those ships, he's timed it to where they'd be leaving soon, so check ships that are leaving port now."

Fifteen minutes later, Aubrey, Jack, and Agent Brewster were speeding over the water in a helicopter, waves crashing below them. Her hunch had paid off, and it hadn't taken long to learn that a Charles Ramsey had booked passage on a cargo ship heading for Ecuador.

Aubrey closed her eyes for a moment, giving herself permission to simply breathe and not think for the first time all day. But her mind wouldn't stop, and instead shifted to the man sitting across from her.

Jack.

She glanced at his familiar profile, trying to ignore the crazy thoughts swimming through her head as the helo sped over the water. She'd purposely not let her mind go back to their conversation yesterday. To thoughts of the two of them, and the possibility of something romantic developing between them. How was it even possible she'd missed what he was feeling all those years ago?

But today? How would that work? They both had busy schedules and jobs, making a relationship difficult. Her mother had always told her that if you love someone, it was worth making any sacrifice to make it work. That a relationship should always come first.

And did she even want to open the closed-up sections of her heart and figure out what she really felt about the man sitting across from her?

The cargo ship came into view beneath them, while a storm hovered on the horizon. She stuffed her feelings away again as Jack leaned toward her.

"You ready for this?" he asked.

She nodded, focused once again solely on the task at hand as the helicopter landed on a freighter with hundreds of shipping containers and beyond that the blue sea. They filed out of the chopper and onto the ship's helo pad, leaving the pilot to wait for their return. The captain was already waiting for them. This was going to be her final confrontation with her father. And as much as she hated being a part of it, this was the only way to put an end to all the madness.

"How big is the ship?" Jack asked, after introductions had been made.

"Three hundred yards long. We're carrying over forty-five hundred shipping containers."

Aubrey frowned. There was no way off, but there were thousands of places for him to hide.

"How many people do you have on board?" she asked, shouting above the noise.

"Twenty crew members and twelve passengers."

Brewster looked out over the bow of the ship. "And the quickest way to find him?"

"I could sound a general alarm. Passengers are required to go immediately to their assigned muster station."

Jack nodded. "Do it."

They headed inside behind the captain, then down a narrow flight of stairs and a narrow corridor. "Watch your step. The ship has no stabilizers, so the pitch and roll can be strong."

The captain relayed his orders, and the loud horn bellowed across the ship, seven long and seven short blasts, sounding a general alarm. Aubrey stood behind Jack and Agent Brewster at the passengers' assigned muster station, waiting for her father to show up.

Six of the passengers had already gathered by the time her

father stepped onto the deck. It only took him a fraction of a second to realize his mistake.

"He's running," Aubrey shouted.

Jack scrambled to the stairs. "Where does he think he's going?"

She held onto the white railing as she ran after him up the narrow staircase toward the upper deck. Engines roared in her ears as she watched him disappear around a corner. A second later, he was gone.

"Where is he?" she yelled.

Jack shook his head. "I don't know."

Aubrey frowned. They could only play cat and mouse for so long. Eventually this would end, one way or another.

"We need to split up," Brewster said. "Keep your com lines open."

She walked down a narrow corridor, past a small dining room. Suddenly she spotted him, starting up the stairs to another deck.

She unholstered her gun and pointed it at him. "Drop any weapons and put your hands in the air."

He paused, then turned around. "Aubrey . . . what are you doing here? Why couldn't you just let this go? It doesn't have to end this way."

"I'm not going to let you do this."

"Do you really think you can stop me?"

"There's nowhere left to run."

How had it come to this? The final unraveling of a flawed relationship. She always had hope for some kind of redemption for the relationship, but now here they were in some kind of final showdown.

"Put your weapon down," she repeated.

"And then what?"

"You'll pay the price for betraying your country. It was you all along, wasn't it? Rachel was telling the truth. But you thought you could use me and the FBI to get the Russians and Chinese off your back so you could disappear with their money. A clever plan, but it didn't work."

"You're wrong—"

"Am I wrong about your involvement in Sean Christiansen's death?"

"I didn't kill him. I told you, he was alive when I left."

"Still, you might as well have pulled the trigger. You tried to blackmail him. But you never think about the fallout, do you?"

She glanced up as a woman came down the staircase behind him.

"Get back!" Aubrey shouted.

But it was too late. Her father grabbed the woman and held his gun to her head.

"That helo you came in," her father said, taking a step backward. "You're both going to help me get on it."

"They'll never let you off this ship."

"Then I'll kill her."

The woman whimpered, her eyes wide with terror.

"No," Aubrey said, keeping her gun level. "This time, it's over."

She heard the clang of footsteps on the stairs behind her father. He turned, momentarily distracted.

She shouted at the woman. "Get down, now!"

As soon as the woman hit the ground, Aubrey fired, hitting her target. Her father dropped to the ground.

She tried to keep standing, but her legs were shaking as she realized what she'd just done. She'd shot her own father. She dropped to her knees, trying to stuff down the nausea.

"I shot him," she said when Jack ran up beside her.

"You did what you had to do, and you saved more than one person's life."

She let him hold her on the corridor floor, thankful when he didn't say anything else. Because there was nothing he could say that could fix this.

She might have saved lives, but at what cost? A daughter wasn't supposed to stop her father with lethal force. It never should have come to this.

CHAPTER THIRTY-TWO

AUBREY STARED OUT the window of the hospital waiting room at the parking lot below, unsure why she was even here. Why it mattered what the doctor was going to tell her.

But Charles Ramsey was her father, and no matter what he did or how he treated her, a part of her still somehow longed to have him show up in her life, tell her he was sorry and that she was important to him.

Which made absolutely no sense.

He never truly cared for anyone but himself. He'd walked out on her and her mother and betrayed his country. Things like that could never be erased or forgotten. And yet here she was, drinking bad coffee, pacing the floor, and praying he made it through surgery.

One of the doctors, still wearing scrubs, stepped into the room. "Aubrey . . . I'm Dr. Gregory Mantel. I want to give you an update on your father."

She tried to read his expression as she walked up to him. "Yes."

"We were able to remove the bullet and patch up the damage. He's still not out of the woods, but at this point, unless he develops a secondary infection, I believe he should make a full recovery."

After which he'd be taken into FBI custody. Aubrey frowned at the thought, wondering how she could still feel sorry for him despite everything he'd done.

And everything he hadn't done.

"Thank you. I appreciate it."

"There's one more thing," the doctor said. "He's still a bit groggy, but he would like to see you."

"I . . ." The request hit her squarely like a punch in the gut. "I'm not sure I can do that. The last time I saw him didn't go so well, and besides that, I'm not sure I have anything to say to him. I was just . . . just waiting to make sure he got out of surgery okay."

She took a step back, unsure of why she was explaining to the doctor her reasons for not wanting to see her own father.

"It's your decision. I just wanted to give you an update and pass on his request."

"Of course. Thank you."

She moved back to the window as the doctor left the room, trying to untangle her emotions. No matter how hard she tried to let him go, Charles Ramsey still had a hold on her.

"I'm sorry I took so long." Jack stepped into the room with two cups of coffee. "Any news yet?"

"Yes." She pushed back the looming wall of emotion. "The doctor just stopped by. My father's out of surgery and, given time, should recover."

"Good. I know my boss will be glad to hear that. We need his testimony." He handed her one of the coffees. "I'm sorry . . . that didn't come out the way I meant it to."

She shook her head. "You're fine. Even I'm not sure if I should feel sad or relieved or mad . . ."

"Whatever you feel is okay. I don't think there's a precedent for something like this."

"I guess they don't make sympathy cards for finding out your father was a spy and a traitor?"

Jack chuckled. "You've still got your sense of humor. I'm guessing that's a good sign."

"I suppose. But there is something else." Her smile faded. "He wants to see me."

"And I'm guessing you don't want to."

"I don't know." She took a sip of her coffee, wishing this wasn't so hard. "Do you think I should?"

"I can't make that decision for you, but I do know that sometimes forgiveness is more for the person who needs to forgive than the person who needs to receive it. Even if that's all that's left to be said."

She knew he was right, but how was she supposed to forgive the one person who'd hurt her more than anyone else?

I just don't know how to do this, Jesus.

She sat down in one of the cushioned chairs, thankful the small waiting room was empty. "I know we're supposed to forgive, seventy times seven, and yet this time . . . I don't know if I can. When I think about what he's done—the lying, the betrayal of both my mom and me, and on top of that of his country. How am I supposed to forgive that? How am I supposed to act like nothing happened?"

"Forgiveness doesn't mean forgetting everything that happened. It doesn't mean that everything will suddenly be okay again, and it certainly doesn't automatically wipe away the hurt. It probably won't even mean your relationship is repaired. But it might bring you the freedom you've never found."

She heard the emotion in his voice and knew he was thinking about what she needed, but forgiveness wasn't something she could simply dole out like a vending machine.

"I know I should, but I'm so angry with him, Jack. And somehow forgiveness seems like I'm giving him an easy out. Like he can just skip the consequences, and everything will suddenly have this happily-ever-after ending because he asked for forgiveness. But for me, it doesn't change anything."

He sat down beside her and waited for her to continue.

"What bothers me the most is that I thought I was over all of this. Thought I'd dealt with all my father issues years ago, but now I find out I haven't. His coming back into my life has been like ripping off a scab I didn't even know was there. And now . . . now I don't know how to react to the emotions seeing him brings up."

Jack set his coffee cup on the table beside him and pulled her into his arms. She nestled her head against his shoulder, breathing in the calming sense of his presence. For a moment, she could almost forget why she was waiting in the hospital with her father only a few doors down, and instead imagine what it would be like to delve into what Jack had told her last night. Their conversation was interrupted, but she hadn't stopped thinking about what he said. Hadn't been able to avoid wondering what might have happened if, all those years ago, he'd told her how he felt.

But she knew all too well that she couldn't change the past.

She also wasn't sure she was ready to deal with the confusing feelings passing between them. For the moment, she simply needed him to be there for her.

"My advice," Jack said, "is to remember that this is all going to take time to deal with, and in the meantime, don't be so hard on yourself. I have a feeling God understands this is a process. It's all a part of your healing."

"Thank you for listening and understanding me." She blinked back the tears, then looked up at him. "For walking me back from the ledge—more than once."

"Always. I know this has been hard. I know you're exhausted and probably haven't even had time to process all of your emotions, but that's okay. Because you wouldn't be human if you didn't hurt, Bree. And the bottom line is, you don't have to go in there."

"But if I don't, will I regret it?"

"Only you can answer that."

She nodded, trying to pull up her last reserves of strength. The past week had sucked everything out of her both emotionally and physically. But this . . . having to deal with her father had pulled her to a place she didn't want to go. But she needed closure, and she knew that the only way she would get that was to see him one last time. To forgive him, and then somehow find a way to move on.

"I'll regret it if I don't go see him," she said.

"Do you want me to come with you?"

She shook her head and stood up. "Thanks, but I'll be fine."

Aubrey drew in a deep breath as she walked down the hallway to her father's hospital room. She stopped at the foot of his bed.

He was asleep, giving her a few moments to prepare herself as she listened to the constant beep of the monitors surrounding him. But the deep-rooted anxiety refused to leave her alone. She turned to leave.

"Aubrey . . . wait. Don't go. I didn't think you were going to come by."

Her stomach clenched. She shouldn't have come. "I didn't mean to wake you up."

"I'm glad you did. I wanted to see you one last time. There are so many things I need to tell you. I know you're probably not going to believe me, but I never meant for any of this to happen."

"Never meant for what to happen?" She sucked in a deep breath and felt her anxiety increase. Where did she even begin, after so many years of silence between them? "Never meant to run off with a younger woman and break my mother's heart? Never meant for me to be raised by a single mom who struggled to pay the bills? Or are you talking about betraying your country—"

"Stop."

"Why? It's all true."

"I know, I just . . . I never meant to hurt you in the process. You're my daughter."

"No, you gave up that right when you walked out on me and Mom, and nothing you say now will change anything. Did you never think about how your choices were going to affect so many other people?"

"I just . . . I made one bad mistake and then another and before I knew it, I had lost everything. And everything I did after that just made things worse."

"But they were all your choices, and you decided not to stand by your commitments. All I ever wanted was a father. Someone who came home at night after work. Who showed up at my ballet recital and high school graduation. That was enough for me. I wanted it to be enough for you."

"I'm sorry, Aubrey."

"And you know what's really sad? This is what's left of your life. You're going to spend the rest of your life in prison."

He stared straight ahead, avoiding her gaze.

"Just tell me why."

"Why I left your mother? Why I went and messed up my life? Why I hurt my only daughter?"

She paused, surprised by his response. Not only had he admitted he'd hurt her, but the defiance he'd had in his eyes for so long was gone. Still, she wasn't sure she believed him. He made his living lying and deceiving those around him. Why would this time be any different?

"If I didn't know better, it almost sounds like you regret your choices," she said. "Or maybe you just regret getting caught."

"If I were to do it all over again . . . honestly . . . I don't know what I'd do. But I do know one thing." His hand trembled as he lifted it and held it out toward her. "I just . . . I need you to forgive me, Aubrey."

She crossed her arms in front of her, fixated on a spot on the wall just above his head. She knew Jack was right, but it seemed far too late for forgiveness. Nothing would give her back the lost pieces of her childhood or fix her mother's broken heart.

And after everything he'd done, did he really think that he could simply ask her to forgive him and everything would somehow magically be okay? His demeanor had completely changed from the last time she saw him. On the boat, he still seemed cocky and arrogant. Certain his plan was going to work out. But now he had no place to hide.

She turned around, ready to walk out. There were memories that haunted her for years. Memories that faded over time as she learned how to move on with her life, but to truly forgive him after all the hurt he left behind? How was she supposed to do that?

She could hear Jack's words, pulsing through her head. Forgiveness wasn't only for her father's benefit, it was also for hers. But she wasn't sure she knew how to do that. How did she just forgive the man who never spent a day thinking about anyone but himself?

But maybe none of those things were what was at stake right now.

Maybe her own heart was at stake. Maybe finally letting go was the only way she was going to be totally free of her past. Free of the bitterness that could overwhelm her if she let it.

He'd made his decisions. Now she was going to make hers.

She turned back around and faced him. "I'm deciding to forgive you. Because while you were off doing . . . whatever, we made it, Mom and I. We made a good life for ourselves, and in the end, you were the one who missed out on all the things a father is supposed to be a part of. You thought there was something better out there. But I choose to forgive you, because as imperfect as I see you, I'm just as imperfect."

A feeling of peace washed over her as she spoke. She'd lost out on having him as her father, but she'd been given so many other things in return. And it was time to start living again.

CHAPTER THIRTY-THREE

AUBREY PULLED HER LEGS up beneath her and stared out across the gray-blue ocean. A ship was crossing the bay in the distance while seagulls dotted the sky above her. The past week had thrown her into a tailspin emotionally, and she just now felt as if she could start to find her way out of the whirlpool she'd been thrown into. Like she could finally believe that life might get back to normal one day. Whatever normal was. Maybe she'd never completely shake the feelings of loss over her father. Maybe that was okay.

The waves rolled in, one after another. A piper hunted for food in the sand in front of her. Closer to the water's edge, a scattering of jellyfish had washed up along the shoreline. She breathed in the familiar scent of salt water. The winter wind was cold, but not cold enough to completely counteract the rays of the sun.

She closed her eyes and let its warmth embrace her. It was over—at least the flood of arrests—but emotionally it was going to take time to find her equilibrium again. Her father's arrest had taken her back to a place she didn't want to go. A place where dark memories continuously swirled around her. She'd slept until noon yesterday, and ten o'clock today. Something she never did. But the doctor she'd talked to told her that it was simply a physical reaction to all the stress she'd been under. And that given time, she'd have the energy to go back to work and life again. Her boss back at the precinct had agreed, insisting she not come back to work until she was ready. And maybe they were right. Maybe it was time she took the time off she needed and actually rested.

"Bree?"

She opened her eyes, looked up, and smiled. Jack stood over her, holding a paper bag and looking down at her. Her heart stirred at the sight of him. Jack Shannon, the one boy who could always make her laugh and feel safe. She'd missed him, but now that he was back in her life, she wasn't sure where he fit anymore.

"I thought I might find you out here," he said.

"Sit down." She patted the sand next to her. "I guess it's not the first time you've tracked me down and found me in this exact same spot."

He always was good at sensing her moods and used to tease her about how he could always figure out what she was thinking. Maybe he was right.

"You don't mind, do you?" he asked.

Aubrey shook her head. "Of course not. I just needed a bit of quiet away from the busy house, and this seemed like the perfect place."

"I'll admit, it is a bit hectic now that the senator's back home with most of his kids and grandkids."

"That's an understatement, though I know he's loving every minute of it. We have a lot to be grateful for."

He settled in next to her and opened the takeout bag he was carrying. "I brought us milkshakes. Oreo with extra chocolate."

She took the offered gift, stuck in a straw, and took a sip. "You were right. You really can read my mind."

"I thought you might need a pick-me-up."

"I do, and I've secretly been craving one of these."

"How are you doing?"

"My father's lawyer called me. The judge denied bail. Said he was a flight risk."

"How do you feel about that?"

"I think he was right."

"You don't have to talk about this, but you never told me what he said to you in the hospital. I guess . . . I guess I was hoping some of this could bring you some closure. You've needed it for a long time."

She stared at her drink for a few long seconds, set it down, then turned to him. "He asked me to forgive him."

"What did you say?"

"That I did forgive him, but it was the hardest thing I've ever done. He's probably going to spend the rest of his life in prison, and all he asks of me is my forgiveness. What gets me though is that he never said he was sorry for anything he's done until he was caught and lost everything. It's like he's seeking atonement to somehow make him feel better, but me . . . what about everything I lost because of him?" She drew in a sharp breath. "I feel guilty about being irritated, but am I supposed to forgive him and simply brush off all the pain and disappointment?"

"You have nothing to feel guilty about. I know that it couldn't have been easy, but in the end, you will be able to move forward because you didn't let bitterness consume you."

"You're right." She dug her fingers into the sand beside her, then let the granules filter through her fingers. "As hard as it is, there's one thing I've learned about loss and betrayal."

"What's that?"

"My father walked out on me, but in the end he's the one who really lost out on so much. And what he did doesn't change who I am. A child of the King."

He reached out and took her free hand, lacing their fingers together.

"I feel like I can finally move on. Like I found peace for the little girl inside me. Closure."

"You've been looking for that for a long time."

She nodded. "And found it in a place I never would have imagined—in the middle of all this chaos and pain and hurt. Somehow God met me right there. I will still have to testify at the trial, something I'm not looking forward to, but forgiving him doesn't mean I'm going to let him control me anymore."

"I'm proud of you."

She shook her head. "I'm not like a hero who chose to run into a burning building to save someone. I was the one inside the building who somehow managed to get out alive."

"That's an interesting analogy, but I think you're wrong." He took a sip of his shake, still holding on to her hand. "You've spent your entire life fighting for justice, and even though this case was personal, you were still a part of the solution. Even when things got hard—you never ran away."

She squeezed his hand. "You were just as much a part of all of this as I was. And you'll never know how grateful I am that you were here with me. There are still a few loose ends to wrap up, but at least all of this is over for the most part."

"It's not completely over." Jack set his shake down next to him and turned to her. "We never got to finish our conversation."

She avoided his gaze, suddenly feeling awkward. Which was crazy. "The one about how you never told me how you really felt all those years ago?"

"Yes. That one." He ran his thumb across her hand. "And the one where I told you I still feel the same way right now."

Her stomach flipped as he stared down at her with those beautiful blue eyes of his. She hadn't been able to stop thinking about what he'd said. But too much had happened since he arrived, and she was still struggling to process what she felt. No. There were too many emotions tangled up inside her for her to look at things objectively. But on the other hand, was love ever objective? Or even easy? Ever black and white?

Maybe not.

Relationships were complicated and sometimes hard to maintain. She'd learned that from personal experience. And it had made her think about something else as well. She'd always believed that her reluctance to move forward in relationships stemmed from the fact that she watched her father walk out on her mother. Because men—in her life anyway—had a habit of walking out.

But what if that wasn't the only reason she never settled down? What if she never gave her heart away because she'd already given it to Jack years ago?

She searched for what she wanted to say. "You care about me, I get that, but a lot has gone on the past week, and whatever you're feeling . . . it's probably just your desire to protect me and keep me safe. You were always like that, but, Jack, so much has changed between back then and now. Neither of us is the same person we were when we lived here. And I'm not sure it's possible to regain those feelings."

"Here's the bottom line, Bree. I know now that I never stopped loving you. And I was a fool to never tell you. Maybe if I had, we'd be sitting here together, watching our kids playing out there in the sand, building sand castles and playing in the surf."

She stared out across the white sand, startled by how real that image seemed at the moment. "I always imagined that day would come. Married with three kids, a dog, and a mortgage."

"So, you want three kids?"

She laughed. "Maybe. Someday."

She always figured that marriage would be a part of her life. That and kids. But was Jack really the one she'd been waiting for all these years? She'd dated on and off, found herself with a man she thought at the time might end up being the one she'd settle down with, but something always stopped her from even getting close to that. But maybe in an effort to save her heart, she never admitted the truth to herself.

"At least say something. Even if you don't feel the same way. I just need to know what you think."

"You're really serious, aren't you?"

"You think I was just kidding?"

"No, but . . . I don't know. I almost always have something to say, but this time . . . I honestly have no idea how to respond."

She shifted on the towel, trying to sort through her churning feelings. Emotionally, the past few days had drained her, but she hadn't missed the unexpected currents that had passed between them. Or that her pulse quickened when he walked into a room or touched her hand.

She loved Jack.

The thought shot through her, unexpected.

She loved him.

He brushed his fingers across her leg. "Just tell me what you're thinking. That whether or not you felt this way back in college, you feel something between us now. And that maybe there's a chance for us." He held her gaze. "What are you feeling right now, Bree?"

"My head is telling me to run away as far as I can go, because I'm going to end up getting hurt." She broke away from his gaze and stared out across the water. "I think I've managed to run from men and relationships my entire life. Always afraid that I'll end up like my mother, in a toxic relationship."

"But your heart? What's your heart telling you about me, Bree? About us. Together."

She turned back to him. When had friendship turned into love? And if that was true, how was she supposed to keep her heart from being betrayed again? She shook off the fear. Just because there was heartache in the journey didn't mean you ignored love in order to avoid pain. Maybe life was worth taking risks. Worth following your heart even when it took you to an unexpected place.

Like realizing you were in love with your best friend.

She dropped her gaze to his five-o'clock shadow, then to his lips, remembering all the times he'd made her laugh and how much she'd missed that.

"Honestly . . . ," she said.

"Yes. Honestly."

"My heart is telling me that I want you to kiss me. Very badly."

"Can I?"

"Yes."

"Good." He shot her a broad smile. "Because I've been wanting to kiss you for a very long time."

He leaned toward her, but she put her finger on his lips and leaned back as a wave of panic struck. "Wait a minute."

"Wait a minute?"

"As much as I'm wanting to kiss you right now, I need to know what we're starting, Jack. Because I'm not the kind of woman who goes around kissing men. Or giving her heart away without knowing what their intentions are."

"And I certainly wouldn't want you to be."

"In all seriousness, I need to know that if this is really love—if that's what we're both feeling—then I want to jump in with my eyes wide open and play this out to the end. You walked out on me once and never looked back."

"I think I was always looking back at you."

"But this can't be some emotional reaction to everything that's happened," she argued. "I can't watch you turn around and leave for Denver in a few days and leave me here."

"Like I did last time."

She nodded, wishing she could find a way to better explain what she was feeling.

"You know I would never do that," he said.

"I just . . . I don't know how we are going to manage this . . . us. We don't even live in the same state. We both have demanding jobs."

"I've done a lot of thinking about that lately."

"You have?"

"Oh yeah . . ." He trailed his thumb across her jaw. "I actually have a friend at the Houston field office. An old buddy of mine from the academy. He recently told me about an opening there, and apparently I'm a shoo-in if I want the job."

"How recently did you talk to him?"

"This morning."

"This morning? You've already started looking for another job?"

"I knew that if I was really serious about you—which I am—I had to find a way to show you we could make this work. I'm not interested in a long-distance relationship."

"I don't know what to say."

Jack laughed. "And I'm not used to you being speechless. Just tell me you love me and that we can make up for a decade of missing each other."

She smiled, knowing without a doubt she felt the same way. "I love you and want to make up for a decade of missing you."

"Do you mean that?" he asked.

"With all of my heart."

He shot her a grin. "Does that mean I can kiss you now?"

"Oh, yeah." She leaned in and brushed her lips across his. "I'd say it's long overdue."

READ ON FOR A PREVIEW
from **BOOK 1** in
the **US MARSHALS SERIES!**

CHAPTER ONE

THERE IS A RAZOR-THIN EDGE between justice and revenge, where the two easily blur if left unchecked. Five years after her husband's murder, Madison James was still trying to discover which side of the line she was on—though maybe it didn't matter anymore. Nothing she did was going to bring Luke back.

Her pulse raced as she neared the final dozen yards of her morning run, needing the release of endorphins to pick up her mood and get her through the day. At least she had the weather on her side. After weeks of spring rains, typical for the Pacific Northwest, the sun was finally out, showing off blue skies and a stunning view of Mount Rainier in the distance. Spring had also brought with it the bright yellow blooms of the Oregon grape shrubs planted widely throughout Seattle along with colorful wild currants.

You couldn't buy that kind of therapy.

Nearing the end of the trail, she slowed down and grabbed her water bottle out of her waist pack. Seconds later, her sister Danielle stopped beside her and leaned over, hands on her thighs, as she caught her breath.

"Not bad for your second week back on the trail," Madison said, stretching out one of her calves. "It won't be long before you're back up to your old distances."

"I don't know. I'm starting to think it's going to take more than running three times a week to work off these pounds." Danielle let out a low laugh. "Does chasing a toddler around the house, planning my six-year-old's birthday, and pacing the floor with a colicky baby count as exercise? And don't forget Dad will be here tomorrow."

"That absolutely all counts." Madison stretched the other side. "And as for the extra weight, that baby of yours is worth every pound you gained. Besides, you still look terrific."

Danielle chuckled. "If this is looking terrific, I can't imagine what a good night's sleep would do."

"You'll get back to your old self in a few weeks."

"That's what Ethan keeps telling me."

Madison stopped and put her hands on her hips. "Honestly, I don't know how you do it all. You're Superwoman as far as I'm concerned."

Danielle laughed. "Yep, if changing diapers and making homemade playdough are my superpowers. You, on the other hand, actually save lives every day."

"You're raising the next generation." Madison caught her sister's gaze. "Never take lightly the importance of being a mom. And you're one of the best."

"How do you always know what to say?" Danielle dropped her water bottle back into its pouch. "But what about you? You haven't mentioned Luke yet today."

Madison frowned. She knew her sister would bring him up

eventually. "That was on purpose. Today I'm celebrating your getting back into shape and the stunning weather. I have no intention of spending the day feeling sorry for myself."

Danielle didn't look convinced. "That's fine. Just make sure you're not burying your feelings, Maddie."

"I'm not. Trust me." Madison hesitated, hoping her attempt to sound sincere rang true. "Between grief counseling and support from people like my amazing sister, I'm a different person today. And I should be. It's been five years."

"Despite what they say, time doesn't heal all wounds."

Madison started walking toward the parking lot where they'd left their cars. She'd heard every cliché there was about healing and quickly learned to dismiss most of them. Her healing journey couldn't be wrapped up in a box or mapped out with a formula. Loss changed everything and there was no way around it. There was no road map to follow that led you directly out of the desert.

"Did you go to the gravesite today?" Danielle asked, matching Madison's pace.

"Not yet."

"You usually go first thing in the morning."

"I know."

Except this year. She slowed her pace slightly. Every year on the anniversary of Luke's death, she'd taken flowers to his grave, but for some reason, she hadn't gone this morning, and she wasn't even sure why. She'd been told how grief tended to evolve. The hours and days after Luke's death had left her paralyzed and barely functioning, until one day, she woke up and realized time had continued on and somehow so had she.

She wasn't done grieving or processing the loss—maybe she never would be completely—but she'd managed to make peace with her new life.

Most days, anyway.

"You know I'm happy to go with you," Danielle said.

"I appreciate that, but I'll be fine. I'll go later today."

Danielle had always been the protective older sister for as long as she remembered.

Her sister pulled out her water bottle again, took a sip, and stared off into the distance. "Want to head up on the observation deck? The view of Mount Rainier should be stunning today."

"I need to get back early, but there is something I need to talk to you about."

"Of course."

Madison hesitated, worried she was going to lose her nerve if she didn't tell her sister now. "I've been doing a lot of soul searching lately, and I feel like there are some things I need to do in order to move on with my life."

"Okay." Danielle stopped in front of her and turned around, hands on her hips. "That's great, though I'm not sure what it means."

Madison hesitated. "I've asked for a transfer."

Danielle took a step back. "Wait a minute. A transfer? To where?"

Madison started walking again. "Just down to the US Marshal district office in Portland. Maybe it sounds crazy, but I've been feeling restless for a while. I think it's time for a fresh start. And I'll be closer to Dad."

"Wait a minute . . ." Danielle caught her arm. "You don't

have to move away to get a fresh start. And there are plenty of other options besides moving, the most logical one being that we can move Dad up here. I'll help you look for a place for him like we talked about, and we'll be able to take care of him together—"

Madison shook her head. "He'll never agree to move. You know how stubborn he is, besides—he visits Mom's grave every day. How can we take that away from him? It's his last connection to her."

"He needs to be here. You need to be here."

Madison hesitated, wishing now that she hadn't brought it up. "Even if Dad wasn't in the equation, I need to do this for me. It's been five years. I need to move on, and for me that means finally selling the house and starting over. I've been dragging my feet for too long."

"I'm all for moving on, but why can't you do that right here? Buy another house in a different suburb, or a loft downtown if you want to be closer to work. Seattle's full of options."

Madison's jaw tensed, but she wasn't ready to back down. "I need to do this. And I need you to support me."

"I get that, but what if I need you here? I know that's selfish, but I want my girls to know their aunt. I want to be able to meet you spontaneously for lunch when you're free, or shopping, or—"

"It's a three-hour drive. I can come up for birthdays and holidays and—"

"With all your time off." Danielle shook her head. "I know your intentions are good, but I'd be lucky if you get up here once a year."

"You're wrong." Madison fought back with her own objections. "I'm not running away. I'm just . . . starting over."

Danielle's hands dropped to her sides in defeat. "Just promise me you won't do anything rash."

"I haven't. I've just been doing some research."

Danielle glanced at her watch. "I hate to cut things off here, but I really do need to get back home. I didn't know it was so late. Come over for dinner tonight. We can talk about it more. Ethan's bringing home Chinese takeout. Besides, you don't need to be alone today. I'm sure the anniversary of Luke's death is part of what's triggered this need to move."

Madison frowned, even though her sister's words hit their target. "You know I love you, but I don't need a babysitter."

She blinked back the memories. Five years ago today, two officers had been waiting for her when she got home to tell her that they were sorry, but her husband had been shot and proclaimed dead at the scene. They'd never found his killer, and life after that moment had never been the same.

"Is it enough that I love your company?" Danielle asked.

"I was going to spend a quiet night at home."

"Maddie—"

"I might be your little sister, but I'm not so little anymore. Stop worrying. I'm good. I promise. I just need a change. And I need you to support my decision."

"Fine. You know I will, even though I will continue to try and change your mind. We could go house hunting together. In fact, there's a cute house for sale a couple blocks from my house that would be perfect—"

"Enough." She reached out and squeezed Danielle's hand.

"Whatever happens, I promise I'll still come up for the fall marathon, so I can beat you again—"

"What? I beat you by a full minute and a half last year."

Madison shoved her earbuds in her ears and started running. "What? I can't hear you."

"I'll see you on Wednesday."

She flashed her sister a smile, then started sprinting toward the parking lot. She breathed in a lungful of air. Memories flickered in the background no matter how much she tried to shove them down.

For her it had been love at first sight. She'd met Luke in the ER. She'd been the patient with kidney stones and an allergic reaction to pain medicine. He'd been the handsome doctor she couldn't keep her eyes off. Ten months later they married at the church she was a part of. They'd spent their honeymoon taking the ferry to Vancouver Island and holing up in a private beach house with a view of the ocean. After the honeymoon, their biggest problem had been schedules that always worked against them. An ER doc and a police officer about to be promoted to detective made for long hours and crazy schedules. They'd fought for the same days off so they could go hiking together at Snoqualmie Pass, Mount Rainier National Park, and the Olympic Peninsula. And when they managed to score an extra couple days, they'd rent a cabin in Lakebay and ditch the world for forty-eight hours.

Marriage hadn't been perfect, but it had been good because they'd both meant the part of "for better or worse." Which meant divorce had never been an option in either of their minds. Instead, they'd plowed through rough patches, learned to communicate better, and never went to bed angry. Somehow it had worked.

When they started thinking about having a family, she'd decided that after the first baby was born, she'd pursue teaching criminal justice instead of chasing down criminals so she could have a regular schedule and not put her life in danger on a daily basis. Luke decided to look for opportunities at a local clinic that would give him regular hours.

But there'd never been a baby. Instead, in one fatal moment, everything they planned changed forever.

Madison's heart pounded as she ran across the parking lot, trying to outrun the memories. Five years might not be enough time to escape the past, but it was time to try and start making new ones.

Tomorrow, she was going to call a realtor.

She was breathing hard when she made it back to her car. She clicked on the fob, then slid into the front seat for the ten-minute drive back to the house she and Luke had bought. It was one of the reasons why she'd decided to move. No matter where she went, memories followed her. The starter home had become a labor of love as they'd taken the plunge and moved out of their apartment to become homeowners. A year later, they'd remodeled the kitchen and master bath, finished the basement, and added a wooden deck outside. Everything had seemed perfect. And now, while moving out of state might not fix everything, it felt like the next, needed step of moving forward with life.

Inside the house, she dropped her keys onto the kitchen counter, then looked around the room. She'd made a few changes over the years. Fresh paint in the dining room. New pillows on the couch. But it still wasn't enough.

No. She was making the right decision.

She started toward the hallway, then stopped. Something seemed . . . off. The air conditioner clicked on. She reached up to straighten a photo of Mount St. Helens that Luke had taken. She was being paranoid. The doors were locked. No one had followed her home. No one was watching her. It was just her imagination.

She stopped just inside her bedroom.

It was lying there. On her comforter. One black rose, just like she'd found every year at her husband's grave on the anniversary of his death. But this time, it was in her room. In her house. Her heart pounded in her chest. Five years after her husband's death, she still had no solid leads on who killed him or who sent the flower every year. If it was the same person, they knew how to stay in the shadows and not get caught. But why? It was the question she'd never been able to answer.

She'd accepted Luke's death and had slowly begun to heal, but this . . . this was different. Whatever started five years ago wasn't over.

Lisa Harris is a bestselling author, a Christy Award winner, and the winner of the Best Inspirational Suspense Novel from *Romantic Times* for her novels *Blood Covenant* and *Vendetta*. The author of more than thirty books, including The Nikki Boyd Files and the Southern Crimes series, as well as *Vanishing Point* and *A Secret to Die For*, Harris and her family have spent almost fifteen years living as missionaries in southern Africa. Learn more at www.lisaharriswrites.com.

The **HEART-POUNDING ACTION**
doesn't stop until the very end."
—*Interviews and Reviews*

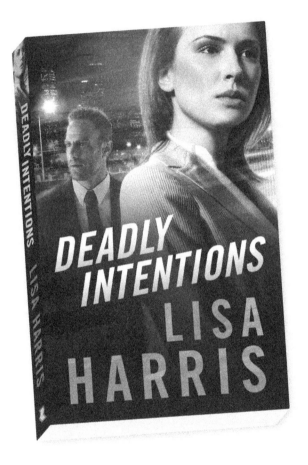

Detective Josh Solomon always believed his wife's death was the result
of a home invasion. But when he is pulled into a case with striking
similarities, it doesn't take long for him to realize the chilling truth—
the attack that took his wife's life was far from random.

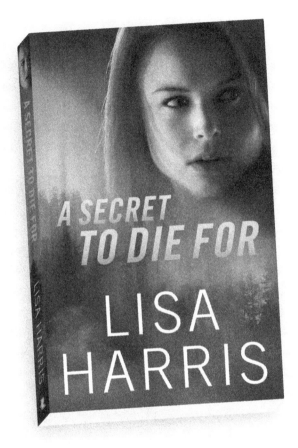

RIDE ALONG ON
NIKKI BOYD'S ADVENTURES . . .

Christy Award–winning and bestselling author
Lisa Harris puts you right into the action in
these fast-paced thrillers.

CHECK OUT
THE SOUTHERN CRIMES SERIES
FOR A THRILL RIDE FROM START TO FINISH!

R Revell
a division of Baker Publishing Group
www.RevellBooks.com

Available wherever books and ebooks are sold.

meet
LISA HARRIS

lisaharriswrites.com

AuthorLisaHarris

@heartofafrica

CPSIA information can be obtained
at www.ICGtesting.com
Printed in the USA
LVHW111924120520
655460LV00010B/179

9 780800 737764